WHEN
WE WERE
ALIVE

C.J. FISHER

Legend Press Ltd, 175-185 Gray's Inn Road, London, WC1X 8UE
info@legend-paperbooks.co.uk | www.legendpress.co.uk

Contents © C.J. Fisher 2016
The right of the above author to be identified as the author of this work has been asserted in accordance with the Copyright, Designs and Patents Act 1988. British Library Cataloguing in Publication Data available.

Print ISBN 978-1-7850799-0-0
Ebook ISBN 978-1-7850799-1-7
Set in Times. Printed in the United Kingdom by Clays Ltd.
Cover design by Simon Levy www.simonlevyassociates.co.uk

C.J. Fisher has a Master's Degree in Film from Exeter University, since graduating she has worked as a video editor, movie critic, social media manager, and creative content producer, as well as presenting talks on new media to charities and brands.

In her free time she is an avid writer, illustrator and online content creator. C.J. vlogs at the YouTube channel Old Hot Radio, which has over 30,000 subscribers.

Her first novel, *When We Were Alive*, was inspired by events in her own life.

For all the latest news, thoughts and announcements, visit
C.J.'s website:
oldhotradio.com

or twitter:
@opheliadagger

For Moopy

Mum,   24/01/2011

I haven't got cancer. Not that I know of. It could be growing
in me right now, as I'm sitting here talking about how I don't
have cancer, but it probably isn't. I read somewhere that
everyone would get cancer if they lived long enough, which
is kind of like saying we're all going to die so long as we're
alive. Cancer is a division of cells that shouldn't be dividing.
It's just a cell malfunctioning. And we have so many cells.
100,000 billion, I think. We have 100,000 billion cells and we
age so severely. It's hard to keep 100,000 billion of anything
in check for moments, let alone a lifetime. The other day I
overheard someone say that they had a nap and then they
woke up, and it annoyed me as it was such a superfluous
thing to say. That's kind of how I see the thing about everyone
eventually getting cancer.

   I think about death far too much but then I also think
about really good last lines for novels a lot, too. No one ever
asks me about either and it makes me wonder what they think
about. Maybe they also think about death and last lines for
novels, but I don't know because I never ask them. Maybe
we're all just walking around thinking about endings and I
think about death the average amount. Anyway, I found a
receipt in my pocket earlier, and on the back of it I'd written
bullet points about why I supposedly wanted this shitty job
as a cashier ready to fill out an application I'd just picked up,
and it made me laugh because I don't know how to cry about
things.

When I was eight I had this friend, Sam, who would always say things I've never heard anyone else say. Which seems obvious and not obvious at the same time. I haven't heard the smallest fraction of all the things that have been said; if all the things that have ever been said were divided between stars in the universe, I wouldn't have heard a single sun. Also, lots of people say things I haven't heard anyone say, as there's a lot of different ways to arrange all the words in our language, even just to say the same stuff. But, even now, it seems to me that Sam said things other people never even talk about, no matter how they arrange their words.

I met Sam at the dentist. I was pushing coloured beads around coloured wires, you know, the toy which only exists in waiting rooms, when this little kid walked over and said, 'I want to taste Christmas.' Those were the first words Sam ever said to me. I thought it was pretty weird, but I knew what he meant. A few years later he told me he wanted to 'Live in the distance', after seeing a photograph of the Manhattan skyline. Then, in high school, he said he wanted 'A girlfriend who is a vintage postcard'. Sam was always wishing for things. We were seventeen when he died. Cancer, obviously. I wish I could remember all the things he used to wish for.

I held Sam's hand when he was dying. Sam died for weeks, all in a single room. The cancer room. Imagine a room that looks like somewhere designed for people who were about to die by people who still thought they would live for ever; that's what it looked like. All cold and muted and empty and clinical. It was a nothing room. A room calculated by people who were afraid and dismissive. If Sam had designed that room, his very last place, it would have at least been *something*, but it was designed by someone without acute lymphoblastic leukaemia, so instead the room was a void.

Sam had these grey eyes by the time he lived in the void, all the colour had drained through them and the red in his lips had hidden itself up inside the cracks. He looked like this low saturation version of himself, so I told him as much because that was the year I tried to have an interest in photography. He made some retort about being overexposed and I laughed, mostly out of politeness because I don't always understand the jokes people make, but then I realised I was laughing at how vulnerable cancer had made him, so I stopped. Immediately. As if someone had flipped a switch and turned me off. He looked directly into my eyes during that loud silence and it felt like he was seeing too much of me, so I reached for his hand and clumsily squeezed his fingers. My palm was slippery with sweat and I realised all the words had gone. After a minute or so Sam grinned, this awful skeletal scratch across his skin, and he asked me why I was holding his hand. I felt embarrassed, avoiding his gaze as he waited for an answer. All I could think was that maybe I had been holding his hand for too long, or maybe he had been dying for too long. Then, instead of having conviction, instead of saying any of the things Sam would have been so good at saying, I excused myself by explaining it was what I had seen other people do. Sam smiled a different smile after I said that.

When Sam was nine he ate a book. I asked him why and he said it was because he had wanted to become the story. Sam ate a book and eight years later he was dying so I held his hand. I guess that's what life is. People really liked Sam, they don't always like me so much.

I don't know when to start telling you about the things you might want to know. I already know everything so it's hard for me to think of how to tell you it all in a way that isn't confusing. My life has been fairly short but it's still the most time I've ever spent doing anything, so it has a lot of details. For example, I want to tell you about the Tiny Cemetery that The Monster has the key to. I want to tell you what happened to me there, but I also want to tell you about the history of the cemetery because it's interesting. At the same time, I know you're now probably also wondering who The Monster is, but he isn't really important. Not to me, anyway, and maybe not to anyone but the kids who tell stories about him.

I thought writing my first letter to you would be weird but it's not. Not really. I've met a lot of people who turned out to be kind of disappointing so I don't care all too much about first impressions. Maybe you're the same.

I hope everything is all right with your life,

Myles

Potential last lines for a novel:
    I want to live in the distance.
    And then they met.

Chapter 2
The Things We Love Before and After We Love Them
September 1936

Lowering himself onto the rug beside his wife's haberdashery cupboard, Jerry Sinclair's thoughts escaped to the trenches. It had been fifteen years since he last held a rifle, but time still obstinately convulsed between rich and terrible memories without trigger. The day he returned from service, Jerry told his wife they should have a child. Two predictable things had happened at that moment; the swollen gunmetal sky of the English Midlands began to empty above them, and she said yes. Their first year of trying for life bloomed with hope and exhaustion, the second withered, and the third became a bitter, silent exchange. Eventually, lonely years lost, the couple mourned what was almost and what almost was, crossing into their forties accepting their fate as a handsome and empty duo. It was then Anna fell pregnant. And it had been exactly thirteen years since Bobby's birth, all fat and pink, when he crawled inside Anna's haberdashery cupboard and started to weep.

To his parents, evolutionarily imbibed with poor judgement, Bobby was a peculiar soul. The good peculiar. The peculiar that at best could go on to invent something mediocre but widely used, or at worst something brilliant yet too niche to be of any practical application. But Bobby was an outcast to those more impartial. During his very first week of school, every kid in his class had been designated a label; a tag unanimously agreed upon during the tussle of playground hierarchy. As soon as one chubby hand had pointed to Bobby as a pariah, the sticky-fingered rest eagerly followed suit. They were safe as long as he wasn't. Eight years later and Bobby functioned happily under the illusion he had ostracised them; he simply found his own company far more interesting than that of his peers. Bobby was, however, impressed by how uncharacteristically intuitive his classmates had been in picking up on his desire to be left alone. And he mostly wanted to be alone. Especially now, as he contorted his body into the cupboard and theatrically sobbed over a tragedy far too profound for his parents to possibly comprehend.

'Would you say Benjamin was a majestic creature of tragedy or an evolutionary outcast?' Anna asked Jerry, who grunted, turned his head downwards, and embarked upon plucking dust out of their rug.

Anna had been writing when Bobby bolted into the cupboard, slowly followed by Jerry, who had taken up position on the floor.

'I'd say he was the last Tasmanian tiger because that's what he was.'

'Of course you would.'

'Then why did you ask?'

'I don't know.' Her husband excavated something from the rug and examined it. 'I thought maybe you would surprise me.'

Jerry pointedly eyed the insect carcass held between his fingers and, as if in response, it began to disintegrate. He brushed at the brittle debris. Tiny limbs sprang away from him at unpredictable angles, and the body shattered under his hands until the pieces were so small they no longer resembled a life. Jerry kept brushing anyway, swiping at where the creature had been, his mind swelling with all the innocuous questions Anna had asked him just that week. All the mundane occurrences of which she made him take note. All the annoying happenstances she insisted on regurgitating. Her incredulity over hearing the word 'wanweird' twice on

12

Monday. He closed his eyes, recalling the night before.

#

'Jerry!' A yell from downstairs.

'Yes?' he allowed a corner of his newspaper to fall forward.

'Jerry!' Footfalls on the stairs.

Watching the door, he held his breath. The steps grew louder.

'Jerry!' Anna thrust herself into his study. 'I've burned the fish!'

'Oh...'

'Well?'

' ...dear.'

'Come look.'

'Look at what?'

'The fish.'

'The burned fish?'

'Yes. It's entirely black!'

'Well, yes.'

'Well, yes, what?'

'Nothing to be done about it,' Jerry flicked the corner of his newspaper upright, obscuring his wife from view.

'It's stuck to the pan.'

'Maybe leave it to soak?'

'What about the supper?'

'Well,' he bit, 'do we have any more?'

'That was the only fish! Come look, it's dry as sand. Pop down and look,' Anna gestured in the direction of her kitchen.

'I believe you.'

'I don't know how it happened.'

'It was too hot for too long. The same as all burned things.'

'But I'm usually so careful.'

'Do we have anything else?'

'Like what?'

'Like *food*,' he chewed the words. 'Like something we

13

could swallow?'

'Oh, onion soup? I could heat up some onion so...'

'Perfect!' he rippled the newspaper with a flourish.

Staring at the headline in front of her husband's face, Anna opened her mouth, closed it, and turned, clumping heavy-footed back downstairs. Wincing at the noise, Jerry began flicking through skinny pages until something caught his attention: a short reflection upon the American presidential campaign. The writer was predicting a second term for Roosevelt. Jerry, having read of Alf Landon's weak opposition, began to concoct a cocky argument for his hypothetical vote against the Governor. A terse speech of self-righteous aggression started brewing in his mind. Working over the details, he grinned... he was on a podium now, spitting a counterargument at a trembling opponent before an awed crowd...

THWACK!

Jerry started, the crowd vanished from before him, and the cool sweat of anticipation stung his underarms.

'*Look*,' Anna stood in front of him holding out a tray of burned fish, her lips drawn into a line, her eyebrows raised and her elbow locked. Jutting the tray of fish beneath his nose, she again demanded, '*LOOK!*'

#

He waited. Elbows bent. Splayed fingertips buried deep into the rug, nails caught against the pile. Jaw tightened. A tap emanated from his left. A second tap. A third, fourth, fifth in quick succession. She was writing, again. He propelled himself through the air from all four limbs. A shared illusory pause hung between them, just before Jerry's weight collided with Anna and her typewriter, in which he saw her eyes opened wide in terror and she saw his mouth set hard with resolve. The almighty crash of man on typewriter on woman on chair, all tumbling onto a hardwood floor, was just enough of a distraction from Bobby's existential horrors to necessitate his emergence from the cupboard.

'Surprise, Annie, isn't always virtuous,' Jerry whispered.

The sharpness in his stomach indicated her beloved typewriter was wedged between them. Part of him hoped it was broken so she could no longer incessantly record their lives with her absurd fairy-tale prose, whilst another part of him already felt the guilt of a man who had become the dragon instead of the knight.

'Daddy?' Bobby's voice choked, thick and raw.

'Yes?' Jerry had yet to clamber off the pile of wood and woman.

'I feel uncomfortable with you doing that to Mum whilst I'm standing here.'

Jerry steadily turned his head to face Bobby. Anna shook beneath him.

'We weren't fighting, Bob. Just playing.'

'Oh, no, I didn't think you were fighting. But you know Jeremy Walters?'

'No?'

'He's the greengrocer's boy,' Anna mumbled, smothered.

'Oh, what about him?' Jerry manoeuvred himself away from his wife.

'He told me, although he is prone to lying, that when a man is on top of a woman it is doing, well, *sex*,' Bobby blushed, pinching a grin from the corners of his mouth.

Laughing, Jerry inadvertently glanced in the direction of his wife, only to discover she was no longer in the room. The chair had been up-righted, but her typewriter remained obtusely askew on the floor.

'I can assure you that what you just saw wasn't us *doing sex*,' he gestured for his son to come closer. 'Besides, I didn't think you liked Jeremy Walters?'

'I don't, he's a prize idiot. But it seems everyone else doesn't care all too much about that.'

'Well, then they must be idiots too, eh?'

'Bunch of ruddy idiots, too right,' Bobby crossed his arms.

'So, are you ready to open your presents now?'

'It's a leap year, Dad,' he sucked at his lip.

'That's just coincidence, Bob. Good things have happened too, you're just noticing the bad stuff because of your silly superstition.'

'I just wish I knew how to think about it.'

'Think about what?'

'Benjamin,' started Bobby. 'Benjamin was the last ever Tasmanian tiger and he died. Today. On my birthday. There aren't going to be any more of them for ever. For ever, Dad. No one will ever know what it is like to live in a world with a Tasmanian tiger ever again, even if we couldn't really feel them making any difference. All these things, they just keep stopping, completely, and I don't understand. They'll be forgotten until it was like they never existed, and how can the world be the world if it doesn't know what parts it is made of? When I have a son he'll live in a different world to me. And I just really don't know how to think about any of it.'

Bobby was almost crying again, but a disobedient feeling of hope wrestled with his cynicism. Wiping his nose on his sleeve, he waited for his father to explain that which he never could. Jerry stared without focus, briefly allowing time to curtail space, sighed and scooped his son into his arms. The kid was all twigs and paper. Four steps carried them to the rocking chair sitting ceremoniously in the corner of the room. Nestling them both into the wide seat, Jerry could feel his son's heart run unsettled in his chest. It still seemed strange, how his lap could be so full with a life he created. This was the child he raised. This scrap, this almost-person, who was so much bigger than before and yet still so small. Rocking them back and forth, Jerry didn't see the unusual, gifted boy who filled him with pride. Instead, he saw the confused, scared kid he had fallen in love with whilst he was no more than a pip in Anna's stomach.

'Dad?'

Looping a finger through one of Bobby's curls, Jerry considered possible answers.

'Sad things can be beautiful, too.'

Bobby squinted. The older man's face was so close to his own he could see the silver shrapnel scar across his father's cheek trace a river in the light. He swallowed the urge to reach out and touch it.

'Huh,' Bobby frowned, digesting the six words he had been given to dismiss his demons. The musky scent, which always clung to his father, slowly wrapped itself around him. '*Daaaaad?*'

'Yes, *Suuuuun?*'

'Do you think my magician's name is stupid?'

'Brilliant Bobby the Breathtakingly Bombastic?' Jerry grinned.

'It's alliterative.'

'That can definitely be said about it.'

'So you do think it's stupid.'

'You want me to be honest?'

'I'm thirteen now, Dad. I think I can take it,' his entire body stiffened.

'I think there's a little room for improvement, yeah.' Silence. 'You all right, kid?'

'Yeah, yeah. I was just wishing I had known this before I performed in that stupid talent show.'

'They probably didn't even notice your name because they were so distracted by your breathtakingly brilliant tricks.'

'I HAD A NINE-FOOT BANNER!' shouted Bobby, his sudden movement sending the pair into a fitful rocking motion. 'It took me all week to paint it!' He noticed a peculiar contortion to his father's mouth, the scar twisted into a crescent moon. 'And they're not tricks, they're illusions.'

Sitting tucked around each other, listening only to the gentle grind of wood below them, both considered what had changed since the year before. To Bobby it had been a lifetime ago, to Jerry it was yesterday.

#

Arriving at the theatre, worn by fat rain, they silently digested the words freshly stamped across the poster in front of them: MASKELYNE'S MAGIC SHOW CANCELLED.

'He's... he's gone, Dad. He's gone!' Bobby crumpled to the cobbled road, one knee submerged in a puddle, tears swelling against his eyelashes and breaking on the sharp wind.

Jerry looked quickly between his son and the theatre, eyes skipping between advertisements. Above the doors, thick black letters announced an am-dram production of *The Band Wagon* where Maskelyne's name had been the night before.

'How about that, Bob? How about we go and see a musical instead?'

Bobby shook his head, crossing his legs in front of him and settling further into the cruel road. Anxious air, thick with rain, whipped whispers as strangers took up vague positions in the rambling ticket queue.

'Come on Bob, I'll take you home. We'll see him next time he's in town?'

Silence.

'Look,' Jerry squatted next to his son, placing one hand on a shoulder and the other on a sodden knee. 'I'm sorry he's not here, but at least you got to see him once. I promise we'll see him next time, yeah?'

Bobby sniffed, twirling a damp shoelace.

'All right,' Jerry mock-sighed. 'When we get home I suppose I could show you how to do a nifty card trick, even though Granddad made me promise never to tell anyone how it was done.'

He deigned a tearful glance at his father.

'And I guess we could buy you your own wand this weekend... I mean, only if you think you might have the talent to be a magician yourself.'

Bobby's stomach fizzed; could he be the next Maskelyne?

18

Maybe, maybe not, but his own wand would be an exquisite first step and he'd be a fool to squander it. Climbing slowly to his feet, he attempted to compose his face into a look of cool nonchalance. A look which faltered as a tittering of applause swelled from out of view. As his father dipped a sly bow, Bobby spun around, face aggressively scrunched, but he was met with only a scattering of folks cowering beneath umbrellas or fascinated with their shoes. Turning back to Jerry, he found raised eyebrows and an outstretched hand.

'Come on, kid,' Jerry took Bobby's palm in his and turned into the wind. 'Let's go get dry.'

Bobby was mid-step when an unseen slap stole the colour from his world. Everything went dark. The skin on his face felt twice as thick and newly fierce. Yelping blindly, he snatched his hand back to avenge his vision. Clawing at his cheeks, he felt only a string of cold, peeling divots, as his eyelids drowned heavily beneath a pulp cloak. His mouth was free. He gasped fresh breath. Raking his fingers down from his scalp, he managed to snake a grip on his attacker.

'Aaah aha!' he yelled, pulling a windswept rag into view, and analysing it. 'Dad!' he alerted, holding the thing at a safe distance. 'Look!'

Jerry eyed the stained sheet. Across the torn midsection was the grinning sepia face of Jasper Maskelyne.

'Hey!' Jerry nodded to the fly poster. 'Aren't you a fan of his?'

'It's a sign, Dad!'

'Well, it was.'

'Huh?'

Mum,   30/02/2011

Frank called today. Frank is one half of the couple who
adopted me. They were always honest with me about that,
well, at least as far back as I can remember, which I suppose
is as good as always. When I was little, I refused to call them
Mum and Dad, and they couldn't bear to have me call them by
their first names, so I called them my no-parents. I never really
thought too much about this until my friend Mira said that they
probably felt hurt every time I said it. It was too late by then,
though. Like if someone had suddenly told me Mira's name
was something else, Claire or whatever, I'd still accidentally
call her Mira all the time. So for a little while I said things
like, 'Can you pass me the ketchup, no-Dad-sorry,' but they
said that was worse. They said instead of sounding like I was
apologising for not calling them Mum or Dad, it sounded like
I was apologising to them because they weren't those things.
Anyhow, now it's now, and Frank has been travelling for
a couple of years. He doesn't really care where he goes, he
just wants to be anywhere no-Mum isn't. Although he could
probably manage that even if he stayed in the house because
she doesn't come out of her room all too much these days.

They were fighting for about a year before Frank left. Mira
says it was probably longer and really their fighting had just
gotten so bad that they gave up trying to hide it from me. I'm
not entirely sure why they would fight, but I have a feeling
it was because I stopped being enough. Like maybe I wasn't
a good enough illusion anymore. For a while I wondered if

I had called them Mum and Dad maybe they wouldn't have separated, but it wouldn't have made anything any more true. So Frank rang today and he didn't ask about Julie. I knew he wouldn't because he never does, which is always a relief because ever since she stopped coming downstairs I haven't really had all too much to say about her. I could tell him I hear her crying sometimes. I could say that one time not too long after he left she got really drunk in the day and went out and got her hair cut the same way it is in their wedding photo, or how she then took their wedding photo down from above the TV and put it in a drawer. I could say that now someone has moved it from the drawer, too. I could say that when I have seen her, coming or going from the bathroom, she hasn't really been there. But instead he tells me where he is and I tell him how I haven't got anything worth saying. I don't think Frank has anything to talk about either, because no matter where he is he never has any stories, and that makes me think that, for the most part, wherever Frank goes he's still here, in this house, not-existing with no-Mum.

I don't know if Frank calls out of obligation or because he's lonely. I suspect he loves me, but I think he probably resents me as well, either for being the way I am or for not being like him. Whichever it is, he is fixated on something else now and he brings it up each time we speak. He tells me how he still hasn't found 'It'.

When Frank says 'It' he means this feeling he had a few years back when he visited Sanzhi. Sanzhi is a place in Taiwan where they were building this futuristic-looking resort, but they never finished it because a bunch of the guys working on it died, for one reason or another, so they just stopped. They just left it there, all those giant pods, half finished. It became pretty popular with photographers because, you know, it was this giant fucking anomaly in the landscape. Anyhow, some guy Frank used to work with said he was going to Sanzhi and Frank decided to go with him. Frank had turned his office into a darkroom that year because I had said

21

I wanted to be a photographer, and he got really eager about how photography was an interest we could share. By the time Frank left for Sanzhi, I was bored of focusing, pointing and clicking at things (but mostly I could never find anything worth remembering), so he pretty much had the darkroom to himself. I think this made his resolve to go on the trip and become some sort of great photographer even stronger. As though maybe he thought I'd realise I'd made a mistake in giving up, or maybe he just wanted me to be proud of him.

When Frank came back from Sanzhi he didn't really care about the dark room anymore. And perhaps that was when things began to change. When he started talking about 'It'. Frank's really well travelled, even as a kid his parents would fly him all over during school holidays, so he'd already been to a lot of places, seen a lot of different horizons. But Sanzhi really affected him. Frank would tell me how he enjoyed the heavy quiet of history. He'd been to the Pyramids and Rome and Auschwitz and this little medieval ghost town in Italy I forget the name of, you know, all the places people go, and he said that they were the kind of places with feelings language doesn't have the ability to explain. He said he could best fail to describe it as a form of elegant melancholy. Sanzhi, though, Frank was in love with Sanzhi. He said that it made him nostalgic for the future, but a future that was dead like the past. He would stammer when he tried to convey this idea to me, as though all of what he had and was would never be enough to justly portray this sublime concept. And that feeling, that absurd and unusual feeling of insignificance and wonder he had become infected with in Sanzhi, was 'It'.

They tore down Frank's sublime concept in 2008.

Myles

Potential last lines for a novel:
And so they were nowhere, closest to everywhere.
I began in reverse.

Chapter 4
Beginnings Are, and They Are Not
October 1936

For the eleventh time that hour, as the sun savagely attacked both his vision and patience, Bobby ambled down from the hot ladder to survey his creation. His week of labour was finally finished and, more importantly, it was perfectly horizontal. He knew this because he had balanced a marble on the top several times only to have it roll over one of the sides. But not this time. This time it remained perfectly still, refracting the afternoon sun in a contortion of illuminations across the grass.

'Bobby Baker the Illusion Maker?' a voice came from behind.

He turned, his chest electrified.

'Nice to meet you, ma'am,' Bobby ambled a few uncertain steps, limply offering his hand to the young girl belonging to the voice.

'Bobby Baker the Illusion Maker?!' she repeated, a smile flickering at the corners of her mouth as she erratically shook Bobby's fingers.

He followed her eyes to the sign and back again, squinting at her audacity, 'It rhymes.'

She squinted back at him, equipping a quizzical frown, one eyebrow arched higher than the other. Bobby met her frown and positioned his hands resolutely on his hips. Wordlessly, faces as weapons, they entered a stand-off. He was the gallant defender of his front lawn and she became a nomad of everything but. Manoeuvring his mouth into a wide smile whilst maintaining a maniacal frown, Bobby watched as the girl, in turn, arched her tongue up towards her nose and raised both eyebrows. Barely acknowledging his contender's move, Bobby slid his pinkie fingers into the corners of his mouth and stretched his eyes downwards with his thumbs. Absorbing his attack and nodding slightly, she rolled her head from shoulder to shoulder. The fingers in Bobby's mouth slackened in anticipation. Deftly, the girl flipped her eyelids inside out, dropped her mouth gormlessly open, and nestled her chin deeply back into her neck. Bobby stared in equal amounts of revulsion and awe.

'You look like a foot,' he said plainly, careful to not show any admiration in his indubitable defeat.

Behind Bobby, hidden by the sun's glare across a windowpane, a net curtain shifted. Observing the scene with trepidation, Anna wore a weak smile. She would not yet allow her hopes to inflate at the potential of her son making a friend. He had been thirteen years without one, and she had mostly come to accept this. Her heart now only prickled every time she heard laughter from troupes of children dotted around the town, but it hadn't been that long since the nights spent lying awake, infested with anxiety over the solitude of her only child. On the floor above Anna, separated from her by wood and cladding, air and dirt, paint and plaster, and a space larger than all of these things, another face appeared at another window. Jerry glanced at the unfolding scene and beamed.

Bobby had been working on his sign all that week, an endeavour which was paired with Anna dutifully moaning about stains not coming out of his school trousers and Jerry picking at the vivid yellows and purples drying in his hair. Looking down into their modest autumnal garden, Jerry observed the muted dance between children, grinning at their tiny arms flapping in wild gesticulation. The girl scooped a lemony lock of hair through her fingers and Bobby elaborately flung a hand skywards, indicating his stage name balanced atop a rickety forest of broom handles.

'Look!'

The girl cackled, doubling over and rendering Bobby momentarily mute. At his silence, she began half-heartedly attempting to compose herself, wiping her hand across her eyes and absently brushing tears onto her jumper. Bobby shook his head.

'A thousand men couldn't knock it down!'

The words were just loud enough to enter the house.

Jerry choked a hearty pulse of laugher, and Anna closed her eyes as the beatific sound resonated mutely through the floorboards and distantly down the staircase; he was watching them, too. She thought briefly of how two people could share both so much and so little, flicking a dull beat of contemplation towards when this could have happened – when growing together became growing apart – and concluded nothing but the glumly foreseeable osmosis of any one strong emotion into a tepid many.

Upstairs, Jerry leant an arm against the window. His cheeks were flushed with joy, still lost to the action below. The girl stepped towards one of the supporting broom handles, glancing briefly at Bobby's face transforming into a wide-eyed gawp. He anticipated her move. Mouth slack and gaping, his head slowly shook, left to right and back again, only once. Impishly, she smiled, raising her foot and swinging her leg forwards. He reached out hopelessly into the too-wide space between them, laughter tumbling from her throat at the sight of his marionette body. Then she stopped. Immediately. Supporting ankle wobbling only slightly as her foot hovered, abruptly frozen, an inch from the sign. He gawked at her raised leg and she winked back, gently tapping the post with the tip of her patent leather shoe. The wood barely quivered and he cried out, grasping the back of his skull. Bending over, the girl rooted a glass marble from the grass.

'Where on earth did this come from?!' she asked, analysing the sky.

'You're terrible!' shrieked Bobby, rubbing his hand over his head.

'I'm Rose Hartley,' she said, stubbornly. Then, softening her face and sighing, 'My parents just moved here from a county over. Nice to meet you, Bobby Baker.'

'My…' Bobby looked at Rose through watery eyes. She smiled coyly. Aware of a hotness in his cheeks, he continued, 'My name isn't Bobby Baker.' He looked towards his feet, 'My name's Bobby Sinclair.'

'But your sign…'

'Yes. I know what the sign says,' he snapped. 'But nothing rhymes with stupid Sinclair.'

'Pin-, bin-, fin-, lin-,' Rose reeled off nothing words until she fell silent, mutely continuing to mime syllables. 'No, I suppose it doesn't.'

'I told you so.'

'Well, I guess no one would call themselves Bobby Baker the Illusion Maker if they didn't have to.'

Bobby went to protest, but she was smiling at him and he found he was already grinning back.

'You should have heard my name before this,' he laughed. 'It was ridiculous!'

'This one's ridiculous!'

'You think of a better name then!'

'And what would I get out of it?' she rolled the marble between her fingers.

Bobby thought, his eyes holding hers.

'I'll show you something you've never seen before.'

Rose studied the strange boy standing in front of her, and she believed him.

'How do you know I've never seen it before?' she toyed.

'Because, Rose, no one has.'

Mum,   26/03/2011

I went to the Tiny Cemetery today. I let Iris come along
because she finds everything fascinating, but also because
Mira asked me to take her. Iris is Mira's grandmother, so she
falls somewhere between the ages of sixty-five and ninety. If
I was older I'd probably be able to guess her age a little more
accurately, but things in the distance are always hard to judge.
Iris says things like, 'When I was a girl, music came from the
heart, not computers,' and, 'Everything changes, strangers
become stranger.' Although, the thing about how everything
changes might have been a result of her Alzheimer's. Iris
hasn't said that she has Alzheimer's disease, but sometimes
she says things I don't understand so I assume her brain is
probably deteriorating.

Iris brought Mira up because Mira's mum died when she
was little, so whilst Mira had the mute sadness of growing
up without ever knowing her mother, Iris had the sadness of
complete emptiness, which is something that Iris says only
comes with losing a child. I don't know much about any of
that, but I think Mira mostly likes me because, as you know,
I've never met my parents either. Mira's dad left straight after
Iris offered to take her in. He was still quite young when
Mira was born. Iris says people make mistakes when they're
young but I'm not sure if she means his mistake was Mira or
choosing to leave her.

Mira is a lot like her grandmother, but her grandmother
is a lot like Mira, too. Which sounds like the same thing but

it isn't. I used to think about that a lot, well, not about Mira and Iris, but about free will. When I was fifteen I'd have these panic attacks. At the start I'd get hung up on whether I liked the things I liked for the things themselves or because of how they were seen by everyone else. Then I thought how everything I did and thought was caused by the constructs of society and language, how even the thoughts about how my thoughts were constructed by society and language were constructed by society and language, how I could never be anything outside of what I knew and I could never know anything outside of what I was, and then, well, I guess I eventually thought about all those connotations so much that I didn't exist anymore. Frank and Julie made me tell some doctors about my feelings because once I didn't stop screaming for a really long time. They put me on tablets and I stopped thinking so much.

When we got to the Tiny Cemetery, Iris didn't really say anything, she just stared at the three graves for a really long time. It's kind of strange how in a lot of ways it feels sadder with just the three of them there than it does when you're standing in the main city cemetery looking over generations of the dead. It's the same as when someone is murdered and you hear all about it on the news and it seems like a big deal, but then hundreds of people will get killed in a war and they're just a number. I think it was Stalin who pointed that out. I suppose our brains can't process something so terribly big. Sometimes I think if we could understand what it means to die, like if we could conceive of infinity, our hearts would just stop.

There's this black iron fence about a foot taller than I am that runs around the Tiny Cemetery. It would be ugly, that fence, but the Tiny Cemetery is this island of grass about the size of a large parking space at the end of a cul-de-sac, so it would just be surrounded by concrete and bricks and strangers anyway. Everything is relative. When we arrived the gate was unlocked. It's always unlocked. The Monster

28

threads the bolt across and places the padlock in a way that makes it looks shut, but he never presses it closed. Mira says it's so people won't try and get in but so the dead can still get out. She's always saying idiotic stuff like that. She's also the only real friend I have, unless you count Iris. I'm not disappointed about that.

There's a bench in the Tiny Cemetery. It's so small that if you sit on it with someone you should know them really well because your hips and shoulders will touch. The Monster keeps the Tiny Cemetery pretty well tended around the graves but there is wild grass growing up around the legs of the bench so you can't tell where the earth ends and the bench begins. It has the kind of effect that when you sit there you fade away.

When Iris had been sitting on the bench in silence for long enough for me to feel awkward, but also for my legs to ache from standing up for ages, I asked her what she was thinking. 'Everything unordinary', she said, without looking at me but at the graves. This wasn't an example of Iris' probable Alzheimer's disease, but the inscription on the plaque that has begun to sink into the wood of the bench, as though the oak is still a living, consuming thing. I sat down next to her, she smelt like fusty lavender and warm cinnamon, and we talked about 'Everything unordinary.' Iris thought it was marvellous, that plaque, and she believed it, too. She said, 'This tiny cemetery, it's a family of the dead living amongst the living dead.' I suspected *this* might be the Alzheimer's and nodded in agreement so she wouldn't get confused. Really I just thought 'Everything unordinary' seemed like something someone would say about what they had lost, because the type of lying people do when they romanticise something is the type of lying other people forgive them for. Then we left the Tiny Cemetery and Iris made us stop for burgers on the way home. I put too much ketchup on mine and Iris said, 'Did you want any burger with that ketchup?' and I laughed, which was right.

I'll write again soon.

Myles

Potential last lines for novels:
  And that was the last first time.
  I will.

Chapter 6
A Gargantuan Silence
December 1936

Bobby and Rose had been working on the show every evening for two weeks. That is, they had been working on the show whenever they were not amidst a battle of one-upmanship. A few days into their preparation, and moments after a heated discussion around the logistics of stage illumination, a fretful confession gushed from Rose; her parents, marginally dubious and wholly paranoid, were becoming suspicious as to her continued whereabouts.

'What if they won't let me help?' Rose panicked. 'All of our hard work would go to waste!'

'I could probably manage most of it alone,' Bobby shrugged, anxiety tearing at his stomach. 'But I suppose if you really want to help I could ask my father to speak to your parents.'

The click of the gate snapped closed, Rose's heel turned into the street, and Bobby hurled himself upstairs into Jerry's office.

'Dad!' he exploded, breathless. 'Rose mightn't be able to be my assistant if you don't speak to the Hartleys and tell them we're all right. That we won't kill her, or kidnap her, or maim her, or...'

'Slow down, kid,' swivelling in his chair, Jerry rested his hands on top of Bobby's shoulders. 'What's the problem with the Hartleys?'

'They won't let Rose come over anymore, they…'

'Probably want to meet your mother and me?'

'Is that… can they? Meet you, I mean.'

'I'll write them a letter. You can pop it over there tomorrow.'

'Thanks, Dad!'

'You're welcome,' Jerry turned to reach for a sheet of writing paper on top of his desk.

'Dad?'

'Yes?'

'What's the note going to say? Do you need any suggestions? Make sure they know we're not dangerous, say we're not dangerous.'

'I'm just going to invite them over for supper on Sunday. They can ascertain threat levels for themselves,' Jerry winked at his son, who furrowed his eyebrows and bit his lip.

'Don't…'

'Don't what?' he slid a fountain pen from his breast pocket and smoothed out invisible creases in the paper.

'Don't… don't tell them we're going to saw Rose in half.'

'Pardon me?'

'I meant to ask… we might need your help with that.'

#

Anna bustled, readying a selection of raspberry and apricot sandwiches on a granary loaf, cutting sausages into thirds and wrapping them in miniature bacon blankets, sugaring a bowl of strawberries, pouring a pot of cream, putting water on to boil for tea, and filling a pitcher of fresh lemonade. She finished by arranging the various platters delicately over a gingham oilcloth. Bobby walked into the kitchen, observed his mother's arrangement, and frowned.

'Have you entertained before, Mother?' he stared at her intently.

Anna looked from her son, to the supper she had just prepared, and back at her son, who raised his eyebrows.

'If my hard work doesn't meet your exacting standards I could always tell the Hartleys not to come after all.'

'Oh, no need!' Bobby's eyes widened. 'No, look at all this!' he raised his arms with exaggerated triumph. 'Besides, the pips in the lemonade will surely add a rustic quality.'

Lily and John Hartley arrived three minutes early with a Victoria sponge. The evening commenced in a convivial tone, with Jerry proving to be a genial host, noting appreciation for his modest lot in life and sprinkling a gentle wit throughout the conversation. After the initial pleasantries and perfunctory dialogue, it transpired Jerry and John had been in neighbouring battalions during the war. For Lily and Anna, this similarity was an abrupt catalyst into sisterhood, allowing them to transcend seamlessly from please-and-thank-yous to nattering all at once about fear and loneliness and relief.

Jerry, sore to his wife's ease at divulging his past, used the opportunity to steal John away from the women and into his mildly crooked shed. Jerry's shed contained nothing of Anna. No fastidious organisation, no tap-tap-tapping. No repetition. Amongst its less notable items, the shed held an oversized hodgepodge bookcase spilling well-thumbed encyclopaedias onto the bare floor, a toolbox hidden beneath a quilted blanket, an assortment of cigar boxes even though Jerry never smoked, and Jerry's collection.

John was three steps deep into Jerry's sanctuary, when he noticed the unusual assortment of found feathers, butterflies and moths pinned to every spare inch of wall space.

'Wow,' he nodded loosely toward the walls.

'Oh,' Jerry nodded. 'A passion of mine. Started with one,' he gestured to a chequered skipper pinned delicately above the window, 'and before I knew it I was surrounded.'

'Huh,' John turned slowly on his heels.

'Sit down,' Jerry nudged at one of the wooden chairs. Placing a basket on top of the blanketed toolbox, he began rummaging through its scavenged contents. He had swiped various bottles, glasses and utensils from the kitchen after he had stolen John from their wives. 'Drink?' Jerry manoeuvred the tops away from two bottles of Mather's Black Beer. He was friendly with the pub landlord and would often find various bottles left on his doorstep with hastily scrawled notes attached: *These just came in, let me know if they're mediocre enough for my rowdy bunch – Pete.*

Jerry and Pete had known each other since they were both children kicking a worn leather ball across Devil's Dyke. Each would secretly hope the other would hit the ball into the ditch and therefore have to venture into the dank water, which, to their short legs and young imaginations, was seemingly bottomless and undeniably treacherous. Since then the years had passed in a parade of staunch indifference, slowly luring the friends into a new routine. The current manifestation of which saw Jerry and Anna inviting Pete for dinner on the last Sunday of every month, with every dinner becoming a shadow of the last; Pete would talk about his dead wife whilst he sliced up his potatoes and they would nod silently as they cut into theirs.

Surrounded by remnants of both the dead and living, John and Jerry clinked the necks of their beers together and proceeded, as those on the precipice of friendship often do, to talk in strict edits about their lives, to lie about their wives, and reminisce, as honestly as nostalgia and memory permitted, about their childhoods. The war, the gargantuan black hole in the middle of their timeline, was not discussed. Both men aware their silence encapsulated everything words would so savagely smother.

By the time John left the shed that evening, Jerry had also neglected to mention the obtuse wooden construction propped up in one of its corners: the coffin he was building for John's daughter.

#

Jerry had been helping Bobby and Rose construct the coffin.

They didn't have the resources available to enable a practice run, so the live show would be the first time Bobby got to perform the illusion to completion. In actuality, the coffin was no more than a wooden box with brass handles, but to Bobby it was a casket fit for a god. Whilst Jerry constructed the coffin and Bobby helped as best he could by criticising and questioning, Rose had set about creating a papier-mâché sculpture of everything below her knees. Anna had melted hardened butter and cream remnants together over the stove and decanted the mixture for Rose, who rubbed it all over her legs in order to prevent the paste and paper from sticking to her skin. Bobby watched silently as his friend tore at newspapers, ripping streamers off the week's stories and shuffling the strips into neat piles, merging the beginnings, middles, and ends of the articles, rewriting history.

Rose giggled as she glued the paper strips around her legs. At first because it was cold and tickled, and then because the sensation of the paper hardening made her feel like she was turning into an android.

'Every time,' Rose slurred at Bobby as she concentrated on folding a strip behind her knee. 'Every time we go to visit Nana Blanche she moans about King George. She gets up on her high horse about the state of the country and questions my parents as though it's their fault. I get so bored and mad because no one ever tells her that her king is dead. So one time,' Rose stretched for another strip of paper, 'after Nana Blanche asked, "What exactly does the king think he's doing?" I told her he was rotting. She looked at me like I was evil and I'd stolen something from her. Like I shouldn't say such things about her precious king she loves to hate. After that, Mum and Dad bought me a whole bunch of sci-fi to read when we visit so I don't get bored and join in with the conversation, and with all this gunk my legs kind of feel like something from one of the stories. It's like they're mine but they're not made of me.'

'I'd like to read one of those stories one day,' Bobby

called to her as he stuck his face in close to Jerry's. 'Is that right, Dad?' he questioned. 'I'm not sure if you know what you're doing.'

An hour later, as Jerry went about sanding the exposed joins, Bobby diverted his attentions entirely to Rose, who began carefully cutting herself out of the casts. He gasped as she lifted the first one away. Newspaper print had stained in licks and curls along her calves.

'Rose,' he laughed. 'You've got a ransom note on your skin!'

Mum,   05/04/2011

Do you ever get scared about what's underground? Not the
soil and rocks and lava, but things that are unexpected. Things
like monuments. Things like the foundations of fallen cities.
Large things. Discovering the heads at Easter Island had
bodies concealed underneath really terrified me and I don't
know why. I didn't like knowing there was this huge hidden
mass. I hate the blue whale at the Natural History Museum,
too. And ships out of water. I don't know if that's the same fear
as the fear of hidden things, but it feels similar in that it's the
opposite. Knowing there was a really big statue in the ground
under my feet would make my knees weak. There's a smaller
version of Christ the Redeemer in the ocean somewhere and
I hate it passionately. This is why I didn't go on the school
trip to Stonehenge; what if there are extra bits they never
found? I guess I just hate knowing there's always so much
more unknown beneath the surface, and the idea of seeing it so
completely is overwhelming. Also whales are unnaturally big
and the sea is a mistress best left to her own devices.

Yesterday, Mira texted me saying, *I just cried whilst
reading the lyrics to 'Star Spangled Banner', time to buy
some tampons.* Which elicited two reactions in me. One:
why the hell is she texting me that? Two: I should read the
lyrics to 'Star Spangled Banner'. So I googled 'Star Spangled
Banner', as well as googling *spangled* separately because I
don't think I've ever seen it used to describe anything else.
Then I googled *spackled*, because I wasn't sure if it was a

word. It was. I tried it for all the vowels; *spuckled*, *speckled*, *spockled*, *spickled*, and found only spackled and speckled existed. That leaves three pieces of prime lexicon real estate unused. I'd love to be the person who gives words life. Why aren't we using all the iterations? There's always more ways to think and feel, maybe today I feel spuckled. Spuckled: the ironic longing for a more vehement sadness.

My biggest secret, a secret I've never said out loud, is that I'm afraid I won't be sad enough when people die. When Sam died it was weird, and I was numb and quiet, but he'd had cancer for so long that death became a part of our friendship. The same way you might put up with someone who is a close-talker, or someone who doesn't wash very much, because you like them. To be friends with Sam was to be friends with death. But I'm scared that a family member or a friend will die without warning and I'll go on as though nothing happened. I'm scared that if I'm not with them when they die I won't notice any change. Like eternal object permanence. And, really, if I never go and visit them after they're dead and see the space they've left behind, how would it be any different than them just being somewhere else forever?

I've imagined Frank and Julie dying, and I don't feel very sad about it. I feel guilt. I feel guilty about my fear of not feeling enough, and I'd feel guilty after they died that their son wasn't destroyed by their deaths. I'd obviously feel guilty about their lives, too. About the smallness of their lives. The loneliness. The averageness. The nothingness. But I don't think I'd be sad. For me or them. When people break down and sob at funerals, are they crying for themselves or for the dead?

The other part of my secret is how I'm scared that when someone dies I'll feel so sad, so completely and complexly sad, that I won't be able to do anything ever again.

Myles

Potential last line for a novel:

    I kept digging, and cried and pressed clumps of earth into my clothes and hair and face, and I knew that this was it… this dark.

Chapter 8
Things in the Dark
December 1936

The hall was so dark and silent that he was finding it difficult to believe it was still full with people. A slight shuffling traced its way around the room as those who found their limbs numb or itching moved to compensate themselves. He was running late, and there had been the background buzz of multiple in-between conversations thick in the air as he cut the lights, conducting a silence. His audience, having been taught that time makes things sweeter, traded their impatience for anticipation. They were quiet with expectation. He was silenced with fear.

'Bobby!' Rose whispered sharply.

'Sorry,' he said. 'I don't think I can go out.'

'I thought you'd done this before?'

'I have... I. This is different.'

'How?'

Bobby looked towards her voice. Heart on fire.

'It's too late to back out now!'

'I could run away.'

'You wouldn't last a day without clean sheets!'

'That's... well, that's true,' he shook out his arms and legs.

'Bobby!'

'Okay! Okay.' He swallowed, 'Here goes everything.'

'Ladies and gentlemen,' Rose boomed over the Tannoy. 'Please give a rapturous round of applause for the illustrious

Primo Chicane!' Bobby never let on to Rose how much he liked the name she had given him, and Rose never told Bobby he didn't have to, she already knew.

A wall of applause built to meet Bobby, shuffling his way through the darkness to the middle of the well-worn stage. Slowly feeling in front of each careful step with the tips of his toes, he attempted to locate the bucket he had placed centre stage before the show. His left foot came into contact with the tin first, causing a gentle tinkering as the bucket scooted a few inches forward. Reaching downwards, he grasped the rim with his fingers.

'Now!' screamed Bobby.

Rose flicked a switch, illuminating the young magician. With the light engulfing his platform, Bobby thrust the bucket forward, alleviating its contents over the crowd; a poorly distributed cloud of glitter, tiny balls of rolled up crepe paper and sequins dowsed itself over those in the audience seated front and centre. The cloud dispersed almost as immediately as it began, revealing Bobby and bucket standing in front of a large painted mural, elaborately displaying the words *Primo Chicane*.

For the most part, Bobby's show went smoothly. Silk flowers bloomed, coins danced and cards revealed themselves on cue. The small audience, perched across the community room's fold out chairs, was politely receptive, gently applauding or cheering at Bobby's grander feats. Only one small error was made; Bobby accidentally revealed all of his playing cards to be red during a flamboyant shuffling sequence. His mistake spurred muffled laughter to puff towards him like gleeful smoke from the front row. Giving the hall a brief glance, he was relieved to note no one further back had noticed. Those laughing were still flecked and glittering from his opening sequence.

The evening's crescendo was to be the fruit of the last three weeks' work. As the lights dimmed once more, Rose wheeled the coffin, settled atop two adjoining steel tables, onto the stage. The squeak of rusty wheels screamed obtrusively into the dark with every rotation, eerily disguising the rustle of Bobby sharply wiggling his arm back and forth so Rose could navigate the stage safely towards him.

'I'm ready,' whispered Bobby, receiving the coffin and rolling it into its final position.

Shimmying onto the lid, Rose dangled her legs over the side and raised one arm into the air, 'Me, too.'

A pair of sneezes screeched out from the back of the hall.

'Well, turn the lights on then!' shot Bobby from the side of his mouth.

'I thought you wanted me sitting on the coffin when it started!' she hissed.

'I do!' he paused, realisation smacking into him. 'Rose, we didn't think about the lights!'

'You reckon?!'

'Well, get off and go do it!'

'You go do it!'

A cough from the audience was followed by a gentle tittering to stage left.

'I am Primo Chicane and you are my assistant, turn the lights on!'

'I am Rose Hartley and I am your friend, *Bobby Sinclair.*'

Bobby's shoulders sagged, but a small smile parted his lips, 'You're my *best* friend, Rose.'

He had never told her that before. The words trailed off towards her disembodied voice and the darkness was his courage. He believed the things people did in the dark were done by the parts of themselves they kept best hidden. *She's not saying anything. Why isn't she saying anything?* His heart scrambled higher in his throat just as illumination brought the collective shadow of the audience looming before him. Bobby recoiled. As his eyes adjusted to the light and his mind scrambled to resume its previous thoughts, a tiny figure scurried in from stage left, jumping neatly onto the coffin in front of him. The scene struck him as momentarily ominous.

Rose was already raising her arms in the air. Shaking his head sharply, forcing the now into focus, Bobby walked around to the front of the coffin and arranged his body into the most grandiose position he could muster; he puffed out his chest, rolled his shoulders backwards and held his hands out slightly to the sides, palms facing upwards.

'Tonight, fellow appreciators of the extraordinary and lovers of the unlikely,' he awkwardly flourished his arms, 'I will cut a woman in half!'

The audience pantomimed *ooh* and *aah* as Bobby twisted Rose and her coffin around 180 degrees, careful not to expose the bottom end to the crowd. Jumping down, Rose gestured emphatically to her friend and his new toy, conducting another small burst of applause. Bobby propped the wooden lid up towards the audience, shielding the interior, and affording Rose the opportunity to climb in. A smile caught on his lips as he saw the poster he had tacked to the inside; the battered face of Jasper Maskelyne grinned back at him.

Bobby ran his wand through his fingers, shuffling his feet as Rose lowered herself down into the coffin. She slid the moulds of her legs, which had been concealed inside and adorned in socks and plimsolls to match her own, through the holes at the foot of the casket. Then, waving her hand out over the lid toward the audience a final time, she sunk onto her back. Inside the coffin, Rose's fake legs were attached to strings of elastic, which were then hooked over a pair of brackets, threaded out through a hole in the bottom, and back through near the top.

Rose twisted the elastic around her fingers and stuck her head through the biggest hole, a large oval Jerry had carved into the top section of wood. Bobby closed her inside. The audience cheered, and she beamed at them, her fake legs subtly moving up and down from the elastic pulley system. Maintaining a smile, Rose started slowly curling her body up into the top half of the coffin. Jerry had attached a thin wooden ridge around the inside so she could feel when she was

43

tucked away neatly enough for Bobby to commence sawing. Rose was slight and young, but she was no contortionist, so Jerry had ensured the coffin was plenty big enough for her to comfortably curl up in. The coffin was so big, in fact, that the illusion would have been entirely suspicious if it wasn't for her ever-moving feet sticking out of the bottom.

'Are. You. Ready?!' Bobby marshalled a mildly booming voice and his audience greeted him positively.

'Yes,' Rose whispered, tracing her finger around the half-way ridge.

Bobby began sawing the coffin along a thin pencil line drawn around the outside. Jerry had traced it so that it sat a couple of inches below the inner ribbing, and parallel with the gap between the tables. The audience waited patiently as Bobby cut into the wood and Rose pretended to flinch beneath the oncoming blade.

As the minutes passed, Bobby's sawing slowed and Rose's squirming lost its urgency. The audience began to murmur. Bobby had yet to reach the halfway point and his arm was becoming increasingly tired. Simultaneously, Rose's screams became less intense, her voice cracking under use. Bobby didn't dare look up. He could feel sweat lining his eyes, drenching the bridge of his nose and dripping off of his chin. He kept sawing.

A few minutes more and Bobby had cut down almost to the table on both sides. Only the thick bottom panel remained. His cheeks flushed red from exertion and embarrassment under hot lights, his hand throbbed, his wrist ached, and his elbow cried tight and heavy. Chubby tears started pushing themselves free from behind his eyes. He was exhausted. It was taking too long. It *had* taken too long. He wanted to run off stage and leave everyone behind. He wanted to sit in his cupboard and hide until no one remembered who he was or what he did.

A conversation slowly bloomed from a few voices to the front-left of Bobby, and another to the back of the hall.

He strongly suspected most of his audience were no longer paying attention. Perhaps no one was paying attention. Or worse, perhaps everyone was awaiting the perfect opportunity to begin jeering, mocking his incompetence, and ridiculing his interests. The idea of giving up was becoming an icy glass of water on a hot day. If he walked away now it could all be over as quickly as it had begun. His hand began to shake. He glanced towards the stage exit. His feet quivered an imaginary step to freedom.

A single, loud slap burst from the midst of the sprouting discussions. Then another. Again. Bobby stole a quick glimpse upwards but the spotlight and his subtlety stopped him from detecting anything of consequence. However, the brief movement was enough to displace the sweat gathered on his forehead. Streams of liquid rushed towards his eyes, forcing them shut. Bobby began fitfully blinking in an attempt to clear his stinging vision. He was still sawing, jagged and weak, but he was going to leave, he was going to leave now. *Right now.* A bleating gasp rang out from the girl below him.

He stopped everything. Browned his white sleeve wiping it across his dripping face, and looked up. There, a shadow in the middle of the room, was Jerry. His father stood staring directly at him, clapping. Bobby frowned slightly as the sight of the lone man silenced some of the nattering. And, in turn, the fast quiet of the few caught the attention of the many, who quickly followed suit and shuddered to a quiet. Staring at his father, an accidental collection of tears thudded from his chin and onto his magician's scarf. Just as the beat of a second salty cluster landed, darkening the violet fabric to purple, he saw John rise beside Jerry. John briefly patted Jerry on the shoulder, and raised both hands, applauding along with his friend. Bobby looked down at Rose, who twisted her head towards him, a massive smile across her face.

'C'mon, Primo!' she urged, trying to wink at him against the restricted angle of her neck.

Bobby gritted his teeth and inhaled deeply, his heartbeat

was heavy in his ears as it chased itself through his body faster and faster, dog and tail. Tightening his grip on the saw handle, he looked back to Jerry one last time, but he was greeted by new sight. Anna and Lily were standing alongside Jerry and John, and next to them strangers were rising to their feet. Most of his father's row were now standing, and the one behind them, and the one behind them. The sound of cheap wooden chairs being pushed back screeched wildly around the room. More and more people were rising to their feet, their hands rhythmically parting and closing in time with Jerry.

'You can do it, son!' yelled Jerry, clapping louder and faster, the rest of the room keeping beat alongside him.

'Show us what you can do, kid!' came a call from somewhere to his left.

'Primo! Primo! Primo!' a chant started off amongst those in the back right. Bobby recalled a glimpse of Pete sitting there before he had started his act.

Fresh tears ran freely down Bobby's face as he thrust the saw forward with a new wave of vigour, cheers falling into rhythm with his movement. After the last of his strength had abandoned him, and as he was pushing forward with hollow arms, the saw finally fell between loose halves of wood. Slowly sliding the blade out, he unsteadily placed it on the stage floor beside him and flexed his hand, which was stubbornly quivering and resolutely fixed into the shape of the handle.

Adrenaline and exhaustion duelling in his veins, Bobby rotated Rose and the top of the coffin around until her head was facing the audience. He then swivelled the bottom around to meet it, aiming her fake feet into the crowd. As the two ends came to rest beside one another, horror darkened Bobby's expression; the audience had fallen silent. All eventualities for what might have gone wrong ran through his mind simultaneously. He swallowed without looking down.

'I feel awfully peculiar,' Rose announced.

A new applause swelled. Foot stamping and sharp

whistling bounded about the room. Rose's fake feet were conducting a jagged dance, parallel to her face, in the half-coffin beside her.

Eventually, after a stilted attempt at leaving wherein many members of the audience shook Bobby's hot palm and generally steeped congratulations upon him, the six of them walked home. Bobby understood that most of the positive reactions had been because he was young, or perhaps to show good faith to his father because Jerry knew a lot of people around town, but he also strongly suspected that he'd done a pretty spectacular performance. As they walked, he and Rose dawdled a few paces behind their parents, occasionally sword fighting with Rose's second legs.

'You did good tonight, Sinclair,' Rose swiped a leg at the back of Bobby's knees but he jumped out of the way before she had chance to connect.

'You too, Hartley,' Bobby swung a plimsoll laden foot at her face.

Rose ducked and laughed, pushing him gently in the side with her elbow, 'Hey, we had a deal. I came up with the best name ever, but you never showed me something no one else has ever seen.'

'I completely forgot about that, you're going to love it.'

Mum,   19/04/2011

It was my birthday this week, but I guess you knew that. This year was mostly as pleasant as I could have hoped, and would have been entirely lovely if I didn't feel guilty about things. Sometimes I feel guilty about the Tiny Cemetery or about Julie or Frank, but I feel guilty about other things too, things that might not even be things, like if I lose something, or whenever I remember I'm not who I thought I'd be. I told Mira about this once and she said that if I felt guilty about everything for too long then suddenly I'd be an old man lying in a bed feeling guilty about having felt guilty for so long. That didn't help.

Iris and Mira cooked me a huge birthday meal, and they didn't invite Julie as she was still in the bedroom and they didn't invite Frank because he wasn't in the bedroom, but they were there and I was there and that seemed like everybody. Iris made this soup that I love, potatoes and carrots and leeks and onions, which doesn't sound special but it's my favourite so I'd rather have that than a fancy meal with too many forks. Mira cooked mashed potatoes because they're my other favourite, and also because Mira can't cook anything else, then she made the mash into a round trough on my plate and Iris ladled her soup into it. Iris and Mira had potato troughs too, and we all joked about how it looked like a scene from *Close Encounters*. But then we all had to be careful about how we ate it so the walls stayed high enough to keep everything from spilling out. After we'd finished, Mira put the plates in the already full sink, opened the fridge and pulled out a giant chocolate cake.

Iris' kitchen is super small and full of clutter and knick-knacks and mismatched wooden furniture, with two dressers wedged into the only wall space. One is from before Paul disappeared and is full of jars and cups and doilies and photographs, and the other is from the time after that. The newer one is filled with all the same type of stuff, except these things are less faded and dusty. No one ever touches anything on the old dresser. It just sits there like a ghost in the corner whilst the other dresser and its jars and cups are used and cleaned and used and broken.

Mira told me that when Iris was young she and Paul had been really close. Apparently, in secondary school, they had gone on an obligatory trip to an open country estate, and Iris had fallen in love with a dresser she had seen there. Paul had probably asked Iris out about a dozen times before they went on that school trip, and she kept refusing him by saying they were just really good friends, but Mira told me that the real reason was because Iris had a crush on Cary Grant and would joke that Paul looked more like Boris Karloff. Anyhow, one time Iris didn't see Paul for a few weeks so she assumed it was because they had exams coming up and he was revising, although she wasn't really sure and kind of missed him a lot.

Then one day, Paul arrived at Iris' parents' house unannounced, asking her to come outside, and in her garden was a replica of the dresser from the country estate. He had been spending all that absent time making it for her. Iris was overwhelmed and really happy, not just because of the dresser but because Paul was there, then Paul got down on one knee and asked her to marry him. Iris said yes, even though they were too young, because he was her best friend and she had missed him. Paul did really badly in his exams because he was building the ghost dresser instead of revising, but I don't think he could have been spending all that time making it because, if I'm honest, it's pretty ugly.

So that was that for twenty years, until Paul disappeared. Mira's mother was incredibly young when it happened, so Iris had to try and never feel all too much about it for her sake. Thing was, Paul didn't die or walk out on them, and he wasn't hiding somewhere making another dresser, he just disappeared. I mean, he must have done one of those things, but no one has ever known which, or why. Everyone saw him leave work the day he disappeared, but no one saw him come home. One of his friends told the police how Paul had said he was looking forward to getting home for a big dinner that night because he was starving and Iris was cooking steak. There were no signs that Paul knew he was going to leave. None of his belongings were missing, and he hadn't been acting strangely. You know, nothing at all was different that day. He just stopped *being*.

When Mira told me that story the first thing I asked her was if anyone ever ended up eating the steak. She frowned, then laughed at me, but I wasn't making a joke because I genuinely wondered. The steak was for Paul, and Iris had cooked for them both, but then Paul disappeared even though she still had his steak. And Iris has kept the ghost dresser frozen for all this time… like, maybe Iris thought if she still had the steak Paul might still come home to eat it. Or if she threw it away, how did she feel about that, when in some other future that was Paul's steak? I don't know, I guess I just wondered if Iris ever felt the same way about the steak as Frank does about Sanzhi. People are always so different at being the same.

Anyway, Mira pulled this giant chocolate cake out of the fridge – the tray was so large it covered half of the tiny wooden table – and got some plates from the living dresser. There was far too much cake for the three of us, but Iris said it would keep for a few days and that there can never be too much cake. Mira lit the candles that she had sporadically stabbed through the icing, and I blew them out as Iris told me to make a wish. I didn't make a wish. When we had finished eating, Mira said it was time for my present, stacked the crumby plates on top of the soupy ones, pulled a box out from somewhere that seemed like nowhere, and handed it to me as Iris clunked around making a cup of tea.

The gift was signed from both of them, which was a relief as I was already beginning to feel bad for the trouble they had gone to, and I had been mostly preoccupied with when to offer to do the washing up ever since I'd finished my soup. I opened the box and inside was a pen. I could tell it was expensive from the weight. Iris had got *Everything unordinary* inscribed along the barrel. I looked at Iris as I held their gift and she smiled at me. The sunlight from the window behind her was visible through her thinning hair, and I could see the wrinkles on her hands trace themselves around the edges of the tea tray. Her whole life of possibilities had come before this moment and yet here she was, standing beside a ghost dresser in a tiny kitchen, holding a tray of tea out for me, *smiling*. And I felt guilty again.

I think 'possibility' can be a dangerous word sometimes.

Myles

Potential last lines for a novel:
Possibly.
They lived together, but that was all they did.

Chapter 10
Regarding Perspective
November 1939

Rose turned the page and stole a glance a Bobby. She knew he had stopped listening sometime around when Jo told Meg it was Laurie who had written the love letter, but she kept reading anyway. It was their Sunday tradition; she would sit on his bed and read to him whilst he would lay across the floor and sketch out new ideas for illusions. Bobby had amassed an array of well-worn notebooks, full of descriptions scrawled beside drawings of false-bottomed boxes, spring-loaded whirligigs, and intricate cogged contraptions.

'Rose,' Bobby spoke tentatively. 'Do you think that maybe *Little Women* is perhaps rather a bit of a book that might be more inclined towards those of the female persuasion?'

'Do you think that there is perhaps the slightest of chances that you could have maybe made your question even more needlessly drawn out?'

'I just thought that maybe since we have this arrangement that we could read something slightly more neutral, like *Dracula*, or something. Naturally I'd understand if you were too afraid.'

'Quick!' she shouted. 'I must immediately get a copy of *Dracula* to prove to a teenage magician that I am not afraid of fictitious creatures!' She shook her head. 'Nice try, idiot.'

'I hate you.'

'I hate you, too.'

Bobby rolled a corner of his notebook into a thin straw, and then out again.

'You want to do something, Rose?'

'We are doing something.'

'You know what I mean,' Bobby threw a pillow at his friend.

'Like what?'

'I don't know… let's have an adventure.'

'All right, Enid Blyton, what do you suggest?' she raised an eyebrow.

'I don't know,' his tone changed. 'It's just that we're sixteen now, and I think, maybe, we should, well, *feel* more.'

'Are you saying that us hanging out in your bedroom all the time isn't utterly exhilarating?'

'I don't know. It's not even that, I just sometimes think that we should do things that we'll be able to share for ever.'

'I'm not quite aboard, Captain. Could you extend the gangway?'

'I'm just saying that we share all this time together, and that's great and amazing, but then I think maybe one day you, we, we'll look back at this and not really remember it, it won't really be anything. Like, say if you went on a beach holiday with someone else and you had an amazing time, you'd look at that person and remember that time and associate them with that, but we just kind of sit around here, and sometimes I think that one day you'll, *we'll*, just associate each other with nothingness.'

'Don't you think maybe it's the people you can do nothing with who are the ones you'll remember for ever?'

He half smiled, 'All I know is that I'm afraid they won't be.'

Bobby looked at Rose. Not that he needed to; he knew every line and hue of her skin, the tendrils of sky blue amidst the grey of her eyes, the asymmetrical line of her hair. He knew it all and sometimes he got scared that one day he wouldn't. He was scared she'd change and his image of her wouldn't be *her* anymore and, in turn, they would no longer be them.

Sometimes, when he thought about it, when he really thought about it, at night when he was all the things he never was in the light, he wondered who he would be without her.

'In that case, it's lucky for us that you'll always be the boy who showed me something no one else has ever seen.'

'Well, there is that,' he grinned, pulling himself away from his own thoughts and back into the room.

A loud banging shook the house from downstairs. Bobby watched the glass in his window shudder in its frame.

'WHAT WAS IT ALL FOR?!' screamed David, barging past Anna, who breathlessly clung to the door she had hastily opened before it splintered. 'Where's Jerry?'

'He's upstairs,' Anna's voice came out even meeker than usual. 'He's in his office with John.'

David, who had been one man before the war and an entirely different one after, awkwardly marched up the wooden staircase shouting Jerry's name. Bobby and Rose exchanged a look of confusion, quickly scurrying to the bedroom door and competing with each other for the best listening space, all the while shushing each other's shushes as they strained to hear what the commotion was about.

'Dave!' greeted Jerry. 'You've met John.'

'John,' David nodded curtly, and promptly addressed Jerry. 'What the fuck were we doing? What the hell did we do all that for, just for this? We crucified this country and for what? Answer me that, Jerry!'

Rose's nose was inches away from Bobby's and she could feel his breath tickling her cheek. They both had an opposite ear pushed against the door. Bobby smelled the perfume of Rose's hair, and tried to secretly keep it inside of him, memorising the sweet vanilla of her.

'He's talking about the war,' she whispered.

'I wondered when this would happen,' he looked down at his hands, squeezing the blood in the tips of his fingers, trying to think about nothing so he didn't have to think about everything.

'You okay?' she put a hand on his arm.

'Fine,' her touch ran ice and fire into his spine.

'He'll be all right, Bob. Dad's there, Dad seems to calm him.'

Rose was right. Jerry had always struggled to come to terms with his experiences in the war. He never told anybody what exactly it was he went through, but the strength of his relationship with the past never diminished, it just manifested in different ways. Bobby suspected none of Jerry's coping mechanisms had ever provided him with any solace. At first, Jerry had tried to create, tried to make something where everything had been destroyed. Then Bobby was born, and Jerry's anger transformed into a sustained need for retribution. He wanted to blame someone, anyone, for what happened. He thrived off a desire to rise and conquer, he just never had anything or anyone to battle. As the years went on he began to internalise his feelings, often removing himself from the company of others in order to spend time alone. Throughout Jerry's frustrations, he had never levelled his anger against Bobby. Bobby was his talisman of forgetting, of ignoring, of pushing everything aside in order to understand all that he felt as a father.

Regardless of Jerry's attempts, Bobby was still far from ignorant of his father's traumas. His childhood was screams in the night, slights toward Anna, and occasionally discovering pieces of broken china Jerry had missed when hiding the remnants of his outbursts. Things had been better since John. *Since Rose*. Bobby never knew for sure, but he assumed that maybe John was able to shoulder some of the weight from Jerry's past. Maybe John could relate. Maybe John had shared his own experiences. Maybe Jerry had simply swapped his weight for John's, and vice versa. Whatever had happened, they seemed to negotiate their burden between them much better than Jerry had ever done alone.

Down the hall from the door that functioned as a conduit for eavesdroppers, who were patiently straining to catch every word, David launched into a monologue.

'I remember getting home one day, in the last days of winter after the war, and my room smelt of hot sweat and cold chips. Hell, it smelt of despair. The sweat was from a pile of shoes I kept heaped in a corner, the cold chip smell was from the greasy papers that filled my kitchen after I'd bought supper out every night for a fortnight. And the despair? Well, shit, that was me: cheap whiskey and no shower but the rain. I looked around. My fish were dead. They were just there, motionless in their own shit. Cigar ash floating on the surface. *This is it*, I thought. *This is it*. So I limped over to my couch and sat down, dislodging a sheet of dust. And here's the thing, I had a fondness towards my limp, yeah? It was still new. It wasn't time addled yet. It had changed me. Not emotionally or some shit like that, it was just a limp, but this change was in the face of a stagnant decade and I could define myself by it. Like a pin in a map. Life was progressing. I'd done fuck all before that but then the war happened and it brought me to life and it destroyed my knee and I progressed. It was all happening in order. Our bodies are okay at first then they fuck up. It's like, fucking, entropy or something. It just felt like I wasn't so far out of the loop that I evaded time passing all together. We had won.

'So I sat down, unwound the scarf part way from my neck, and thought about myself. I was there with my fucking limp and my dead fish and this woollen noose and I thought fuck it. I was part of something. I had moved forward. I had helped move everything forward. The next day I threw out the chip grease. Since then I've had a history, I had *my* limp and *my* history. And now what? Now they want to take it all away from me by saying that my war didn't mean anything? That we're back where we started? That we're entering another war, and me and my bum leg and my bum life aren't even up for fighting in this one? That we're back at square one, and I'm nothing again? Fuck them... *fuck them*,' David had shouted most of his speech, but whispered his final words.

Sagging and defeated, he looked to John and Jerry for help, knowing there was none to be had.

'This is a different war, Dave,' Jerry consoled. 'Ours stands alone, you were there and you existed. We all did.'

'No war is different,' David countered. 'No war will ever be different until we're different.'

Bobby turned and fell back against the door. The men had left for Pete's to continue their discussion, or to drink until it didn't matter anymore. Rose filliped lint off of his collar.

'Thoughts?' she turned, sliding down beside him.

'I'm just glad I'm too young to be conscripted.'

'Me, too.'

'You're a girl, you wouldn't have to go anyway.'

'No, fool. I'm glad *you're* not old enough.'

'Baloney.'

'What? You don't think I'd miss you annoying me all the time?' she nudged the soft part of his side.

'Really?'

'Of course I would. Who else would I get to cut me in half and ignore me whilst I read them fantastic literature?'

Bobby looked at her, his eyes darted between hers and down to her lips. A soft smile crept up at the corners of her mouth, and his heart helter-skeltered up into his throat. He would never be hungry ever again. *I could kiss her*, he thought. *Right now, I could kiss her, here, in my bedroom, when we're both sixteen and have never known anything greater than each other. Now,* he thought. *Kiss her now.*

Bobby sighed and turned, rolling his head back against the wooden panel of the door. His bravado dissipating as quickly as it had risen. Relief and disappointment flooded him. From the corner of his eye he saw her head lower slightly, and traitorous cells inside him hoped it was in frustration. That maybe she too had wanted to kiss him, *finally*, after three years of everything that comes before. Encouraged, Bobby turned to look at her again, but her face was tilted away. His skull slunk forwards in heaviness and his hand snaked a nail along the floorboards. Scratching the dust out from the grain, he picked the dirt from his thumb and rubbed the curl of grime between his fingers, noticing Rose's hand draped loosely over her knee. Ruby painted nails glistening freely in the air. He swallowed. Reaching out slowly, his palm ambushed by sweat and heat, he gently slid his hand over the top of hers. Freezing for a second – a second that almost never ended, the second before she responded – and melting again as she turned her hand to welcome his. He slipped his fingers between hers, and she held them gently together.

Sitting in silence, looking across the room and through the window at the night sky, they were slowly enclosed in darkness.

Mum,   15/05/2011

I've got an interview next week to work in the City Library, which sounds like it wouldn't be a terrible job, only nowadays you supposedly need some sort of diploma or a decade of experience to be able to understand how to put books in the order they're numbered, so I'm only being considered for the basement. The basement is where they keep all the old books that have been too badly mistreated to keep on the for-loan shelves, or extra copies of books that aren't as popular as they used to be.

During the tour they gave us potential employees, one of the librarians said they don't hand the old books over to charity anymore as it's too much paperwork, or something. I laughed at that but I was the only one who did. Some guy with a mossy beard who smelt like bananas and mould frowned at me whilst I was laughing. He was probably about twice my age and I suspected he might feel worse than I did about being there, so I whispered to him about how books are made from paper so of course it was a lot of paperwork, but he just sort of squinted at me then asked the librarian if there was a coffee machine. There was.

I got a birthday present from Frank. It was late because of logistics, and I wouldn't have really minded if he forgot anyway, so I said not to worry when he called to ask if I liked it and I said there wasn't an it. He apologised, saying there must have been a problem. Frank's friend ended up delivering my present two days ago and I didn't know what to say, or how to thank Frank because I can't call him as I never know where he is, but it's pretty much the best thing I could ever imagine. Frank's friend told me it's a goldendoodle; three parts gold and one part doodle. Twelve weeks old. I don't really know how any of that makes a difference, but I do know that he looks beautiful and simple all at the same time, and smells like hot rain.

I've named him Montecore because I think it's a pretty good name, but also because the first night I had him he would cock his head to one side, look at me, and make these noises that could have been words if they had more sounds, so I looked straight back at him and asked him what he wanted and he said *mooreeeouuree*, which didn't sound entirely like Montecore but sounded even less like anything else.

When I went to sleep last night he was lying at the foot of my bed, but when I woke up his whole body was curled together in a little dirty cream-coloured spiral on the pillow next to my face, and I could feel his breathing against my ear. I already like him more than anything else.

This morning I went and made us sandwiches for breakfast, and we ate them whilst watching a TV show about other people's junk. I don't know why people like sitting in a house of junk, watching other people talk about or sell similar junk, but they must do because this show has been on in the morning for as long as I can remember. Unless everyone is just watching it because there's nothing else on, or they can't find the remote control – like I couldn't – so they just watch it anyway, and then the TV companies think people like it and the cycle goes on and on. That probably happens with a lot of things. It's kind of like that phrase, 'If it ain't broke don't fix it', except nobody knows it's broke so nobody tries to fix it.

I'm going to invite Iris along when I walk Montecore sometimes because she doesn't get out of the house much, and Mira says being in there with the ghost dresser isn't good for her. Iris is alone most afternoons as Mira works at The Other Day. When Mira started working at The Other Day, it was a second-hand bookstore called Book on the Bright Side. Book on the Bright Side had a teapot and a kettle, so they'd say they were a café, too. There was a little triangular table in the corner with these two rickety chairs around it for people to drink at. I remember one of the legs of the table was shorter than the other two, so there was always a copy of some unloved book propping it up to save hot drinks from spilling. It's all changed, now.

The Other Day is a café with a second-hand book section. They have a whole bunch of mismatched tables and twelve types of coffee bean, and there's just this one shelf that runs around the top of the walls, where the picture rail would be, that holds all the old books. For the most part people can't even reach those books. I think the owners like that. I think they just like the books being there for the way they look. All those stories, those characters, that work, it's just sitting there ignored as people consume coffees like it's an activity. And whilst they're drinking they're talking about the junk they saw on the TV that morning. All of it, the drinking and the talking and the junk, it makes me feel guilty so I don't like to visit Mira when she's working very often.

I'm writing this at my desk. Sometimes I'll write to you from here, or from the Tiny Cemetery, or from Mira's house. I used to sit here when I was younger and imagine I was the captain of a ship. Frank and Julie's house is on the top of a hill, so when I look out of my bedroom window I can see the tops of these ragtag grey houses rambling steeply down the tiny road. I used pretend they were waves. My desk is nestled right into the bay window so it gets pretty cold in the winter as we don't have heating upstairs, but I figure a ship's helm would be cold anyway so I don't mind too much. My desk is one of those giant oak ones with the green leather square in the middle meant for writing. I like it because it's old. All the furniture in my room is odd like in Iris' kitchen as it's where Frank and Julie keep all the stuff that doesn't fit anywhere else anymore.

For a long time the top of my desk was empty, but then for Christmas Mira bought me some Artemia NYOS, which are a kind of pet invented by scientists in the 1950s that can be sold to kids in packets. They're advertised as Sea-Monkeys but they don't look anything like monkeys. Apparently they called them this because of their tails but a whole lot of things have tails that aren't monkeys. I think they look more like really small armadillos, but I guess 'Sea-Armadillos' wouldn't sound as good. When you get them, the Artemia, they're in a state of cryptobiosis, which for the most part is the same as being dead except with the potential to come back to life. Stuff can not-live for ever in cryptobiosis, which is the kind of interesting I could think about for ages but never really conclude anything about. Anyway, as I am writing this I have a transparent cylinder of water on my desk containing a bright pink plastic pirate ship and some minuscule armadillo-looking monkeys.

I've never really understood the rules that determine which things matter enough to be told. Mira says she likes that about me because she never knows what I'm going to say, but I said that even though we're all talking about the same things, we never know which thing anyone is going to say or how they're going to say it, otherwise no one would ever say anything. Mira agreed that was partly true, but she also strongly suspected people would keep talking anyway just so they knew they were really there. I thought of all the things that could potentially validate someone's existence and concluded that talking certainly wouldn't be one of them. What with all the lies and quotes and limitations of language and talking about other people's junk. So I told Mira, I said 'What about the lies and quotes?' but I didn't mention the junk, and she simply said, 'How would we be able to tell lies or be influenced if we didn't exist?' Which was pretty valid, but I still disagreed. I also largely assumed that at this point it was our definitions of what it was *to exist* that were different, not what constituted *existing*. Once I realised that, and how that would require us to have an entirely different and much more elaborate discussion, instead of pointing it out I just said, 'Good point do you want to get some chips?' and she said yes because chips are simple.

It's weird, you'd think that the one thing people would be able to agree on would be what it was to exist.

Myles

Potential last line for a novel:
    And then the silence.

Chapter 12
The Size of a Life
July 1941

The magician and his beautiful assistant perplexed the crowds and defied imagination with the grandeur of their illusions. Their mastery of the senses presented itself as a cavalcade of light, misdirection and astonishment, which bled deep into the night. The old day finally died as the performance climaxed; our magician dived from stage to crowd, somersaulting through a cloud of frosted pink smoke and emerging as a dove.

Anna slowly pulled the paper free of the platen and placed it on the pile beside her. When she had started to turn Bobby's life into a fairy tale, seventeen years earlier, she hadn't given much thought as to why. A nice memento of his youth, she supposed, a quaint offering that families who keep milk teeth and locks of hair might appreciate. Tonight, Bobby was out with Rose, performing his latest medley of tricks to entertain those the war had left in limbo. Her son had become quite accomplished in his passion this past year, and it was that, along with his clear devotion to Rose, which began to toy with Anna as she traced an absent finger around the keys of her typewriter.

Bobby was almost a man now, and he had long since been the boy who would cry in her haberdashery cupboard, yet still she sat typing, day after day, recording their lives with fanciful whimsy. Whilst it may have once been for Bobby, she realised, it was now for her. Why, when Bobby was eight, or ten, or thirteen, hadn't she presented him with this token? This gift of a mother's love? She had crafted her magician's young life as an illusion and yet now she was beginning to worry if she had been the only one who couldn't, or wouldn't, see past the smoke and mirrors. Reflecting on her work, Anna couldn't pinpoint exactly when she had stopped writing for Bobby and started writing to keep writing.

She collected up the pile of paper that had accumulated and crossed the room to deposit the new pages along with the rest. Nearing the wardrobe, she caught sight of the distant light in Jerry's shed glowing through the bullet holes of loose knots in old wood. The window to his shed faced away from the house so she could never see him inside, even in the day when the blackout curtain wasn't lowered, but at night the pricks of light let her know he was still there, still alive. Anna unlocked the wardrobe with the small key she kept on a piece of yarn around her neck, aligned her latest chapter atop the lowest tower of paper, and locked the wardrobe once more. She had long since removed the winter coats and dress shirts to make room for all her words. To keep them protected under lock and key.

Anna walked back past the window, stalling to watch the holes of light emanating from the shed dance on and off as Jerry moved inside. She wondered if David was still there. *Most likely*, she thought. It seemed as though he rarely left. He and Jerry spent every night in that wooden box, drinking and shouting platitudes alternating between patriotism and disgust. John didn't visit as much these days; his solemn passivity didn't quite light a fire in Jerry the way David's odium could, and Anna suspected that John had eventually just given up fighting for him.

Sitting back down at her typewriter, Anna threaded another piece of paper under the inked ribbon. *The cupboard is almost full now. Soon there will be no space for our lives.*

The night was cool against their skin, and a welcome change from the heat the afternoon had brought. Rose was drawing eights and infinities in the dirt with her finger. Bobby picked pellets of bark off the broad tree trunk they were sitting up against.

'Mum said she's got some extra eggs Anna can have if she wants them? Luke dropped some off from the farm. He said not to tell anyone, else everyone would be wanting, but she said to offer you as your mum's a good friend.'

'I miss eggs,' Bobby mumbled.

'I miss bacon.'

'Mmmm bacon, toast soldiers with bacon on the side… what I wouldn't give.'

'Shut up, I'm starving!' she laughed. 'We are lucky, though, that we don't live in the bigger cities.'

'I'm not sure comparative luck can necessarily be considered luck.'

'How else would you measure it?'

'I don't know, Rose,' he stopped smiling and stared at the ground. 'I just know this doesn't feel all too lucky. I guess what I hate most about this war is that everything about our lives is measured now, nothing's free like it used to be.'

Rose studied the dirt under her fingernails.

'I suppose when there was loads of food I wouldn't even be thinking about eggs or bacon or toast soldiers, I probably wouldn't even think I was hungry, so I wouldn't be wanting them either. Is that what you're getting at? That the *knowing* we can't feels more restrictive than the restrictions themselves?'

Bobby was quiet, peeling a long strip of bark from the tree and watching through grey air as budding bubbles of sap speckled from the pale wood underneath.

'Sometimes I wish I was out there,' he addressed the darkness.

'What?! You take that back, Bobby Sinclair!' she shrieked. 'I thought you were relieved you were too young to fight?'

'I was. I was relieved, at first, but now I'm just stuck here, not feeling anything, not saving anyone. Not even able to eat a bloody bacon sandwich if I fancied it. Of course I want to go. I want to go and fight for feelings,' Bobby announced wildly, before giggling. 'And sandwiches.'

'You want to get yourself killed over a sandwich? Can you hear what you're saying to me?' Rose's voice rang out into the empty field. 'You'd leave me for a sandwich!'

'And for feelings,' he raised his voice to meet hers.

'What feelings? What magical feelings are you going to concoct in the trenches, eh?' she was gesticulating with a fervour which Bobby feared could become hazardous to his well-being, and he was reminded of that first sunny afternoon they shared together. Her foot-face, her wild laughter, her friendship. Her reinvention of him. 'What are you so desperate for that you can't have here?'

'All right. Calm down. It doesn't matter anyway. I can't go, I'm only seventeen.'

'Not for long! And it doesn't make what you said any less stupid,' she slumped back against the tree.

'Why'd you get so het up, anyway? I was only saying.'

'Well, it just sounded like you'd rather put yourself in mortal danger than spend time with me,' Rose coyly dug into the ground with a small rock she had uncomfortably removed from underneath one of her buttocks.

'I suspect any man would choose mortal danger given that option,' Bobby grinned as she shoved him. 'Kidding, I'm kidding!' he exclaimed as Rose turned away, feigning a sulk.

'Sometimes I don't even know why I'm friends with you.'

'Me either…'

'Huh?'

'I was just thinking. Do you remember for ever ago, when David came around shouting after it was announced we were going to fight the Germans?'

'Yeah, it was the night you weren't listening to me read you *Little Women*,' she dug the rock through the ground.

'Yeah. Well. Yes. But you know later when we were listening at the door?' Bobby was aware that all of his limbs seemed out of proportion. He shifted position but he still felt awkward, so he moved again but his body mismanaged itself and he suspected his balance was considerably off centre. He swallowed loudly.

'Yeah. When you were sensibly glad you were too young to be a soldier? I remember that. It seems you've only digressed in wisdom.'

'Again, yes. But after all the shouting had died down, you remember we just sat in silence?' he felt his words thickening in his throat. She didn't reply, so he continued, 'And, well, we talked about our friendship?' Bobby brushed one of his curls away from his eye and shot a glance at Rose, who was still resolutely scratching away at the world. 'Do you remember that?'

'Yeah. What about it?' a smirk crossed her face at the sound of his discomfort. She was glad she had the veil of the night to disguise the heat in her own cheeks.

Right, he thought. *It's now or never.*

'Well, when I held your hand, that wasn't all I wanted to do,' he swallowed again. 'I really wanted to…'

'Bobby!' Rose yelled, twisting and routing around in the ground beside her.

'What?' he asked, dejectedly attempting to peer into the complete darkness cast beyond Rose.

'Look!' she turned, smiling in the moonlight, presenting him with a small, muddy tin box.

'What's that?'

'A small muddy tin box.'

'Yes, Rose. But what is it *after* that?'

'*I don't know, do I?* I just found it buried here! Look, I was digging and scratched it with my rock along the top,' she pointed to a silver line that shimmered across the rusty

68

picture on the lid. Bobby was reminded of the scar across Jerry's cheek. His frown faded.

'What's in it?'

'I don't know, do I?' Rose stressed the repetition. 'Did I mislead you into believing I had psychic powers?'

'No, but I thought you might be able to hazard a guess with your powers of always being right.'

'Bobby Sin...'

'Open it then!'

'I will do when you stop telling me what to do!'

Bobby inhaled, reached across, grabbed Rose's cheeks between hot fingers and kissed her. His bottom lip met flush with hers as his top lip landed slightly above her mouth. Rose, being caught unaware, had her lips pressed shut.

'What are you doing?!' she gasped, extracting her face from Bobby's.

'I,' *In for a penny in for a pound*, he thought, but the words – the conclusion to his emphatic gesture – only came out as a choked whisper, 'I love you.'

'If you loved me you wouldn't have said you wanted to go and fight in the stupid war.'

'It's *because* I love you that I want to fight in the war.'

'Make that make sense.'

'Because...' Bobby took a deep breath, *Now or never.* 'Because I want you to know I love you. I want you to feel that I love you in an exceptional way. I don't want to be the kid who had a marble fall on his head four years ago... the kid who had just styled himself as Breathtaking Bobby the Brilliant...'

'Bobby Baker the Illusion Maker.'

'Whatever,' the urge for everything he had been hiding to spill from him in that moment, in that dark, was overwhelming. 'Rose, the way you looked at me the night I showed you something no one else has ever seen... you turned to me with an expression of utter innocent astonishment and I was convinced no one had ever seen something as beautiful as you. That was when I knew I loved you. We were thirteen and

I loved you. I've loved you for four years and only once have you looked at me like that. I want to be the boy that shows you something you've never seen *every* day. If I went to war I could spend every day fighting for you. Fighting to save you. And when I came home I could cook you toast and eggs and bacon even when you didn't want it.'

'You present an interesting case,' Rose giggled, her face so deeply flushed she felt sure Bobby would be able to see it in the darkness. 'You may kiss me again, so long as you go about it as less of an attack.'

'Sorry… if I didn't do it quickly I was worried I'd never do it,' his momentum wheezed to a halt. Only thoughts surrounding the potential incompetence of his kissing technique clamoured for attention.

'Kiss me, Sinclair!'

Bobby tentatively rolled his finger around the edge of Rose's ear, tidying away yellow waves of loose hair, and leaned forward, kissing her slowly, gently. He could feel the edge of her lips slide upwards in a smile beneath his as he succumbed to ecstasy and fear. The ecstasy of finally experiencing something he had coveted for four years, the *only* thing he had coveted, the only thing he could ever imagine truly wanting. And yet already creeping into his chest was the fear of one day discovering it had all been taken away from him. He pulled away and looked into her eyes as they glittered grey under the dark blanket of everything.

'Do you think I'm a pessimist?' he asked.

'What on earth happened between your grand speech and kissing me that made *that* the first thing you said?'

'I don't know. I just got scared I'd never be that happy again.'

Rose leaned over and kissed him, 'There,' she said. 'Still happy?'

'Very,' Bobby grinned.

'Good. So you don't have to worry because I'm not going anywhere.'

'Kiss me again.'

'Nah, I think I'm over it,' Rose shrugged.

Bobby stammered unintelligibly, his eyes wide. She cackled.

'Oh, come on! Don't go all fish face on me like you actually thought I was serious!'

'*Women*,' he shook his head and she laughed again, gently pushing his chest and kissing him once more.

'What was it you said earlier? Breathtaking Bobby the Bril…'

Bobby clamped his lips back down onto hers.

Mum,   09/06/2011

I got the job in the library basement. I started last week. It's just me and this other guy, Charlie, working down there. I think Charlie is really old as his skin is weather-beaten pock-marked leather and he wears a perpetually peppery five o'clock shadow, but then maybe it's *because* of all those things that he looks really old, not the other way around. Maybe Charlie used to work as a fisherman and the salt winds aged him prematurely. I haven't asked Charlie his age because we'd still be there under the library, together amongst the ruined books every day, however old he was. Although yesterday he compared the faded pages in the dirty basement copy of *A Handful of Dust* to the static over a wireless, so maybe he wasn't a fisherman.

Charlie is really nice. He started bringing me an extra sandwich with his lunch because I was buying them pre-made every day, and he wanted me to save my money because we don't get paid very much. Obviously I can't eat the sandwiches he brings as I have no idea how clean Charlie's house is, and I'm worried my imagination would make me vomit if I tried to eat one, so I have to surreptitiously throw them away where Charlie won't see them. I feel a lot of guilt about this, especially when he smiles at me as he gets his little transparent lunch box out, and I can see he's carefully wrapped up two piles of sandwiches in tinfoil. He'll gently excavate one of the foil parcels, and his lined, crumpled hands will be shaking because Charlie never stops shaking.

Then he'll pass it to me and say, 'We've got cheese and ham today, kid,' and he'll beam at me as I take the sandwich. Then he'll sit there on the tiny stool, balancing the lunch box on his knees, gently unwrapping his own sandwich. I'll walk away so he doesn't see me not eating, and he'll eat his in silence amongst the unwanted books. I don't think Charlie has any family because he's never mentioned anyone, and yet every day I throw his sandwiches away and sometimes I have trouble getting to sleep.

I leave Montecore with Iris whilst I am at work because they both need looking after, then after I say goodbye to Charlie I walk to Iris', and she has usually already started cooking enough tea for me to join her and Mira. So now most evenings begin with the four of us sitting around the tiny table in the cluttered kitchen. Well, Montecore just kind of lolls around our feet, but Iris always gives him a little plate of scraps so he doesn't feel left out. I think Iris really likes it when the kitchen is full and she doesn't have to think about anything, but if I'm honest I'd rather not be there, at least not every day.

Now, when I wake up, I have to shower and then walk Montecore to Iris', and then walk to work, then I am in the basement with Charlie worrying about sandwiches all day, then I walk back to Iris', and we all have dinner when Mira gets back, and I stay long enough to make it look like I want to be there, then I walk home with Montecore and it's already quite late. And I am tired from all the thinking about what to say and what not to say, but I can't sleep because I am guilty about Charlie and about not wanting to be at Iris', and I feel like this entire week has gone by without me really being there.

I get paid every fortnight, which means I will get paid tomorrow as it's a Friday. I think I am going to buy something for Charlie to say thank you, but I'm worried it will also be a little bit because of my guilt, and if it is because of my guilt then I'll really be buying it for myself, so that won't help the guilt at all. There's nothing I can do about that. I'll get Mira to come shopping with me on Saturday because she is really good at thinking of stuff like presents, even though she doesn't know Charlie. I'll hopefully get to spend Sunday on my own so I can think about everything that has happened this week, like the fact that whatever Mira decides we should get Charlie it won't stop him from being alone, and then Monday will turn me into a flesh automaton again.

Montecore sleeps beside me with his head on my pillow every day now. I suspect when he gets big I might need a larger bed. I like it though, feeling him breathing beside me and knowing that inside he is feeling whatever he shows me in his eyes, which seems to only ever alternate between happiness and hunger and needing to go outside. Last night I had a dream that was the same as being asleep until a man without a face appeared and I heard his thoughts about wanting to hurt Montecore, so I grabbed a rock and hit him over the head with it until his brains spilled out and became everything else, and suddenly Montecore was standing on my shoulders and I screamed out into the black that I'd kill anyone that came near us. Then I woke up and everywhere was the same colour as my dream, and I thought how I'd have to get a rock just in case.

Myles

Potential last lines for a novel:
   How could I be capable of this?
   Everything that was gone.

Chapter 14
I Thought the Birds Didn't Sing Here
June 1944

Bobby fingered the yellow, withered paper clamped between his sharply angled knees, and skimmed his nail along the torn edges. The grime against his hands was so deeply ingrained it no longer brushed off against clothes and clean things, although perhaps it was just that everything he owned had already grown a second skin of dirt. He pinched the tired muscles in his face together, forcing his eyes so tightly closed the space behind them compacted and ached. Pushing the blood fast and heavy behind his ears, he was almost able to drown out the surrounding sound with the scream of his insides, and for a moment he was gone.

'What *is* that?' Bobby didn't hear the question so Fraser put a gentle hand on his shoulder. 'Hey, Sinclair, what's that you're always fiddling with? Love letter?'

'Sort of... It's a story my girl found a couple of years ago. She likes to say the characters are us in a different lifetime,' he kneaded the paper. 'You know how sentimental women can be.'

'Yeah, women eh?' Fraser laughed. 'You say she found it?'

'She did. We were sitting under a tree one night, she was just scratching around in the dirt and discovered this little tin box. This story was folded up inside,' he smiled and adjusted his back against the metal.

'So, what's it about? Why would someone bury that? Do

you know who wrote it?' Fraser scooted his scrap of a body towards Bobby in an attempt to block out chatter around them. His interest piqued both from curiosity and, as always, the cloying desire for distraction.

'We do actually. Know who wrote it, that is. Well, as much as we can know. There were a whole bunch of letters buried alongside it.'

'Go on, I'm not going anywhere.'

That night three years ago, after his magic show, after the tree with historically festooned roots, when they were both sat by vanilla candlelight on Jerry's living-room rug, Rose had made Bobby promise not to tell anyone about their find. Her face had flickered with zealous concern, orange and black against the flames, as she fervently sang on about how they needed to preserve the letters for themselves.

Bobby thought about how heavily animated she had become reading the story; how precious the written history became within her fingers. Rose had argued that other people would want to be a part of James and Daisy if they found out about them, and that they mustn't be diluted. That the story couldn't be decanted into other lives as well as their own or else it, *they*, would no longer be extraordinary. She had gesticulated wildly – the way she always did, the way he remembered her – slicing the old tin box through the air, a blade in a duel, as she insisted this was to be theirs alone.

A promise made in candlelight doesn't belong here.

'All the letters were one sided. They were all signed from this girl, Daisy, and addressed to James. They were love letters, sort of, but really they were letters of desire and frustration. From what we could tell, Daisy was infatuated with James. She would write about her dreams of the two of them together, about her hopes for their lives as a real couple in the future, and about how one day they wouldn't be judged. The biggest problem for Daisy was that James was married to The Stranger.

'We figured maybe she was just this lonely girl who had

developed a crush, but there's a part in the last letter where she talks about how her skin burned under James' touch, "The night that God blessed them." So we thought it stood to reason that James had an affair with Daisy but refused to leave his wife. Then we noticed pieces that didn't fit, little clues that were inconsistent with what we had presumed. I think it was because we had assumed their situation that we initially overlooked it, but then we realised, eventually, that Daisy was just a child.

'We hadn't read the story at this point because we were reading everything in order of date, so we didn't know this was to be roughly confirmed, but our guess is that she was about twelve based on a few of the things she said. We were thrown by some of the mature content, but Rose recognised one of the quotes from Keats' *A Thing of Beauty*, and we realised a lot of the letters were just a regurgitation of what Daisy must have read about love. They're incredible though, the letters. They're passionate and terrifying, and the idea of James and Daisy, well, it should be dreadful but it comes across as this implausibly perfect love.'

Bobby looked at Fraser, wondering if he was still listening or if his capriciousness had instead lead him down another avenue of interest somewhere in the midst of his explanation. What he found was Fraser staring at him so intently Bobby could almost see questions in his eyes.

'But if,' started Fraser, struggling to decide what to ask first, his queries all in a pugnacious battle across the arch of his tongue and collecting at the back of his throat. 'If she was only a girl, what did they do? When he touched her?'

'I don't know,' he had thought about this. 'It could be anything, he may have simply put a hand on her shoulder, or held her, or…'

'But…'

'Yeah, there's always *but*, I'll say it; maybe James made a woman of her, there's no way of telling, but I don't think he did. I think he loved her how she loved him and somehow touching her *that* way would hurt him too much. Rose once put it like this; it's like picking a flower, it's beautiful but if you want it you have to kill it.'

'Maybe,' Fraser paused in thought. 'But I'd like to think he kissed her, just once. On the lips, like a promise he never intended to keep because he thought she'd grow out of it the way girls grow out of dolls. She'd grow up and grow out of him.'

'I didn't realise you were a romantic,' Bobby teased. This was nice, he realised, this fleeting forgetting.

'Hey, we all love, Sinclair. We all got to love.'

Bobby had appreciated Fraser's nonchalant honesty right from the moment the two had met. They had been introduced a month earlier, and Bobby immediately noticed Fraser had this specific way of talking. It wasn't that he spoke with dignity, as such, but more that he always spoke without *in*dignity. Whatever he felt he *really* felt it, whatever he thought he allowed himself to think it. Despite the fact that Bobby knew he was undoubtedly the more intelligent of the two, he frequently felt ignorant in front of his new friend. Bobby would hide behind stigma where Fraser would embrace and shame it, Bobby would try to disguise weakness yet Fraser would confidently announce it, and Bobby would make excuses where Fraser would give explanations.

The negotiation of fear and emotion was a constant source of bewilderment for Bobby, who believed to betray his own limitations would result in emasculation, and yet he saw Fraser readily admit to his own demons time and time again, and he respected him for it. 'To feel is a very simple thing,' Fraser had recently told Bobby, and the statement had been so incongruous with Bobby's own perspective that he briefly felt physically shaken, before dismissing the notion as part of Fraser being a character. His mother always said that about people who were slightly eccentric, or unusual, or vibrant. They were all characters to Anna.

'Sometimes I wonder if he ever touched her at all,' Bobby wiped the salt from his eyes. 'We've only got her perspective on events, and half of them are plagiarised.'

'Why do you even think he loved her, though? You said the letters were one sided. Did she say he did? And if she did she was probably just delusional, right? Unreliable, you just said. And why does your girl want you to play the role of some feller that touches kids in this alternate fantasy she's invented for you? She's not... sh...'

'Rose is my age, yes. Thank you.'

'I'm never going to fully believe you until I get to meet this Rose of yours,' Fraser grinned widely, exposing almost all of his top teeth and the kind of thin lines around his mouth that are reminiscent both of youth and its vulnerability. 'Seriously, though, why is the infamous Rose casting you as some kiddie fiddler?'

'That makes a lot more sense when the story comes in,' Bobby gestured to the paper triggering the discussion. 'It's how we know James loved Daisy, too.'

'I'm on the hook just reel me in, Captain.'

The breath caught in Bobby's throat. Sometimes Fraser reminded him of Rose, and no matter how often it happened he was never ready for it.

'So, the letters are dated up until August 1886, then right where the letters end we get the story, which is marked as September third of the same year. That's the part when Rose decided that we were them. She said that she's got the soul of Daisy and I've got James', and that before they were themselves, Daisy and James were the characters in the story. Rose has an entire spiel about how we've been trying to be together for lifetimes, but that each time we've suffered heartbreak and separation, and that's why she found the box, so we'd know everything we've been through until now. We'd know that we were meant to be,' Bobby paused, he could feel Rose in his chest and at the tips of his fingers and alerting the invisible hairs across his skin. He coughed, and brushed something that wasn't there off of his trouser leg, 'Or something along those lines. Like I said, *women.*'

Fraser was studying Bobby's face when Bobby turned to glance at him, caught his muted green eyes with his own, and immediately looked away. Bobby's focus quickly darted between various distances across the water, his eyes searching for a suitable distraction from intimacy in the void. Instead, all he saw was tens of caliginous flecks careening across the unsettled ocean. The flecks were other boats containing other men, each with their own torn families and their own tapestries woven throughout the past.

'I like it,' Fraser announced. 'Your Rose sounds like a good one, Sinclair. Remind me to buy her a bottle of wine when we get back.'

'Red, she'll love you for a bottle of red.' Bobby had no idea if Rose even liked wine, but it didn't really matter. They all said of a lot of things like that; made a lot of plans for the future. The plans themselves weren't important but nobody ever paid too much attention to that part. Bobby briefly wondered what other sanguine promises were being made at that moment all along the ocean, and how many would be broken. 'I guess it is kind of sweet,' he added, being drawn back into the present. 'What about your other half, she as sentimental as mine?'

'Not exactly, no,' Fraser gave a trace of a smile but Bobby sensed a sadness. Everything always obscured by sadness. 'How did Rose react when she knew you were coming out here?'

'She doesn't know,' Bobby thought back to the way Rose had looked at him when he told her he was leaving. He had planned to be honest with her; he hadn't even considered lying, not until he saw her eyes, not until she made *that* inhuman sound. 'I told her I was going to be stationed along the English coast. I said they needed some of us to stay behind in these fake ice-cream huts dotted across the beaches in case we were invaded. I made her promise not to tell anyone because it was top secret. She said she thought I'd be safe there, she even smiled.' He took a thick, salty breath.

'I told her that's why I wouldn't be able to write or receive any letters, so no one would discover my location.'

'Sometimes I worry that we're safer out here than they are back home,' Fraser was thinking aloud, distractedly thumbing the gold band on his finger. 'I know it sounds silly, but they're back there with the bombs, they're nothing more than ants under the feet of giants.'

'Then what are we?'

'We're still ants, but we're ants with fucking guns!'

He understood completely.

'You never said you were married,' Bobby gestured at Fraser's hand, unable to remember seeing the ring before. Then again he'd never really looked, not with the intent of seeing.

'I'm not,' Fraser twisted the metal about his finger. 'It's more of a promise thing, really. A symbol of commitment no different, but not an engagement, there's no marriage to come after it.'

'Can't be tied down, huh?'

'Oh, I'd be married in an instant, would that I could.'

'Sorry if I'm being ignorant, she isn't ill, is she? I didn't mean to pry. I feel awful, if that's what it is.'

'No! No. It's not that at all. It's just,' Fraser became uncharacteristically quiet. 'Can I tell you something, Sinclair?'

'Of course,' his mind inadvertently alerted him to the leap year and he berated himself for the childhood reflex; he wasn't *him* anymore.

'I haven't got a girlfriend waiting for me at home.'

'Oh, but your ring…'

'Hey, can I read the story?'

'Of course,' Bobby felt a vague, unfulfilled climax suddenly hanging between them and he didn't know why.

Fraser took the bundled up paper and unfolded it as gently as possible with the boat lurching beneath them. His long fingers weaved tidily between the folds, separating the old

81

story with eerie caution. Settling his elbows astride his knees, the paper nestled in his hands, he began to read:

The Castle at the Beginning of the World

When the world was flat and never-ending in each of the four directions, there was a castle with walls so high, and surrounding land so plentiful, that no one ever bothered attempting to travel beyond it. They never bothered because it was almost impossible, as to carry enough provisions for a journey that far, or to climb a wall that high, would have been a weight too heavy for any man alive then or now. For this reason it became known as the Castle at the Beginning of the World, and it was the northernmost point of the small capital city, Small Capital City.

This was a time when only a few pockets of population were scattered across the land. Nests of activity had sprung up around trade posts and, inexplicably, one had appeared around a rather large cave entrance that no one had explored out of fear, but many desired to live close to in case the roof above the sky collapsed and the moon fell upon them. This city was known by two names; those who lived there called it the Final City, believing it would be the last on earth, and those that did not live in the city called it the Foolish City, for obvious reasons. In the Foolish City all houses were designed like large sedan chairs. They were square wooden boxes with no foundations. Instead, they had large sticks jutting out either side so the family could pick up and move their home into the cave at a moment's notice. The Foolish City was a terrible place to live as the cave was so far away from the rich trade in other areas of the land. So far away, in fact, they often had to send one house out, carried by the city's strongest men, to function as a large storage container able to bring back rations from the distant traders. As it happened, the city dwellers didn't mind living on the edge of poverty and often snickered at the thought of those wearing rich gowns, plump with fresh fish and rosy with expensive wine, splattering under the weight of the moon.

One day, twelve of the strongest men from the Foolish City were sent out carrying the house of the Unwise Priest on a journey to collect some provisions. He was known as the Unwise Priest for no reason other than he often did very idiotic things, including telling everyone he was a priest even though the city was still arguing over which religion would best appease the moon. Following a recent incident in which the Unwise Priest had gone missing after he thought he saw the moon shudder, the Travelling Committee had instructed the twelve strongest men to take his house with them for storage. There were many eyewitness reports claiming the priest had run into the cave screaming, but no eyewitness reports claiming he had emerged.

After many days and nights, the twelve strongest men and the Unwise Priest's house ended up in Small Capital City with the Castle at the Beginning of the World. No one knew that the Foolish City was actually located beyond the Castle at the Beginning of the World, and that they had simply walked in a wide circle around the city in order to enter it from the front (nor did they know that they were the only ones who could have travelled so far, as they worked together carrying their provisions in a house and not individually upon their backs), and finally, no one knew a young boy had hidden himself in the Unwise Priest's house as soon as he had heard the trip was to be made. The young boy had decided to become a stowaway very early on in his life, on account of the fact he did not want to live in poverty, and had a strong suspicion that the moon wasn't actually going to fall on them.

The boy watched carefully as the twelve strongest men from the Foolish City finally left Small Capital City, carting a house full of good cheese along with them, and turned to face his new home. The city with the Castle at the Beginning of the World was tiny. In fact, he doubted it could even be deemed a city at all, even a small one. It was simply a very large square with rows of tiny houses on each side, a thin alley (only a single body's width wide) separating each row, and a vast expanse in the middle, which contained an old well, a park, a tavern, a ring of trader's stalls and the most extravagant flowerbeds he had ever seen. Between this, or 'the Middle' as those in the city called it, and the houses, or 'the Ring' as they had come to be known, even though they were shaped in a square, was a very wide cobbled street.

The street looped around the Middle, exited in a straight line through a gap in the south side of the Ring and disappeared out into the rest of the world. Behind the houses on the east of the Ring was a harbour, and the boy could see the masts from the ships there from wherever he stood in the city, and behind the houses to the west of the Ring he could see the front of a rich forest. He liked it very much here. It was simple and sensible, but mostly there were puddings and the children had toys.

Two years passed, and the boy had experienced very few puddings or toys from the city with The Castle at the Beginning of the World. He had made himself a home from scraps of wood at the top of a tree in the easterly forest, which was very small and awkward, but not much worse than what he had called a home in the Foolish City. He would climb down from his dwelling just before sunrise each morning and lurk in the Middle, waiting for the traders to arrive and set up their stalls. This was the best time to steal food, as storage crates were everywhere and often left unattended for minutes at a time. The boy had no capacity to cook food and he didn't want to draw attention to himself with a fire in the woods, so he had settled for a diet mainly of breads, cheeses, and fruit. Sometimes, at night, he would sneak back down to the tavern, and if he lurked outside for long enough he could swipe the scraps of cooked meals from the candle-lit tables on the decking before the plates got tidied away. He was happy here, mostly because he didn't have to suffer the chatter from the Foolish City, but also because he never knew what would happen. The same thing happened every day, it was true, but he liked the possibility that one day it wouldn't, and one day it didn't.

The boy was walking around the cobbled path, chewing on a crust of bread and absorbing the bustle of the city's morning routine, when he turned onto the northern side of the Ring. This side of the Ring consisted entirely of the castle's curtain wall, which reached out far beyond the edges of both the Middle and the Ring, yet had designated a lower, decorative segment as the portion that constituted the city's northern side. There was a pair of grand bronze gates in the centre, wider and taller than any of the houses in the city, and it was through these gates that the city dwellers would enter the castle whenever a feast was thrown, or a rare gathering was held inside the castle grounds.

These instances, of feasts and festivities, were very unusual, as the family who lived in the castle were fearful of the city dwellers, assuming they were hated for their wealth. They were not hated for their wealth, or for any other reason, as the city dwellers were very well aware that if it weren't for the rich family they would see less trade and the city would never have existed. They were happy, nice people without envy in their hearts and also they liked the occasional free feast. But as a result of the family's fear, their youngest daughter, who was not fearful, was never allowed to attend the feasts or gatherings, nor was she allowed out of the castle grounds. She was terribly lonely, and would often sit in one of the windows of the tower in which she slept, watching the people below her laughing or arguing, drinking or playing, hurrying from the Middle to the Ring and back again, or dawdling, passing the time meandering around the market and in the tavern. What luxury, she thought.

One day, the girl was up earlier than usual and she spotted the boy, whom she had never seen before, walking around the cobbled streets and eyeing up the market stalls as the sun was rising from across the harbour. She giggled, watching him loot one stall and then the next, hiding peaches in his socks and bread rolls under his tattered hat. She saw how nimbly his feet danced around the Middle, his hands moving across the stalls as though they were the keys of a piano, his eyes bright and quick, his body slender and his lips mischievously full. She fell in love that morning. She fell in love so deeply, in fact, that every day for the next seven years she sat at that very same window for as much of the day as she possibly could in the hopes of seeing the boy, wishing to talk to him, dreaming of holding his fingers in hers, praying he would look up and notice her. Cursing that even if he did, the two would still never meet. Not until she was old enough to escape her prison.

Often, she would see the boy walking around the flower beds, crouching to study one particular blossom for a seemingly endless amount of time before moving on to the next. Sometimes he would sit for hours beside the yellow rose bush, or the blush-pink peony, and she, in turn, would sit for hours watching him, and then he would leave and she would mourn him until she saw him emerge from a corner of the Ring once more.

The boy had, in fact, seen the girl looking out of the castle window, and had also immediately fallen in love. Knowing that a girl like her could never love a poor boy like him, he simply spent every day watching her watching the city. She did this so often that he was afforded plenty of opportunity to memorise her face, her movements, imagine her smell and the smoothness of her skin. After a few months of watching the girl he could no longer bare to keep all of his love trapped inside of his chest, for fear that it would engulf him, so he took to sitting in the flower beds and writing his love for her in great, detailed verse, on the insides of thousands of petals across the city. Each autumn the flowers would die, along with them his words, and every spring he would rewrite everything he had written before and more, for every year he grew more greatly and deeply in love with the girl in the tower.

He did this every day for seven years, but during the eighth year he could take it no longer. He was almost eighteen, and he was living in a tree house above a very small, square city, and his life had become so very painful not being able to speak to or hold the girl in the tower that he simply had to leave. That spring he wrote of his love for the girl one final time, inside of every flower he saw, before slowly walking away from the Middle along the cobbled path that faced due south. He left the girl and his heart in the city with the Castle at the Beginning of the World, and believed he would never come back.

A few days after the boy had left, the girl's insides were ravaged by pain from missing the boy. Not understanding why he was no longer anywhere to be seen, her hurt had grown more fiercely with every passing hour. It had been exactly one week since his disappearance when her mother entered her room with an extravagant smile on her lips, followed immediately by her father who was carrying so many gifts that his face was entirely concealed behind brightly coloured paper and shiny ribbons. 'Happy birthday, my sweet, sweet girl,' her mother said as she embraced her. The presents were spilled across her bed, there was cake and singing, and generally far too much commotion in such a small amount of space for anyone who was feeling such pain and longing to endure. 'I thought perhaps you would like to accompany me to the Middle later, dear? Pick out a nice dress for your birthday party?' her mother had spoken but the words themselves hadn't registered. 'What?' was all the girl managed to muster in reply. 'Well, you're eighteen now, dear, can't keep you in this castle for ever. I thought we could go to the Middle and buy you something special. Oh, don't be scared,' her mother had added, misinterpreting the look on her daughter's face. 'We'll take Daddy's right-hand man, awfully strong fellow he is, he'll protect us if anything untoward happens.' The girl couldn't believe it, she had been so preoccupied with her pain that she had completely forgotten that she was turning of age, and that she could go out into the Middle and meet the boy she loved so very dearly. She jumped up and ran to the door, 'Come, Mother,' she almost shouted. 'Let us go quickly!' The girl's mother looked at her husband and whispered, 'I didn't expect such enthusiasm, I fear Myrtle's dress selection is going to prove a disappointment.'

The girl spent days after her eighteenth birthday searching the city for the boy, but he was nowhere to be found. She cried every night and most days, and when she stopped crying she drank water so that she could cry again. The girl could not understand where he had disappeared to, or why he had to go when he had been almost within her reach. Even if she could have spoken to him, she doubted he would want a girl like her. He would probably think her spoiled and boring, for why would a boy so free and interesting like him look at a girl like her?

She wrote all her dreadful thoughts of broken emptiness into a diary. So frequently did she end up carrying this diary with her to document her feelings, that her handprint became a permanent fixture across the soft leather cover. One afternoon, the girl slumped amongst the flower beds, smelling the roses as though they were the boy himself, hoping perhaps some tiny amount of him was still there; that she could touch it and surround herself in the invisible parts of himself he had left behind. She thought of how long the boy had spent amongst those petals, the hours and days he had sat within the bloom of the Middle, and she began to pick the flowers. As soon as she began collecting the flowers she had immediately stopped writing. This simple and beautiful flora was her story now, just as it was his. That summer she picked as many of the flowers as she could and pressed them all between the pages of her diary.

Many years later, long after the girl had died (rather on purpose) from sustained heartbreak, the boy returned. He was a man now, and he had been to many of the cities across the land, yet he liked none as greatly as he liked the city with

The Castle at the Beginning of the World. More importantly, he had never even considered loving any of the girls he had met the way he still loved the girl in the tower.

The man walked up the cobbled street at the south of the city, and around the Middle to the north side of the Ring where the castle stood. He felt absurd looking for her now, for surely she would have married, and perhaps even moved away. Even if she hadn't married, he ridiculed himself, she still wouldn't care to look at him. Just then, a small boy walked past him chewing on a crust of bread. The man stopped the boy and asked him about the girl in the castle, to which the boy replied that there had never been a girl in the castle, not that he had known. 'She's gone,' said the man, slumping down into one of the flower beds to weep. He could not stay here, not without his love. The memories were too sore. The boy was rather perplexed and concerned by the man's behaviour but, unsure what to do, he felt it best to just wait there and stare at him. Then the man abruptly stood up, thanked the boy, who said it wasn't a problem, and started to walk once more down the cobbled path that lead away from the city. 'Wait!' shouted the boy. 'Hold up, mister!' The man turned to see the boy holding out a battered book. 'You dropped this, it was in the flower bed,' the boy said, offering it to him. The man told the boy it was not his, turned on his heel, and left for the last time.

The boy looked down at the book, placed his own small hand within the handprint indented on the cover, and sat down to see what was inside. Opening the book, the boy saw it contained a multitude of dried flowers flattened beneath each of the pages. He picked one up and the petals immediately came apart from the stem. It was then he noticed that one of the petals had writing on the inside. He looked at another petal and it had same thing. He broke another flower apart, there was writing on that, too; there was writing on all of them, hundreds of petals covered in tiny verses of love that had never been read.

#

My Dear, sweet, Daisy,   September 3rd, 1886

I wrote this little story for you not a week after your last letter, but yesterday I heard the tragic news of your death. I was absolutely beside myself and completely inconsolable for many hours. Of course, I could not let on to the fact it was because of your passing. I could be saddened, undoubtedly, but to be so vehemently distressed would seem out of place and suspicious. Instead, I took to the country, telling my wife I had business to attend to. I don't know why I am writing this now, perhaps it is from the guilt of never having written to you whilst you were there to cherish my words, and instead letting you suffer the tumult of longing. In many ways I feel this story became a foreboding warning of our love, yet unfortunately for the duration of my writing of the boy and the girl I did not heed their warning of time. For that, I may never forgive myself.

I want you to know that my heart will always be yours. In a perfect world you would have lived on until your early womanhood and we could have ran away together like you always dreamed, like I will continue to dream until I am taken to be with you again.

All my love, regardless of the confines of time,
James

#

Fraser folded the old paper back up along the thinning creases and passed it to Bobby, who had been watching the horizon slowly turning from liquid to land, his chest aching.

'Blimey,' Fraser exclaimed. 'I get it.'

Bobby swallowed meekly, realising Fraser had yet to notice the distance had stopped falling away and was instead crawling forwards to meet them.

'The part that gets me is why he buried it,' Bobby wondered aloud, trying to captivate Fraser's attention within the boat for as long as possible. 'Did James just decide to forget about Daisy, add his final chapter and bury the whole thing, or was it out of pain? All those letters from her just left under the ground like that. You'd think he'd treasure them.'

'He could be an unreliable source too, though, if he's grief stricken. Maybe losing Daisy made him think more of what they had. You don't know what you've got 'til it's gone, they say. Or maybe The Stranger found them and buried them,' Fraser suggested. 'Maybe she found them and made him some sort of deal, like if he stayed married to her and forgot about Daisy then she wouldn't tell all their friends about his secret?' Bobby made a throaty sound, which Fraser took to mean his suggestion was plausible. 'I can't imagine that, though, can you? Living every day as though the love of your life never existed? Perhaps it's just this bloody war, but I think every kind love should be shouted from the rooftops.'

'It does change your perspective on things,' Bobby agreed, looking over at his friend only to see him trying to stand up amongst the men hoarded into the crowded vessel.

'Gentlemen, your attention, please!' Fraser, now attempting to balance whilst standing on the irregularly rocking bench, shouted to the tens of men surrounding them. 'I, Henry Fraser,' he bellowed the words so loudly that even those who hadn't wanted to listen were given no choice. 'Aged nineteen years, from Warwickshire, do very much love my new but already very good friend, Bobby Sinclair!' He gestured to where Bobby was sitting, and was met with a silence so thick and heavy it seemed as though even the sea, crashing against the hull only moments before, became still in anticipation. Fraser seemed undeterred by the lack of response, whilst Bobby, incredulous and briefly distracted from their destination, tried to shrink back into the unaccommodating metal. 'I urge you,' Fraser continued, 'all of you, my comrades, to use this opportunity to tell each other how much love there is in this one, small boat. DO IT NOW!' Fraser screamed. 'Because we're bloody human! And we're bloody British! And the Germans can bloody fight as hard as they want but they'll never, ever destroy the love I have for my brothers!'

Terror racked Bobby's body in the second after Fraser finished his speech. He looked to the floor, to the sea, to one and then another of the men surrounding him. All eyes slowly traced from Fraser to him. His face was hot. He dared to look up to Fraser, who was staring down at him, a resolute smile poorly disguising a sorrow turning in his eyes. *Fuck it*, Bobby thought. *These may be my last days.* He was almost standing when the roar rang out.

'TO BROTHERS!' screamed Jackson, a juggernaut of a man from the opposite side.

'TO BROTHERS!' echoed a staggered, hearty call from around the rest of the boat.

'TO BROTHERS!' yelled Bobby, slapping his friend across the back.

'To brothers,' Fraser laughed, turning and throwing his arms around Bobby; the force of the bear hug causing him to stumble back into the side of the boat, despite Fraser's paper skeleton. Laughter was tumbling out of him uncontrollably; it was the kind of laughter that escapes a person suddenly afflicted by happiness when they were already so full of fear.

'I bloody love you, Sinclair,' Fraser whispered, kissing him loudly on the cheek.

He looked around. Infectious shoulder squeezes and shallow embraces chased each other around the boat at the speed of triggered rat traps between men. Bobby saw each touch as the promise it signified between one son to the next. It was a pledge of assurance, of camaraderie, of support, and the word *brothers* rang out into the air for many moments afterwards, just as the beast twisted out before them.

Fraser was the first soldier from Bobby's section to be killed on Sword Beach. Of course, the tragedy that surrounded D-Day would grow in infamy, and for many years Bobby would live with a constant reminder of the death toll from those few days alone, but he couldn't help thinking how he wasn't meant to die. They weren't met with the kind of resistance their allies faced further along at Omaha, and what's more they were positioned at the back of their battalion. They were the clean-up, the tail, the safety net.

Bobby, arrested by panic or surprise or curiosity, never said a word as he saw the dead German raise his arm and fire a dirty brown bullet directly through Fraser's heart. He didn't say a word as Fraser's body continued running, staring at him lifelessly until it collapsed into a crumpled heap; its left ankle coming to rest behind the right knee, one arm reaching forward, one awkwardly angled below the reddening bullet hole. Face flattened against a sodden regulation footprint. Bobby didn't say a word as he wondered at the speed of it all. This wasn't a hero's death nor was this a struggle; the dance with the void he had envisaged. Fraser had been running beside him, Fraser had been talking about Preston beating Arsenal in '41, Fraser had *been*.

The elimination of his friend had been instantaneous, and with no adjustment period pending, Bobby felt his own brain inadvertently scrambling for meaning. His thoughts dived gracelessly into an assiduous search for something, anything, between Fraser's *is* and *was*, his *has* and *had*, his *will* and *would*. The in-between moments had been ripped away and he had been duped out of the devastating sickness, the goodbye, the gentleman's handshake. He hadn't agreed to this. *He'll never know he's dead*, Bobby thought, excusing himself the obvious. Walking over to the inanimate heap of limbs, he removed Fraser's ring from the left hand, and turned to watch the war machine as it slowly moved further along the beach. His squadron brothers exchanging lives with strangers like rare postage stamps. *No one knows they're dead*, his legs folded beneath him and he wept.

Chapter 15
What is, What is to Take Place
July 1972

William ran a finger below his ribcage, hooking it under the bone like turning a page. His nail tucked into him. He was too infested to eat properly, too distracted by the night. He was distracted by the night because, for him, every night had become *the* night. *The* night that triggered the insomnia, *the* night that triggered all other nights to parade as a dark hours theatre with only one billing; a tragicomedy of the husk that once masqueraded as the apocryphal real boy.

The light had long since been absorbed when William rolled over and propped himself up on an elbow, which immediately succumbed to its own weakness and began rattling under his meagre weight. Instead of adjusting his position, William studied the vibrations from his pinched nerve, intrigued as he attempted to will his arm to be still. He knew this exercise of mind over matter was futile, he'd attempted it many times before; as a kid bored at breakfast, as a teen bored at dinner, but always his bones danced until he physically moved them into calm.

Glancing across at the digital clock, William was thankful its hesitant light saved him from turning on the bedside lamp. Thankful, because under the veil of darkness his vision was exempt from the obtuse floral mustard bed sheets. William had spent many hours contemplating whether the sheets were a penance for past events; an unspoken punishment he unconsciously deigned to serve. *If I suffer these bed sheets I will surely, ultimately, achieve redemption... right?*

William also, and more strongly, suspected that the garish design was calculated by the hotel. It was a clever move, employing these sheets. At first, the design conveys an air of quality, flair, and moderately acceptable taste. Nothing suspicious there. Yet when forced upon someone for extended periods of time, the sheets wear away at the psyche, bit by bit. They were a continual scratching outside the wooden door of the mind. Once inside, they became a tool to exacerbate ennui. These were bed sheets to escape from. Driving guests like cattle from their rooms and into the casino pens below. Then, once siphoned into the enclosures, the cattle start frantically feeding grey-green bills to glutinous machines and card dealers. All hoping to win enough money to buy bed sheets so utterly sumptuous and innumerable in thread count that the memory of these mustard abominations would serve only as a tawdry symbol of what had been left behind. These were bed sheets designed with a sole intent: to inspire superficial ambition, by kill or by cure.

William's arrival at the hotel also coincided with his introduction to the digital alarm clock. One of the digits on his particular clock, in his particular room, was a constant flickering eight. Time could only ever be estimated within the hour. Like the bed sheets, William knew this was intentional. He was in Las Vegas and time was hidden. The bloody lines of illumination currently flashed 05:86. He had been there, in that hotel room, for eight weeks. The maids had stopped trying to clean after a fortnight of his neurotic insistence, but they still emerged every couple of days under the guise of a supply drop. Tiny shampoos, sachets of coffee, single serving biscuits, thimbles of milk, postage stamps of soap, it was all designed for being alone and yet their necessity precluded it. William stuck a scrap of the Bible to his door with *Leave me alone* inked over Ecclesiastes, but discarded it before the tack had cooled.

He knew the maids were really just checking to make sure he wasn't dead or killing things. Checking he was just the necessary amount of legal. He watched them eyeing the bathroom, undoubtedly hoping to uncover a compact pharmacy of narcotics behind the assorted towels. William fantasised about hiding drugs (cocaine and sheets of acid, primarily) in the stuffing of teddies, instructing mule-kids to claim they'd been lucky and won a prize off one of the fixed games. At least, he decided, if he was to covertly deal drugs (he didn't have any drugs) through the children of Vegas (he didn't know any children in Vegas), that's how he would do it. Instead, he watched the maids concoct their own life for him.

Every morning, William peered through the peep hole in his door to observe whichever pair of women happened to be collecting his waste. As far as he could tell, there were five on rotation for his floor: two identical Hispanic women who only ever worked together, an adolescent girl draped in shell jewellery, a woman with seven fingers that were never still, and an old hoary African who made William uneasy. Her ratty eyes constantly darted around like wasps trapped under glass, whilst her mouth hung loose and disenchanted, giving the illusion of two faces as one. She would always inspect his rubbish viciously, eyes flickering to the peephole, staring directly into him and then away as though no exchange had occurred between them. William knew she could see his lone eye, warped small and dry, a bead in the glassy node.

The others tentatively handled his loosely knotted bags, carefully angling his empties away from themselves, as though the pizza boxes and whiskey bottles were hiding tools of degradation. Perhaps disguising objects from fetishist practices, disused needles, or any terrible concoction of materials eagerly awaiting to infiltrate and rot their meat away until they were dust in the desert.

As William lost himself to thoughts of his unfair designation as a source of concern, the lowest common denominator in the hotel ecosystem, he was reminded of a newspaper article that outlined the capture of a paedophilic babysitter with fervent hyperbole. Some kid's parents had gone to pick him up after a Christmas party and happened to see a used condom in the kitchen bin where the swing lid hadn't fully closed. This wasn't incriminating in itself, but next to the condom they saw a soggy pebble of green Play-Doh, tiny fingerprints still visible, and their entire world turned inside out.

William surveyed his hotel room, recognising the shadowed outlines of objects haphazardly strewn across the space. His life was synopsised by his belongings, all lazily heaped into a brazen array of Venn diagrams and Boolean operations. Arranged obtusely, the meaning of his possessions were morphed and tainted by each other; the way a condom is unremarkable until half-sculpted Play-Doh rallies against it.

William noted his pairings were more subtle. A cigarette packet was resting next to a handful of loose vitamin C capsules. The dosage instructions from a box of Aspirin were screwed up at the bottom of a short, fat glass, and bloated with remnants of cheap rum. An almost empty wine bottle had overturned, leisurely bleeding a rusty crimson stain through a once treasured first edition of Knut Hamsun's *Hunger*. Other items rested in solitary corners – they were pie charts with only one statistic – a journal, a tourist guide, a thesaurus, a packet of biros, two used mismatched dinner plates, a book on philosophy, a book on other books, a sachet of vinegar, a paper bag with a soft-core porno magazine creeping out of it, deodorant. Nothing, not really. Nothing of a life.

#

Stumbling out of the lift, sweat dripped down his scorched forehead from where the Nevada sun had relentlessly beaten his meek, meandering body. William had just returned from a slow swerve back up the strip. Wobbling a slalom from the Flamingo to the Stardust, all the while his blood thickened in the heat as the vodka burn screamed in his throat. Turning to face the corridor, the metallic whiz of the lift rushed away from him, and he sagged unceremoniously into an aluminium serving trolley. Squinting, trying to observe his surroundings with clarity, he clung to the metal.

Unsure if this was his floor because all the floors looked the same, and yet right now he recognised none of them, he noted his depth perception had greatly deteriorated. William prodded a sweaty fingertip towards his eyes in case one of them happened to be closed. Both of them were closed, cowering away from his hands, and he could see nothing but a cloak of colour that was both black and white at the same time. All of the colours and none of the colours flashed behind his raw eyelids. William's head came in contact with something cold, the way a lolloping child suddenly comes in contact with the ground, and a clinical lavender fragrance traced into his nostrils, eliciting an urge to wretch. Conceding the use of his legs, he slumped to the floor in a desperate attempt to escape the wretched lavender, and landed in a concertina of limbs, wedged into a nook beside the hotel elevators. He looked up with half an eye. A hazy wicker bowl of tiny square soaps teetered precariously on the edge of the trolley, threatening to fall and assault him with its odorous contents.

'You absolute bastard,' William slurred towards the bowl, as a bubble of hot alcohol roared in his gut and rippled through his throat. He gasped a few times, trying to cool his oesophagus with the stale hotel air. Wondering vaguely what non-specific minute of which hour it was, he gargled. Not that the time mattered. He knew it was still daylight outside, so whatever hour had happened to sneak up behind him he was inappropriately drunk. Time was a snake in the desert.

#

His left eye opened, successfully wrestling against his gound entwined lashes, whilst a bloom of crust cemented his right closed. His functioning eye cowered, and hesitantly opened again as it attempted to adjust to the unwelcome light of the living; the light stabbed through his retina and back into his brain like a shard of ice. William compromised on a squint and picked at the yellow crystals along his dry lids.

'Fuck,' he mumbled as his skull turned to rock.

'My dad owns a magic shop.'

William's heart bolted, and he sat up so fast he thought the propulsion would keep him moving until he was completely folded in half. His eyes, shed so suddenly of sleep, opened widely and blinded in the daylight. His arm shot up to mediate his vision as he attempted to hastily decipher where the intruding voice came from.

'Who, what?' his voice popped and snapped.

He was confused. He hadn't spoken to anyone without exchanging money or keys with them since he'd arrived. He wasn't even sure he remembered how to converse under normal circumstances, let alone with this unknown voice, now, here.

'My dad owns a magic shop,' the female voice came from behind him and he twisted accordingly. A woman he didn't recognise was sitting on a wooden chair he did recognise, her arm resting across the Formica desk which held all the never-to-be-used hotel stationery.

'Why are you telling me that?' *And who the fuck are you?*

'You looked like you could use some,' she smiled.

'Some what? Oh, magic. Sorry. I'm... Could you pass me my trousers?'

'You weren't wearing any when I met you.'

Oh, God.

'There should be some on the floor somewhere,' he swallowed thickly. 'And sorry about that. The trouser-less... ness. And the floor.'

She laughed easily. 'That's not a problem, I was highly amused.' William exhaled to half capacity. 'But you don't have any trousers here. You know this isn't your room, right?'

His eyes snapped across the carpet, desperately searching for his Venn diagrams. His dirt. His beautiful waste. But there was nothing of his blurb here. There was a suitcase closed under folded clothes. A large sun hat on the coat hook. No vulnerable story fallen across the floor; those folded clothes, that sun hat, they were nothing more than a tale on the back of a postcard. A prologue to nothing. This room was tidy, her life was tidy. And it all meant she was correct. This wasn't his room. *Holy hell.*

'I don't. Words. I don't really have any of them to say about this. I'm sorry. I'll go. I can't believe,' William spluttered, attempting to vacate the bed swiftly and without making eye contact with the woman. 'So very sorry, really.' His eyes darted about the floor, still hoping to see his own socks, or journal, or any general debris that could be attributed to him.

'I'm Dawn.'

He heard the smile in her voice. Her honeyed tones were vaguely soothing in spite of circumstance. It was then he realised.

'You're British?'

'From the same county as you, apparently. At least I think that's what you said. You were rather excited about that.'

'Wait, I spoke to you? Functionally? I maintained a conversation last night? Hold on, what time is it?' William rapidly felt different parts his own body for familiarity. He had no memory of this incident. Surely she wouldn't have approached him. He remembered the overwhelming smell of lavender, which still hid at the back of his throat, and nothing more.

'You did, I'd almost say you were more coherent than you are now,' Dawn laughed again, fingering one of the Stardust's pencils. It rolled away across the Formica. 'And it's…' he heard the stretch of her body in her voice as she elongated her last word, leaning out to see the clock he could have just as easily looked at, 'ten fifteen.'

'That's specific.'

'Ah, your clock with the eight.'

'I told you about my clock?' William rubbed his head, and recoiled from the pressure. His skin was on fire. He must have gone outside. There were people outside.

'You did indeed.'

'Were there many other additions to the conversation or did I just impress you with the clock anecdote?'

'Mostly the clock anecdote.'

He felt the thickness of dehydration heave through his veins. He needed water. A thought drifted to how pretty she was. *Why would someone like her talk to someone like me?* Her beige-blond hair was shoulder length, tousled, shorter and lighter around her face. She had a soft – perhaps too soft – jaw, and milky-blue eyes. William saw all corners of her smile at once.

'Don't you find it weird when people describe women as "the girl next door"?' He hated that phrase, he shouldn't have mentioned it, but he hated it. He had grown up next to a busybody whose beauty, if she had ever been blessed with it, could no longer be found in either her aesthetic or abstruse qualities.

'Um, sure...' There was a crackle of white noise and a loud whip of tuning as the radio came to life, and some guy started warbling about being lucky to love. 'Oh! I set the alarm last night in case you had anything to do today,' Dawn explained, reaching to turn it down as William started.

'Yes! I mean, no, I don't have anything to do. But thank you. Excellent idea. I thought maybe, well, whatever I thought it clearly wasn't logical.'

William fumbled with Dawn's identically insipid sheets. His earlier attempt to excavate the bed had inadvertently exposed a large portion of his chest, which was now manifest torment amidst the room's crisp light. Most pressingly, he was all too aware of the shade and size of his nipples, which had seemed perfectly normal in all instances up until this moment. William projected a scene in which he had been able to accept life's abject monotony. He imagined himself sitting in a creased, dull-white shirt, his cheap name badge marginally askew. His elbows resting upon a plastic desk in a tiny cubicle, situated amongst many other replica cubicles containing replica men. He imagined making thousands of calls about insurance for eight hours a day in exchange for an annual wage of £1,500, and he thought how wonderful it would have been to have his nipples under that shirt.

'Do you like this group?' she asked, gesturing slightly to the radio as she elegantly left her chair and began to conduct a grapevine across from the desk to the bathroom, and back again, as the warbler moved on to something about magic spells.

'I, this song's nice. Edison Lighthouse, isn't it? I don't think I know anything else they've done.' *Is this what women do?* he thought. *Do they invite indiscriminate men into their hotel rooms at night and then dance in front of them the next morning?* 'Oh, God,' the flush fell from his cheeks to sicken his stomach. *Oh, the irony.* 'Sorry, I… I don't think I have my wallet. I, it's in my trousers, which aren't here. Apparently. Awfully.'

'Surely you won't need your wallet between here and your room? Or…' Dawn stopped dancing.

'Oh! No. You're right. I don't know what I was thinking,' *That you were a prostitute.* 'I should go, then. Unless. No. Absolutely no unless, is there? You've stopped dancing, it wouldn't be rude. Thank you. For this. And sorry. For me.'

It doesn't matter that I'm embarrassed now, he attempted to mollify his rising anxiety. *I'll never see her again, I'll recover from the shame in a few weeks and the residual memory will only sporadically creep up on me and cause sudden profuse sweating every few months for the rest of my life. It's all fine, normal, really. A perfectly reasonable exchange.*

'You're very welcome,' Dawn was now back at the desk and writing on one of the never-used pieces of hotel stationery.

She's breaking all the rules. 'You were most entertaining. I'll let you go get showered and fed. I'll see you later though, yeah? Half past eight, wasn't it?' Dawn handed him the note she'd been scribbling, it had the familiar Stardust logo printed at the top whilst the rest contained a soft, printed rendition of her less familiar details. 'In case there's a change of plans and you need to contact me before then.'

Mum, 11/07/2011

Montecore drank my Sea-Monkeys. I had to leave him at home whilst I was at work instead of taking him to Iris' because she had a doctor's appointment and couldn't look after him. At first I was relieved because that meant I got to go straight home after work, so I stopped off at the take-away place across from the library and bought a celebratory pizza for me and Montecore. I ordered a double topping and ran home with the pizza box tucked under my jacket so it didn't go cold. Montecore greeted me at the door like he usually does at Iris', but he was even more excited because he could smell the pizza so he kept jumping up. He could jump surprisingly high, and even though he's still pretty small he's already twice as big as he was when I got him. He's really springy, like a jack-in-the-box. I'd call him Jack but everyone calls everything Jack. Why is that? And why aren't more people deterred from calling things Jack when there's already so much Jack?

Anyhow, he was jumping up and I could see beads of water on his tiny white beard. I assumed he'd just been drinking from his bowl, but when I got upstairs the pirate ship was upturned in the middle of my desk surrounded by a thin puddle of water. I looked at Montecore and he cocked his head and looked from the desk to the pizza, like he knew he had done wrong and maybe this meant he wasn't going to get any pepperoni. So I told him he hadn't been bad, not really. He'd only misbehaved by human standards, so I wasn't angry because he isn't human and he wouldn't understand and doesn't have standards. When I was cleaning up, I noticed one of the Artemia was still alive and lying in a tiny pool of liquid, so I refilled the small tank and put the ship and the lone Sea-Monkey back inside and named it Jack.

I gave Charlie his gift this week. He gave me a cheese and pickle sandwich and I remembered I'd brought something for him, too. I'd wrapped it up really nice and put it in one of those bags that make gifts seem more grandiose. He seemed really pensive when I handed it to him, like I'd done something wrong or he was scared. Then he asked me how I knew, so I asked him what he thought I knew, and he said that it was his birthday. I said I didn't know it was his birthday, and explained I got him a present to say thank you for the sandwiches. Then he looked at me, his eyes wetter than it was necessary for them to be, and said that was even better. He said it in a whisper, like maybe I wasn't there. So I wished him happy birthday, and he said yes, yes it is. Then, because he had said that, I felt compelled to say that the gift wasn't really very good and that it just seemed like it might be because it was in a bag and sorry. He said that the gift was the real gift, so I stared at him in case he had Alzheimer's like Iris probably has, and he smiled, so I smiled back, but I was very aware that all my teeth were showing. They were so dry, my teeth. Dry and sticky. My lip wouldn't slide back down.

When Charlie finally opened his present he didn't say anything, so because I was standing there also not saying anything, I felt I should say something otherwise the silence would become too loud. I asked him if he had any birthday plans and he smiled again, without any teeth showing and not with his eyes, and said that he didn't. Then, by accident, my voice asked him why he didn't have any plans, and he said he had no one to have plans with, other than himself, and that he was going to sit in front of the telly and drink a pot of tea. I asked him how far away from the TV he sat, and he said it didn't matter because he never turned it on anyway. I wondered what that meant, before doing some more in-depth wondering about why Charlie didn't ask me why I had asked him how far away he sat from the TV. I concluded there's more I don't know about people than I knew I didn't know about people.

Looking back on it, it was a pretty rubbish gift to get Charlie, even Mira had advised against it. Well, she wanted me to get him this real nice set of Dickens' collected works. They had covers that made them look old even though they were new because people like that. I thought this wasn't the best idea Mira ever had because Charlie worked in the library basement surrounded by all those books all day, including many editions of Dickens, and people are always complaining about taking their work home with them, so why would Charlie be any different? Mira argued that whole, *Do a job you love and never work a day in your life,* Confucius spiel that everybody likes, but if I'm honest, I'm not too much of a fan of his.

When I was little someone gave me a book of Confucius' sayings and one of them was something like *Better a diamond with a flaw than a pebble without,* and then right there on the same page was this other thing, *Everything has beauty but not everyone sees it* and those two ideas always seemed really contradictory to me. The guy says everything has beauty but then he says a diamond is better than a pebble. Why? What if I prefer pebbles? Is it because a diamond is rarer, or because it has been denoted as more 'valuable' by society? So what? Even if I exchanged the diamond for food or shit like that, that's only because society has implemented this economic infrastructure that values these tiny bits of rock that were just in the ground anyway, hiding down there all free and equal to the pebbles and silt and gold. We used to trade in pigs and crops. In some parts of the world a rich man would be the man with the most camels, but here, in a city suburb, a camel would be an inconvenience. That man with all the camels wouldn't be rich, he'd be in quite the predicament.

In other places, in tribes or monasteries or other times, a rich man would simply be the man who was happiest. A diamond is a lot of camels, but it could never be a lot of happiness. Was Confucius a real person, or just a made up man people attribute sayings to?

Anyway, more clothes or food or camels or happiness or whatever, we're all equal, we're all just alive because of sympathetic conditions, and we have developed this inexplicable consciousness that is just the most absolutely mind-blowingly astounding thing conceivable. And what's a diamond in the face of human consciousness? In the face of the fact I can write this to you and you can understand it and contemplate the same things that I am right now, even though we're not even a flicker in the middle of infinity? It's a fucking pebble. That's what it is. Sometimes Mira says I get too concerned with things like this, and for a while I worried about that too, then I saw another programme about people exchanging junk and cared a lot less about what Mira thought.

So, I gave Charlie a snow globe and inside it had this Victorian looking factory and when you shook it instead of glitter these tiny black flecks filled the sky. Even though it's kind of one of those things that has no reason to exist, I'm pretty sure that to him it was better than a diamond or a pebble.

Myles

Potential last line for a novel:
The same thing was on every channel.

Chapter 17
Falls the Shadow
June 1944

'That's not entirely true now, is it, Annie?' Jerry forced a smile.

'I'm just saying what Brenda told me. I don't know either way, but facts don't just start from nowhere.'

'No, that's the habit of rumours, wouldn't you say, John?'

John shifted in his chair.

'I wouldn't like to say, Jerry. Who can really tell? Everything is so up in the air in this war,' he paused, 'all wars.'

'Anna, you must remind me to give you that recipe, it's delicious, although I might say that's due to the deterioration of my taste buds,' Lily interjected. 'Crazy the effects of this rationing, isn't it? I've found myself craving bananas and I never even liked them when I could have them, something about the texture I never got along with.'

She slipped her hand gently over her husband's knee, tightening her fingers around his thigh, and in return he squeezed her fingers soothingly between his.

'Annie would just end up burning it, whatever it was,' Jerry chuckled derisively without the courtesy of mirth. 'You couldn't make a sandwich without burning it, could you, Annie?' He raised an eyebrow at his wife and reached to pick up a mug of weakly strained black tea. His chair rocking slightly against the hard floor.

'It's eggs I miss,' Anna answered Lily. 'And we were luckier than most, what with you getting all those extra from the farm at first, but now... well, you can't make anything without a few eggs, can you? And don't you try to tell me that awful dried packet stuff is the same.'

'How've you found the farm, Lily?' Jerry asked. He barely even listened to Anna at all anymore, and had recently concluded his newly acquired bursts of tinnitus were symptomatic of her presence.

'Our Lil has barely had the energy to take her socks off when she gets home,' John embraced his wife's hand in his lap, his clumsy paws eclipsing her thin, recently toughened fingers.

'He's been giving me foot massages,' Lily forced a giggle. 'If I'd known all I had to do to get a foot massage was work hard labour for fifty hours a week, I'd have done it sooner.'

'I don't think there's enough hours in the week for me to work in order get Jerry to give me a massage!' Anna laughed eagerly, her eyes darting between Lily and John.

The room stiffened in the stilted tension that followed Anna's laughter; the walls shifted awkwardly against themselves, the rug buried deeper into the wooden floor, plaster blushed behind paint, toes curled in shoes, and teeth gritted behind lips, all in the hopes of passing the moment faster. It was Jerry who readied to break the silence.

'Well, perhaps you'd know if you ever did anything, or were you planning on winning the war with all that typing you wrap yourself up in?'

In truth, Jerry was hoping to aggravate Anna's unbearably tireless, whinnying personality in front of their friends. Not to shame her, but simply to illustrate his inhuman endurance of her insufferable character. Jerry maintained the potentially futile belief that a mild nod of recognition, or the promise of a sympathetic ear in the future, may briefly alleviate his purgatorial punishment. However, he was worried that it was the length of time suffered in a relationship that caused the other to relinquish their charms. And consequently, where he would see Anna's mawkish ignorance, John and Lily would see only admirably sweet, if not slightly cloying, concern and affection.

'I'm lucky, really,' Lily shot. 'I mean, I get to come home every night because we live so close. One of the girls who works on the farm, she's only seventeen bless her, she has to cycle six miles in each direction. I think she must be awake before the moon, if she sleeps at all.'

'Perhaps I should just drink my time away,' Anna spoke so quietly there was evident doubt she had spoken at all.

'We get all the biggest potatoes, though,' John added. 'Huge,' he gestured the approximate size of a large potato with his hands. 'Bigger than this, even,' he reassessed, looking at the negative space between his palms. 'Eh, Jerry, imagine that!' John raised his fingers, pressed in a large oval, towards Jerry.

'How's Rose?' Anna addressed the room, convinced that their children may be the only topic Jerry would graciously respect. She knew he missed seeing Rose as frequently as he had before Bobby left. They both did. There were so very many things to miss that sometimes there was no time to appreciate what remained.

'She seems fine when we see her,' John answered, lowering his imaginary potato. 'She's still working up at the munitions factory. We see her at weekends, but I think she prefers it there because they have a bunkhouse for all the girls so she gets to stay with them. She says it stops her from missing Bobby so much. I don't know what she'd do if…'

'*John,*' Lily.

'Sorry. Jerry, Anna. Sorry, I… Have you heard anything?'

'We haven't heard any bad news so we're assuming that's good news,' Anna swallowed thickly.

Anna hadn't really known how to behave since Bobby left. She couldn't remember how she used to fold her legs in order to sit comfortably, how she used to concentrate for so long on reading or writing or being. How she could walk without being conscious of each leg repeatedly moving in front of the other, so carefully, so precariously well balanced. How she could once drink or eat or breathe. Anna could simply no longer remember how it felt to live without fear. All she knew was none of those nothing things – the breathing, the walking, the living – had a feeling until the fear came and took them all away. The nothing things had become something things. Next time, Anna vowed, next time there was nothing she'd make the effort to remember every single detail. Every smell, every movement, every touch, every sound of nothing, she would memorise the lightness until she was so saturated with nothing that she would never again have to be so completely something.

'Bobby might not be as tough as some other boys, but he's got something between his ears that I'm praying will keep him out of trouble. You don't need to be tough when you've got a gun. Bullets don't care all too much about the size of your muscles, they'll rip through that flesh as good as any other.'

'*Jerry*,' Anna.

'*Anna*,' Jerry.

'Well, I hope you both know our thoughts are always with him,' Lily, too far away from Anna to touch her, pressed her fingers to the bevelled edge of the coffee table and rubbed it comfortingly.

'We do, Lil, we do,' Anna matched Lily's hand on her side of the table. 'Please, you and John help yourselves to anything you want from the allotment. There's not a lot but there's too much for just us, and we'd rather you took what you wanted before we handed the spare out.'

'You can't just say, "Help yourselves to the allotment," Annie,' Jerry pitched. 'They haven't come over to go digging around in the mud, *you* must root it up for them yourself.'

#

112

The allotment, much like everything else, had been a source of increasing disagreement between Anna and Jerry. At first, it was ploughed and planted out of necessity. They had borrowed tools from polite, nervous neighbours, and Jerry had dug over the small rectangular area of garden that didn't appear too arid to grow anything. Once the more strenuous labour had been completed – the tough rooted grass removed in rigid dry squares, the hard clay bottom soil broken up and turned – Jerry handed the upkeep over to Anna, who planted the area half with carrots and half with parsnips.

They had also procured a pair of chickens, swiftly and ironically named In and Out. Lamentably, In and Out never once laid eggs, but would frequently eat and defecate, so Jerry eventually got drunk enough to throttle them. Any residual hung-over guilt from the cull quickly dissipated during the week Anna was able to serve chicken with every meal. Whilst the birds were dry in the absence of oil or butter, and flavourless without much seasoning, when Peter had visited for dinner that Sunday they each commented on how particularly mouth-watering In and Out were.

The week of In and Out ultimately served as nothing more than a distraction from the ever-increasing distance between Anna and Jerry, which was manifesting most fervently from that rectangular patch of soil. For the first few months after the allotment had been dug out, Anna unsuccessfully tried to produce anything in the way of sustenance. Jerry found her incompetence irksome yet pardonable; the soil wasn't ideally suited for vegetables, it was her first attempt at having a vegetable garden and, most pertinently, Jerry suspected he would have fared no better himself. However, it was the placement of the allotment that finally brought the guillotine to their relationship. Of course, given the petite dimensions of the garden there was no alternative, but if allotments were to require walls theirs would have been satisfied borrowing its first from the long side of Jerry's shed.

More and more often, Jerry would be contentedly relishing

his evening of bitter and drunken melancholy with David, only to hear Anna outside chirping questions openly to the soil. Irritated by his wife encroaching upon his privacy, Jerry was perplexed by the understanding that if Anna could hear them through the thin wall, then she must realise they could, in turn, hear her. Jerry brewed further hatred for his wife, assuming her infernal drivel was an attempt to garner his attention. Why must she be so needy as to require him to be constantly distracted by her? Was it because she knew he would have to listen, and any response would infer interest? It was presumptuous and selfish. *She* was presumptuous and selfish.

Eventually, under the spite of ex-lovers, the allotment overcame its initial teething problems and blossomed into a stalwart crop, but it was far too late for Jerry and Anna. At the behest of social convention, their relationship had yet to entirely collapse, and instead teased at bare minimum. They became little more than the perfunctory shell of commitment. The allotment had provided the final barrier between husband and wife, for it was the first fruit grown of their love ending. They had undertaken a task together with their minds and hearts separated and yet here, in the form of a few carrots, it was proven; life would go on. Jerry spent more and more time in his shed after the child of their intolerance bloomed, and Anna returned to the room upstairs, filling the wardrobe with words.

Chapter 18
Kekulé's Dream
July 1972

William hated the photograph in his wallet. He kept it hidden in a windowless slot behind a tab of dried out gum, but he kept it nonetheless. He hated all photographs of himself. Tiny suspended fragments of life. He never hated them because of how he looked – who cared if he was too heavy or entirely skeletal, if one eye was closed or his lips appeared too thin – that stuff couldn't really haunt a person. His looks had either been changed, for better or for worse, or they remained, in which case there was no nostalgia to be had for them; they could be tidied away, packed into neat diminutive compartments, and forgotten about.

It was what lay behind his eyes in those photographs that really taunted him. It was the hope and intrigue for the future, the yet-to-be-quashed aspirations, the blank, inflated heart of potential throbbing within his bones before it was burned, blackened and broken. He knew the story of that boy in the photograph and he wanted to warn him. He never felt any pity for his present self, the self with the experiences and ruin, the self who couldn't sleep and wept and hurt. The self filled with hate and disgust. He saved it all for that boy in the washed-out photo. That innocent, pale him who was so misguided about what it would be to try and live.

He wondered if everybody felt that way, wondered if their hearts broke over their own childhoods every time a family album was opened. Wondered if everyone mourned their adolescence, watching in agony for that change from everything they could be to everything they became. Convinced his discomfort was more than the simplicity of ageing, he supposed that perhaps the real disquiet came when considering how all that time had been exhausted and yet still he had no answers for the most precious way to have spent it.

That's the terrible thing about time, he thought. *You spend all of it trying to do the most possible with no ability to measure what 'most' constitutes. The real desire with time is to save it, to do something so completely inconceivable with it, that once it has passed, it is then collated and presented to you as a complete multifaceted article: it is presented to you as that exact time again.* William considered how impossibly he desired for spent time to become a tangible gift, able to transcend the end of his life as a stitch in space. In reality, he knew however he spent his time it would still one day be gone, and he couldn't come to terms with having to possess every second until they all departed. There was no pause button, no rationing of minutes; there was no life other than one spent watching every moment expire in its complete strict definiteness.

He'd adapted to his fear of living by apprehending the morose, prosaic yet-to-be with an ambition to do nothing more than watch it pass. William decided that if he chose to live in melancholy, swollen with disenchantment, if he chose to live in absolute dissatisfaction with stagnant aspirations, then he would surely thwart the system. He would get everything he wanted simply by wanting what he would be given. He would ride his life as a rat and a dead man.

He looked at the version of himself in the photo. Seventeen years had passed and it might as well be someone else. He was sitting chubby kneed and ruddy faced on a gritty beach, his sticky fingers prodding at a red cowboy hat as the dry British summer hung high overhead. Only a parasol and an elderly stranger encroached into the middle-distance between him and the flat, glaucous sea. He couldn't remember that day, but he could remember the ghost of not being the way he was now. When he was very young he had wanted to be a conquistador. He hadn't known what one was, but he had liked the sound of it, *conquistador*, and had inanely repeated the word until it triggered semantic satiation in his parents. By the time he had discovered what exactly a conquistador was, he had lost interest, and the next possible future was beginning to spike in his imagination.

William had lived none of the many futures he had cycled through during childhood, but he had learned to dismiss all of them. He reasoned that all his dreams would have eventually ended up tired and over-analysed, broken down and chewed up as meaningless fractions of a whole. All good would become empty. Any life would slowly change into a list of its components: breakfast every day, commute every day, work every day, and in turn, each of those things would eventually become broken down, too; breakfast would become grabbing the cereal, opening the fridge, pouring the milk and handling a spoon, until each of those things became even further fragmented into beats and seconds; it would be sliding a finger along a cardboard flap, raising it, splitting open the plastic innards, tilting the box over a bowl, watching the cereal cascade into the ceramic, lowering the box, pushing the bag back inside, taking three steps, feeling for the fridge handle, combatting the initial suction release before the door swung open, touching the chill of a milk bottle, hearing the clink of the glass against its neighbour... and then each those things would fragment further... William knew any life would ultimately contract into meaninglessness, the way many years ago *conquistador* had to his parents.

#

'I just hate how we're all the same, don't you? Well, you must do if we're all the same, because if you didn't hate that we're

117

all the same then we'd be different, then there wouldn't be anything to hate in the first place, which would make us all the same again... or don't the minutiae count?'

Dawn thought for a moment, processing the latest coagulation of William's thoughts. The sun radiating off the busy Las Vegas strip mirrored her eyes back at her in the sides of her aviators. She blinked, watching the shadow of her lashes bat against the tinted lenses. William appeared predictably unsettled, shifting his weight in his chair and winding his scraggy arms in a jumper far too thick for the weather.

'Of course they count,' she measured. 'If they didn't we'd be considered not as individuals but as communities or countries or planets or galaxies, because where would we draw the line? What would be seen as an irrelevant detail and what would be seen as relevant? There would be no overriding authority to determine the degree of difference something must have before it became *other*. It's a sorites paradox,' Dawn paused, observing William. In the silence he was tracing a finger around the edge of his plastic seat, his head propped jauntily against his shoulder, his mouth firmly closed and his eyes staring so fixedly at the ground that she doubted he even saw it. 'You know, it's just like that question: if you keep removing individual grains from a heap of sand, you will eventually be left with only a single grain, but at which point did it stop being a heap? Or in this case, at what point do our differences stop resonating as differences?'

William picked at the pads of his fingers. He was surprised by Dawn's response. She hadn't dismissed him in the way he had anticipated, although he should have come to expect that of her by now. It had been four days since he had woken, disoriented and stunned, in her hotel room, and she had yet to walk idly into any of his assumptions. He looked at her. Her face was almost neutral, only a slight resting smile turning the corners of her lips. A thread of her loose hair was delicately pirouetting on the dry dessert breeze. He felt a flicker of envious desire towards those freely dancing

118

strands, his jumper clinging greedily to his neck and arms, boiling his anxiety beneath an itchy woollen shield.

'It stops being a heap when you can see how many grains there are without having to count,' he squinted at the gleam of a passing car.

Dawn laughed openly towards the washed-out Vegas sky. He lowered his chin, watching her through the tops of his eyes, as though conducting covert surveillance behind a newspaper. She was muttering not-quite sentences – *oh Will, you, what did I expect* – between her fractured laughter. A small, uniformly pastel-clad family walked past their table and towards the café, smiling symptomatically at Dawn's infectious delight. William immediately set about fingering his paper straw, prodding the remaining shards of ice in his glass of watery Coca-Cola.

'Excuse me, honey, I hope you don't mind me saying but you look beautiful,' the mother of the pastel family had paused, breaking away from the pack.

William was transfixed by his thumb in his sleeve.

'Oh, you're so sweet to say so!' Dawn replied. 'But it's just the weather, it makes everybody beautiful.' She smiled as the pastel woman squeezed her arm and bustled away into the café after her family. 'What a lovely woman,' Dawn beamed.

'Well.'

'What?'

'Nothing.'

Dawn took a sip of her lemonade. William pretended to have his curiosity piqued by something happening further down the strip.

'My brother studied Philosophy at a university in London. I read his old course books sometimes when I'm working in Dad's shop. It can be kind of slow in there.'

'Oh,' William was unsure how to respond to her arbitrary facts.

'You know, what I was saying about the sorites paradox,' she explained. 'It was one of the first things my brother taught me when we were younger. It's one of those bits of knowledge that everyone recognises because it exceeds the subject, like photosynthesis, or oxbow lakes, everyone knows about those even if they don't know anything else about science or geography.'

'Oh,' William understood.

'Only, with my brother, I think it was the heap thing that piqued his intrigue.'

'This is very unlike England,' William spoke absently, to himself as much as Dawn.

'Why else would we visit?'

'In England we don't talk to each other unless we already know each other. That woman,' he gestured inconspicuously towards the pastel family re-emerging from the café. 'She wouldn't have happened in England.'

'Which do you prefer?'

'I don't think I'm too fond of either.'

'Of course not.'

'In England, if you're in a lift with a stranger you can safely assume neither of you are going to speak. But that's awkward, too. Both people in the lift know that the other can talk, but won't talk, and both people are probably also thinking about being in the lift with another person who can talk, but isn't and won't. So then not only are they not talking, they're not talking about this huge thing they so evidently have in common, which is what people spend their entire lives basing relationships around. So really the whole negative aspect of the situation is intensified by itself. It's vicious circle, using a lift in England.'

'How do you know what other people feel in a lift? You could be alone in thinking those things.'

'Dawn, nobody gets in a lift relishing the opportunity to spend fifteen seconds entombed within the personal space of a stranger.'

'Maybe not, but they could nothing it, *I* nothing it.'

'You don't nothing it.'

'Yes, I do.'

'You can't nothing something, because to know something is about to happen is to apprehend it in some way, even unconsciously. You could even argue nothing-ing something is to something it.'

Dawn shook her head slowly, biting her lip to try to hide a burgeoning grin.

'All right,' she conceded. 'My unconscious response to apprehension when getting into a lift is to nothing it,' she teased, labouring William's words back at him.

'Well,' started William, beginning to sink into the vague comfort of their new dynamic, his mind betraying him as it considered the softness of her skin, '*you* would nothing something.'

'...And you would something nothing.'

Mum,   15/08/2011

I am sitting on the bench in the Tiny Cemetery as I write this. Montecore is lying nearby, nipping at the hawkbits blooming under the bench to meet the summer. I feel kind of light and I don't know why. The best I can guess is because the sun is shining, Montecore is at my feet, and I'm here, in the Tiny Cemetery, and whilst I'm here I feel like everything else matters a lot less, if it matters at all.

I noticed Charlie taking some of the books from the basement today. We're not allowed to take the books, so I asked him what he was doing because he could just check the same titles out upstairs as we were both given library cards when we started working there. I think the library likes to engender a passion for reading in its employees, which makes sense. Charlie laughed when I told him this and opened his bag to show me what he was taking; it was full of Roald Dahl and Enid Blyton. I blinked a lot instead of saying anything because I wasn't sure what conclusion he wanted me to make. Then Charlie said the books weren't for him, so I told him he didn't have a family, and he said he knew that.

Charlie said he was taking the books from the library because once a book gets put in the basement it never leaves the basement, so thinking this was a terrible waste he decided to take it upon himself to surreptitiously deliver the books to a charity for underprivileged kids. He said the charity never really has all too much money, and even though these books weren't new anymore, the stories were timeless in the way

122

that everything rich and wonderful and full of imagination is. He said the library works in conjunction with the university here, so they're spending all their money on textbooks and fancy volumes on Art History that no one will ever read. Then, in turn, the art books will make the library look good to prospective students so they will decide to come here with their tuition fees, which the university will then donate to the library so they can buy even more pretentious texts and upgrade the computer suite so even more students will come, and the cycle will go round and round.

Apparently, Charlie has been sneaking books out of the basement to give to the kids' charity pretty much since we started working together but I never noticed before, which made me think about the other things I must not notice, and that's really an impossible thing to think about. Charlie said he sneaks the books home and cuts out the pages that have the library stickers on so that no one knows where they are coming from, and then takes them to the charity. I made a joke that Charlie was like Robin Hood, and he said not quite but then he smiled.

Anyway, I wanted to tell you more about the Tiny Cemetery, not Charlie. I just told you about Charlie because one day maybe I'll say something else about him and it's important to know lots of different things about a person so you can interpret the intentions behind their other actions more easily. Like, because I know that Charlie doesn't have a family, my brain is making me think he's taking books to poor kids to compensate, but if he did have a family then I wouldn't invent a reason for why he was doing it. I'd just assume he was being a good guy. Or maybe I'd just invent a different reason, like he feels guilty because he has a family.

There are a few different rumours behind the Tiny Cemetery. Different guesses for who could be in the graves and why. Mira used to say they were the graves of characters from books that have always been real, only no one knew they were real, so they were buried in unmarked graves. That way the stories about them could continue for as long as there were people to write the stories. Mira said because of this the secretly real characters could essentially live as close to for ever as anyone could. I explained to Mira that mathematically, even if people wrote about them until the extinction of the human race, they wouldn't live any closer to for ever than us, which prompted her to argue that time didn't exist if there wasn't anyone to observe it. I laughed until I realised she wasn't joining in. I was unsure as to whether she was being modest by not laughing at her own joke or actually being serious, so to test I made a counter-joke asking her if that meant her for evers were finite. She said of course for ever could be finite, so I stopped arguing because I realised she was being an idiot, and you can't argue with an idiot.

Like what Mira believes, the rumour that circulates amongst little kids is that the Tiny Cemetery is home to the graves of Goldilocks' three bears, which is probably some story parents tell in order to buffer the truth because the official rumour, the rumour that has become local legend, is a whole lot creepier. I like the legend though, because I think it offers the most human answer to why the graves have no names, which is kind of ironic.

If you start walking away from the heart of the city and keep going through the thin alley past the Tiny Cemetery, you will eventually arrive at the home of the upper crust. This is essentially a long winding street lined with these impossibly green hedges and an armament of trees and other over-sized foliage. Sporadic wrought-iron gates are dotted throughout the leaves. This abundance of fleshy nature acts as a barrier between those that live in the houses beyond it, and those of us who will probably never step inside a home so large it has entire rooms that have been forgotten.

The legend says there was a rich woman who used to live in this part of the suburb, in one of those houses that can't be seen from the road, and that she was lonely. She had once been married, but when it transpired she couldn't have children because her womb was dry and bitter her husband stopped telling her he loved her. A few years passed and the husband decided to leave. Only he had bided his time; he waited until his wife was old and insecure before he left to punish her for never giving him a family. He waited for her to fade and crinkle, her hair to thin and her skin to blot, and then he walked away. People say that he abandoned her for a much younger woman and this new woman gave him children, and the husband sent photos of himself with this new woman and these new children to the old woman who still lived in one of the sprawling hidden houses.

So all the heartbreak, the loneliness, and all that other stuff that plagues people whom only own cold things, it just chewed her away for days and weeks and years. Until one day she bought a doll. She bought an expensive doll that looked like a little girl, and she dressed it up and pushed it around in a pram and curled its hair and called her Sal. A couple of years passed and she bought a new doll, she gave it the same name and treated it the same way. Almost everything about this doll was the same as the last but this one was bigger because Sal, according to the laws of time and biology that otherwise escaped her, was older now. Two years later and a yet another new doll was bought. The same process applied. This went on and on in the giant empty house, as throughout the rest of the world an entire generation grew up, until eventually the old woman was living with an adult-sized Sal. She'd sit with Sal and conduct one-sided conversations, read Sal books and manoeuvre her up to the dining table having cooked her a meal. She even bought Sal birthday and Christmas presents. But then the woman got scared. She became worried that Sal would leave her. She worried that Sal would become restlessly bored being a young woman cooped up in a lonely house with only an old lady for company, so she bought a disused mannequin; she bought Sal a husband. She made them up a bedroom with his-and-hers end tables, and made him a whole bunch of suits and invented a job for him and named him Freddie.

This guy, John or Jeremy or something, he was the postman for that rich old woman, and he told people that one time when he went to deliver her mail he saw these two full-sized dolls, Sal and Freddie, propped up fully clothed on the swing seat in the garden. He said it unnerved him as they were rocking slowly back and forth whilst he walked up the path even though he couldn't see anyone else around. Anyway, by now the old woman was living with Freddie and Sal and I guess she suddenly freaked out, like maybe Freddie would leave Sal if she didn't give him a kid. Which makes sense to me, well, within the context of the situation anyway. So she bought Sal and Freddie a little girl: a baby doll that cried when you rocked it (a cry people still claim they hear coming from the smallest grave in the Tiny Cemetery). I don't know for sure but, naturally, there have been speculations that the old woman staged Sal giving birth with red dye and such. People embellish everything.

By this time, the old woman was living in that big empty hidden house with Freddie and Sal and the baby, and it really got to her, you know? Her husband left her and suddenly she's living with this perfect family and she realises they don't need her; she realises that she's entirely redundant to that functional little unit and she panics. She develops this paranoia about the doll family she lives with, the one she spent all those years nurturing, and she convinces herself that they're going to leave her. So one day she just flips out and kills them all in their sleep before they can abandon her. Well, she smashed their plastic skulls in whilst they were positioned, still spooning, in the bed she placed them in, and smothered the fake baby in the real crib she had so carefully lowered it into only hours before. And there you have it: three bodies for three graves.

The woman was rich and she'd bought the plots in the Tiny Cemetery, which I guess wasn't initially intended to be so tiny, for her family years before. She bought it before the cul-de-sac was built up around it in the fifties, before what was left of the grass was slowly eaten away, metre after metre, by garages and concrete parking spaces, and before she knew she was barren. People say that's why there are no names on the graves. That she did it to punish Sal and Freddie for wanting to leave her. She stripped them of the identity she had given them and made it as though they never existed. Maybe 'Everything unordinary' is actually just an old woman's spite.

It's a funny thing the power of a name, how so much attachment and endurance can be formed alongside something so intangible and common. Loads of people are called Myles. Perhaps less have my second name as well, and of course there's the surname on my original birth certificate, your maiden name, but there are still seven billion people in the world and more dead, some of whom will inevitably share my name. I find it kind of strange how the name of something is so inherently emphatic that once it's given it becomes inseparable from the thing itself.

There's a photograph of a man, you may have seen it, and he's alone, kneeling down at the 9/11 memorial. His head is angled downwards resting on the parapet, his arm outreached with his fingers clutching at the inscription of his son's name. It is a position of complete anguish. Yet his son never even knew about that memorial. He was killed, along with the 3,000 other names, in the terrorist attack on the World Trade Centre. Yet a father is there, kneeling before the name of his son – his own name – and he is completely vulnerable. All of those names, each and every one crowded within that tragic space, they conjure a little more weight, a little more empathy and shock and hate and sorrow and disbelief. *Three thousand* people died, but we see those names and learn one of them was named Ben. Maybe two or ten or twenty of them were named Ben. But you see a name and suddenly the death isn't symbolic of *one*, instead it's a real multifaceted life. Ben: a man who grew up and grazed his knees and didn't like carrots and had a first kiss that was awkward and read *Catcher in the Rye* four times because he thought he was meant to like it but really he didn't get why everyone loves it so much, and then many seasons passed, and he got rejected from his top choice university so he went to his backup and didn't study enough whilst he was there anyway and proposed to a girl who wasn't his first love but who packed his lunch the day the plane hit the North Tower. Ben.

I think names would be much more special if they were numbers. Montecore and I watched this film all about a lack of freedom and identity in this grey dystopian future where everyone has their name taken away and is instead assigned a number. I thought that was great, how no one else would ever have the same name as you because numbers are infinite. Mira said the idea was awful, she said if she was called 628948 (I don't recall the actual number she said), then she'd be constantly reminded that she was exactly the same as the 628947 people who had come before her. I said that the number would actually be much, much higher than that, but also that she was being silly, as there are probably thousands of Miras in the world right now, but there would only be one 628948. So she looked me right in the eyes for a second, which I've learned is what she does when she thinks she's right, and she said, 'What about the Sea-Monkeys? What about *Jack*?' There was a lot of emphasis on *Jack*. Admittedly, Mira seemed to have a good argument, until I replied, 'People aren't Sea-Monkeys, Mira.' Then she got high-pitched and said that wasn't the point. I was getting bored, and I don't like listening to squeaky Mira, so I decided to win (and therefore end) the conversation by saying, 'Jack doesn't have an identity because he is called Jack, he has an identity because he is an individual, which he became by being the only survivor of the Montecore incident.' Turns out I was wrong; being right didn't end the conversation.

I don't know what the truth is about names or graves,

but I do know if it wasn't for the Tiny Cemetery, I would never have met Mira. Anyway, I think Montecore is getting hungry. He's eaten two hawkbit heads and is looking at me as though he has been wronged. I think I'll leave now and get us another pizza.

Myles

Potential last line for a novel:
The war ended just as the war began.

Chapter 20
Ebb and Flood
July 1944

David paced, one foot heavier than the other, flattening the fibres of the rug against the floor beneath, and overtly checked his watch at each end-of-room pivot. Anna and Rose sat behind the low coffee table, eyes following David on a pendulum. His brisk movements were kicking up a dust, which twisted and whirled throughout the shards of light dividing the room.

'He said he'd be here by now,' David spat.

'I know. Sorry, Dave. I'm sure he'll be here soon. Sit down,' Anna waved a hurried hand at a chair. 'Do you want a snack? I might have something left…'

'I don't want a fucking snack, Anna.'

'Have you heard any news from Bobby?' Rose asked Anna for the second time that day.

'No, dear,' Anna smiled at the young girl. 'I'm sure we'd know, though. If anything bad happened, we'd feel it.'

'Well, did he say where he was going?' David interrupted, pieces of his saliva cascading heavily through the dust and light.

'He can't have gone far, why not take the weight off your feet until he gets here?' Anna gestured again to Jerry's rocking chair.

'I'm not a cripple.'

'I didn't mean to suggest you were. Please, Dave, just sit

down. Relax is all I meant, I wasn't even thinking about your leg.'

'No, of course you weren't thinking about my leg. Who cares what I lost, right? Who cares about me when the incredible Bobby and all the little boys are out fighting the *real* war and I'm cooped up here with the fucking women.'

'Shut up,' Rose's whisper was slight, but it had a polished edge.

'Excuse me?'

'You're lucky Bobby is out there fighting for you,' she met David's stare directly; the softened, waxy fat of eyelids draped over his stumpy lashes.

Rose had never believed Bobby when he told her he was going to be camped away somewhere along Britain's beaches, but the look on his face when he explained he was leaving spoke louder than the sentiment stunted between his lips; he needed her to believe him. And he needed to believe she wasn't going to worry herself sick, to believe she wasn't going to be completely alone with fear, and that he wasn't doing something as typical as breaking her heart. So, as her chest tightened and her knees buckled, Rose told Bobby she was glad he was going to be safe. Rose had smiled the first time her world ended.

'I'M LUCKY?' David bellowed incredulously as his awkward pacing came to a severe halt, his cheeks reddening under the pepper of stubble. 'What the fuck are you talking about?'

'Oh, let's not make a fuss. We're all very lucky and grateful for everything everyone's done, Dave. Whether it be now *or* then. Let's just be thankful we still have each other, yes? Sit down, please, you'll feel better.'

Neither Rose nor David acknowledged Anna's plea as she nervously looked from one to the other and then desperately towards the clock, praying her husband would get home quickly to appease his friend.

'You're lucky,' Rose spoke louder now, 'because if those

men weren't out there fighting then this entire country would be nothing more than smoke, bones and twisted metal, and your little *raison d'être* would be barely more than dust.'

'Don't you *dare* disrespect me, child,' David growled. 'I've been you.'

'You've *been* me?'

'I didn't just crawl out this way.'

'Regardless, you know nothing about me.'

'I know youth.'

'Age doesn't define me,' he had stolen her intrigue.

'Needless sentiment? Unapologetic hope? I'd say it does, sure as shitting and war. Both are diseases cured with time.'

'Or killed by bitterness.'

'Don't mistake symptoms for cause,' David smiled, assured in his convictions; she would believe him, if not now then one day. Life was its own punishment.

'You say I'm disrespectful, do you find all *truths* to be disrespectful or just that one specifically?'

David paused, his eyes narrowed, incensed as his teachings were left to hang, ignored without trial. Rose took a sip of water and placed the glass back down on the coffee table without breaking eye contact.

'Oh, you're a pair,' Anna laughed nervously, placing Rose's glass back onto its coaster.

'You're a spiteful little bitch. No wonder that kid left, probably just wanted to get away from you,' David's teeth flared towards Rose. He hated this.

'And how is your adoring wife, David? Or did you never marry? I forget...'

'Don't you push me, you little whore.'

He was leering over the coffee table now. Stretching his full height in an arch towards Rose, who feigned calm as his finger prodded against her face. Sweat traced around his receding hairline. The pungent aroma of stale alcohol crept out on his breath and crawled through his skin.

'Now, now, everyone, haven't we had enough of war not

to bring it into our own homes?' Anna tentatively traced a hand across Rose's back. 'We're all on the same team here!'

'So, no? Is that a no on the wife?' Rose gently sang her question towards the mountainous man. She held her voice and kept her breathing steady. Her insides whisked a storm through her chest. Bobby had gone to chase one monster, the least she could do was defy hers.

David's entire body shook at a resolutely stoic Rose. She politely took another small sip of her drink and placed the glass neatly back on the coaster, acknowledging Anna with a quick smile. Anna could feel blood vigorously driving at her throat as the tension thickened. Nervously twisting a cushion tassel between her fingers, a quiet *nnhmmm* escaped her lips as she tried to meet Rose's smile.

'Why don't you wait in Jerry's shed, Dave?' Anna tried to swallow but emptiness caught on the dry of her mouth.

'Shut up, Anna.'

She recoiled.

'Now, that was rather disrespectful of *you*, wouldn't you say, Dave?' Rose balanced a delicate weight with each word.

'YOU!' David lunged towards Rose. His palm met her throat. His knees cracked against the coffee table, sliding the other side forcefully into Rose's shins and upturning the glass of water, which spilled across a pile of papers and the plate of dry biscuits. 'Fucking bitch.'

Anna saw her nothing turn into something.

'LET HER GO!' she screeched. Leaping to her feet, the unprecedented volume in her voice catching both Rose and David by surprise. David stilled, observing the quivering woman. Shaking, Anna stood wielding a dripping wet plate. Soggy biscuits scattered wildly across the floor. Rose remained seated, forcing calm so she could push small breaths past the thick, meaty fingers grimly hooked around her throat. 'I said. Let. Her. Go.' She spoke through the teeth of a cornered animal.

'What the hell are you going to do about it?'

Nothing moved in that moment, only the nervous energy pulsating through Anna as the plate vibrated in the air.

'If you lay one more finger on that woman, I'll rip each and every one of them off.'

Their bodies waxworks, all three turned their eyes towards the living-room door.

'Jerry!' chimed David.

'Let go of that girl, Dave.'

'The little bitch was mouthing off about…'

'Let go of that young girl, David.'

'You should have heard her, the cunt…'

'Anna, you can put the plate down now, love,' Jerry smiled towards his wife, who meekly stood back in simultaneous relief and apprehension, lowering the damp plate to her side. Jerry walked the stunted paces of a gunslinger across the room. 'If you don't take your hand away from that wonderful young woman's throat, I'm sure both she and Anna will happily agree that the actions I'll be forced to take were in self-defence.'

'You don't scare me,' David roughly let go of Rose's throat. She gulped for lost breath.

'You should leave now.'

'Don't you fucking start, Jerry, not over these whores,' David pushed his shoulders backward, swivelling his bad leg to face his friend, who stepped forward to equal him.

'Get out of my house.'

Anna saw it first. David had reached for the wireless radio beside him, and the arc of his swing was heading right for the side of Jerry's skull. Jumping forward, she positioned her body between the men, hoping the extra obstacle would halt the conflict long enough for them both to calm. David intercepted by shoving her backwards towards the coffee table. Jerry ducked and charged, hurtling David backwards into the wall.

It was Rose's scream tearing through the house that stopped the men dead.

Chapter 21
Knights and Knaves
July 1972

'He doesn't know I'm here,' she pushed her fingernails against the rim of her glass, watching the pink fade to white as the blood scampered away.

'What made you leave?'

'It's strange, I suppose I must just be really good at ignoring or justifying what happens to me, but as soon as it happens to someone else…' Dawn gave an empty laugh. 'It was my dad. I came home with a black eye once too often and he worked it out. He broke down and cried right in front of me. It was the first time I'd seen him really show any sign of weakness and it was my fault. I'd broken his heart and it hurt me more than any of the abuse from Danny.' William silently nodded, refilling his drink. 'All the lies, the cheating, the put-downs, I'd excused it all… but my dad's face when he worked it out… I couldn't be the cause of that.'

William unhooked a small painting from the wall of his hotel room and studied the card backing, holding it rigidly in one hand whilst nursing a stout glass of whiskey in the other. Dawn brushed out a crease in his bed sheet with a flick of her wrist, watching him meander uncertainly across the carpet, the painting obscuring his vision.

'What…' William took a sip of his drink, holding the glass to his mouth and allowing the ice to numb his lips. 'Why did you two get together in the first place?'

135

She was surprised to find him staring directly at her. 'I don't know... He wasn't the same person then. He seemed vulnerable or, I don't know. I think that he just didn't know how to love me, that's all. Maybe he was afraid of losing me so he pushed me away.' William's eyes darted away under a frown. 'Or, you know, maybe he was just an asshole. I don't know, I was young, I'm *still* young. Stuff happens,' she shrugged.

Sitting down at the little Formica desk, William allowed a bare whimper to crawl off his tongue in agreement. He had quickly tidied his room after Dawn invited herself over, and whilst doing so he had felt the twinge of apprehensive unknown that typically fills teenage lungs with each breath of clumsy love. He hadn't felt it in many years. He was only twenty-two, but he had aged at a violent speed.

'My dad,' William began, shifting a glance into the small desk drawer and fingering the crisp Bible inside, 'he cries.'

'What do you mean? Like, easily?'

'Yeah. Well, he never used to. But then Mum died and he started crying and, I mean, he stops sometimes but that's only when he isn't feeling anything at all.'

'I'm sorry, I didn't know.'

'He exists but that's *all* he seems to do. He just exists and walks and breathes and eats, but it's like the whole world is a part of something he isn't.'

'How so?'

William exposed the corner of a sad smile into his glass.

'One day, after Mum had died, Dad told me how his life just felt like one really long World Cup final, only he wasn't watching.' Dawn made a sound like she wanted to understand but didn't. He cracked ice between teeth. 'You know the fervour that clung to everything and everyone when England beat Germany in sixty-six? The camaraderie that ravaged the streets so... vibrantly, so triumphantly, that suddenly, momentarily, we were all a team and it felt as though we'd all somehow, I don't know, earned that victory together?'

She nodded.

'Now imagine that, how incredible the air felt that night, but being locked in a box with no television, no radio, just the sounds from the cheers and the streets and the parties spreading like a weird virus across the country. Imagine observing that amount of joy but being stuck behind glass, banging, really screaming, and no one can hear you. Dad said he felt like everywhere had become a celebration, and he could hear all these voices connecting around him just never through him; the world was a secret victory and he wasn't in on it. He said the feeling only stopped when he slept.'

William drank.

'I like how true that is.'

'How *true* that is?'

'Don't you think things can have levels of truth the way things have levels of beauty?'

William put down his drink, inadvertently presenting Dawn with the illusion of contemplation. 'No.' Dawn saw his glass was empty again. 'I think something is either the complete truth or it is a lie.'

A banging on the door startled them both. William eyed the clock; it was 22:81. More banging, then voices. No, just one voice talking to itself. Now talking to him.

'I know you're in there, little lamb,' the words snaked through the door. 'I followed you.'

He should have expected this but he hadn't been thinking clearly. He should have insisted they went to her room, or out to the casinos, or bars, or even the fucking desert. The desert was consuming and vacant enough to be a thousand things to an optimist. She was an optimist, she would have written the meanings. He had a copy of *The Wasteland* somewhere; he could have read her that in a sea of dust. They could have played at being young and engorged with promise. She would have liked that. She liked everything.

Instead he was here. In a room that had abruptly grown so very small, so inescapable, so suffocating, so like home.

One or the other, never both. He frantically looked between the piles of hastily tidied belongings, then at Dawn, then the door, unable to formulate a plan that would cause an outcome vaguely preferential to the one staggering before him.

'Oh, Willy-Willy-William, come out, come out to play!' the voice was an incantation.

'I can't today, Earl,' he hardly heard himself. 'I'll come and see you soon though, yeah?'

'Will-you-now, Will-ee-am?' Earl sang the syllables from his station in the corridor. William's mind conjured the image of other hotel guests creeping from doors, or pushing eyes to the cold rims of peepholes, hungrily observing the scene.

'Of course, but I'll come and find you, don't worry about coming all the way over here,' William, standing on the far side of the room, directed his words towards the door with as much calm as he could muster. Still, his voice spiked, his cheeks darkened, and his heart ran tribal. 'Just a friend I met here,' he whispered to Dawn, pouring another whiskey and unsteadily offering her the bottle. Dawn reached out, but he put it down before she could accept.

'Why don't I believe you, Billy?' Earl toyed.

'Hey, it's not like you don't know where I live!'

'Tell me, what would I do if you left and accidentally forgot to say goodbye to your good old Uncle Earl?'

Fingernails scratched along wood. A giggling cloaked in heavy breathing came slowly hissing through the crack between door and frame. William threw his drink into the back of his throat, choking on the bite. Dawn, who had patiently watched him unravel, slowly unbuttoned her blouse.

'I wouldn't do that to you!' William's voice splintered and wetted as his throat rushed saliva to meet the burn of alcohol. 'He must be drunk,' he clarified with a nervous titter, not looking at Dawn, and she wondered if this charade was for him as much as her.

'See, I think you would, babe. And I don't fancy you walking out on me because I've become accustomed to your obedience. The way I see it, do you want to know how I see it, William?'

'Earl, I…'

'Do you want to know how I see it, William?'

'Yes,' he massaged the bridge of his nose between his thumb and forefinger.

'The way I see it is you're mine, and I feel like the longer you make me wait out here the rougher I'm going to be. You won't like Earl when he's mad, princess, his teeth come out,' a slow, metronomic tapping began rattling through the peephole.

Dawn was unlocking the door before William noticed she had moved from the area he had placed her in earlier; an area he had specifically designed to both accommodate Dawn and compartmentalise her view of his room, leaving him at a manoeuvrable advantage. All too late he saw her blouse hanging in loose drapes at her hips, the door swinging wide open, and her propping one hand defiantly against the wall. He half crouched forward. His natural instincts torn between ducking behind the bed in pitiable refuge, and dragging Dawn away from the door. He wanted to scream at her, ask her what the hell she thought she was doing, but at the same time he wanted to shelter her from Earl, from all dark and ferocious things. His hesitation caused him to stumble over the conflicted directions of his feet. Grasping at a corner of the mattress in an attempt to steady himself, William crashed gracelessly to the floor.

'Who the hell do you think you are, interrupting my time?' Dawn gestured wildly, indicating her body objectively towards Earl. 'I don't come hammering on your door when you've got your hands on him, now do I?'

'Huh?' Earl.

'You going to take any more of my hour or are you going to pay it for me?'

'I… fuck it, I just thought he was…'

'Yeah I know what you *just thought*, but he's fucking

busy. So if you don't mind.'

'Tell that tidy piece of meat I want him later, or maybe Earl won't be so patient next time.'

'Don't put me off,' she slammed the door.

William had scrambled into a scrappy, cross-legged arrangement, wide-eyed and flushed, in the middle of the awful mustard bed sheets. The half-empty bottle of Jack Daniels sat between his thighs, his hand gripped around the neck so fiercely his knuckles were white. Dawn took a step towards him. Her shirt still unbuttoned. William wasn't looking at her chest, but he noticed the white lace of her bra cradling her breasts like paper cases around peach cupcakes. She raised her eyebrows toward him, puffed out her cheeks, and folded her hair behind her ears. Her body shimmered in the glow of the lamplight.

'Blimey!' she lightened.

'You know?' he managed, quietly.

'I know,' she nodded, gesturing to sit down beside him.

'Don't move.'

'What?'

'You know?'

'Yes. You told me the night I met you. I thought maybe...'

'Why the fuck didn't you tell me?' louder now.

'I thought you knew I knew!'

'No, you didn't.'

'I...'

'Why didn't you tell me?'

'When? When was I meant to bring it up? Oh, by the way, you know I know about...'

'Oh, I don't know, *any time*? When we were eating dinner, or talking, or drinking, or any other fucking time during the last week,' the words tumbled as wounds through his teeth. 'Any of those occasions ring a bell?'

'I didn't, I... Did you want me to just drop it into casual conversation? It doesn't make any difference to me.'

'Well, it makes a lot of difference to me.'

140

'Look, William,' quietly.

'Get out,' quieter.

'Don't be...'

'Get out,' a whisper.

Dawn delicately lowered herself onto the bed beside him, her hand moving to soothe his thigh.

'It's going to be all right.'

William jerked, launching his bottle at the wall. The thick glass bounced off the stucco disappointingly, skidding to a gentle stop at the bathroom door. The anti-climax of his outburst racked his body with frustration. He jumped off the bed and kicked the cheap wooden chair away from the desk, electric tremors of pain ricocheting along his left shin.

'GET OUT!' thundered.

Mum,   25/09/2011

There were some flowers in the kitchen today. Real dead flowers like from Valentine's Day and graves. I have no idea where they came from or why, but they were on the sideboard between one of those old-fashioned flat irons that people love to display (even though it is essentially the same as someone in the future using a Morphy Richards as decoration), and a photo of me as a kid holding a cat. I think it was meant to look all loving and cute, me cradling that cat, but I've never really liked cats and it's apparent from the way I've gritted my teeth and pancaked the cat to my chest, whilst one of its front legs claws at my shoulder, that this has been the staged photographic dream of an adult. I must be about five or six in that photo. I still had a bit of puppy fat on my bones and my hair is gossamer shiny in the sun.

So, the flowers were sitting there between these two romanticised histories, one that was kind of ours and one that wasn't, and they had been arranged nicely in this lilac vase that was usually vacant so I guessed they were important to someone. I would have asked Julie about it but obviously she was in the bedroom, so I checked the calendar and it wasn't her birthday. I wonder if they're from Frank. Maybe he's given up searching for 'It' and is coming home. Can people do that? Just slot back into lives as though they never left? Anyhow, I sniffed the flowers, which predictably smelt of sweet and fresh things, then went to my room. Montecore and Jack were waiting for me, which was great because I keep expecting those two to have another altercation. I'm more attached to Jack now there's only one of him, and although I wouldn't care all too much if he died, I'd still feel a bit guilty about it. Sometimes I call Jack 'Captain' because he's now the sole owner of the pink ship, and then I get amused because I notice Jack has no idea how camp the whole thing looks, which reminds me of something else that happened this week.

Charlie was sitting on the wooden crate that's aligned with the back wall between the two farthest basement shelves. Charlie is always sitting there. Especially in the late afternoons when there's really no more work to do. He sits there every day and reads his paper and sucks on those little round white sweets with the red lines in them, the ones that look like cross-sections of a stick of rock. I'm not really sure if it was Tuesday or Wednesday, but it was a day of the week that wasn't better than the others because it wasn't near the weekend. I was putting a couple of books in the 940-949 section, which is where European Military History and late-afternoon Charlie live, and I noticed that Charlie looked kind of sad. Well, he always looks a bit sad because of his thick, beaten skin, but he looked morose. I didn't say anything. I just attempted to slide an ambitiously giant textual analysis of the Battle of Stalingrad on to the shelf as casually as possible, but the space between the other books wasn't *quite* big enough. Instead of giving up or moving some stuff around, I decided to push it really hard in order to wedge it into position, but the dust jacket had air trapped inside so it went in about half way before the air caused the plastic to balloon out at the spine. The cover puckered and crackled and stopped. I attempted to inconspicuously slide the book back out as though there wasn't a problem, so I could leave Charlie in peace, but the book was jammed in place, half in and half out.

I could see Charlie engrossed in his newspaper. It would have been as though I wasn't there at all, except his eyes weren't moving, they were just focused on one spot.

143

He wasn't reading, he was just waiting for me to go away again. I gave the book another gentle tug but it was steadfast. I resolved to try once more before giving up. This time I yanked it with a short, sharp jerk and it shot away from the shelf faster and easier than I had anticipated; I must have loosened it a bit the first time. Anyhow, the back of my hand smacked into my face, followed immediately by the force of Stalingrad, which is when I felt the blood start streaming out of my nose. I suspect this must have disturbed Charlie because his hand came up silently from behind the paper holding out a handkerchief.

As I took his handkerchief, I told Charlie what had happened. I hit myself in the face with this book about the Battle of Stalingrad, I said. Charlie remarked that it happened to the best of us, but I maintained a strong conviction that it didn't. As I mopped the blood off my face I noticed that Charlie's eyes were wet, and Charlie must have noticed me noticing because he wiped at them with his knuckles. Don't worry, I said, I'll be all right! I said this to pretend as though I thought Charlie was crying because Stalingrad attacked me, and it worked because he smiled and nearly laughed. I thought this was a good way to leave things, and went to walk away, but Charlie gestured to the newspaper he had been holding, so I had to look at that instead.

It was an article about a boy in Wales who had killed himself because of bullying. The paper wrote how he had been bullied for years but just before he killed himself there had been a 'stand out incident' where a group of other teenagers had pinned him down and tortured him. They said that the torture consisted of some teens burning him with lighters whilst others kicked him repeatedly, and wrote *FAGGOT* across his forehead in permanent marker. Apparently the boy was gay, but he was also ginger, which the bullies took additional exception to. The article said one of them cut at his hair with a penknife until his scalp had patches that were bald and bleeding. When I had finished reading the story, I didn't say anything, but handed the paper back to Charlie. Charlie looked at me for a while. I think he was trying to gauge my reaction to what I had read, but instead I was thinking about how I *should* react, and how closely Charlie was looking at me, and how much I wished that Stalingrad hadn't happened so that book had never been written and I wouldn't have been standing there.

What do you think? Charlie eventually asked, but I didn't have to say anything yet because he kept right on talking about how fucking disgusting it was, what those kids did, how it made him sick and angry and sad and vengeful all at the same time. When he had finished saying how repugnant everything was, it was my turn to talk. I said I didn't really understand how someone being ginger or gay could make someone else so angry. Charlie said neither did he, but then he said all that stuff people always say in defence of homosexuality. How it doesn't hurt anyone, how it's their human right to love, how they didn't choose to be gay, and how it didn't change who they were as a person. What Charlie said was all well and good, but I don't think that regurgitating the standard gay rights speech is really very interesting to someone who doesn't hate gay people. I don't hate homosexuals, so my brain stopped listening.

Whilst Charlie went on stating things that seemed very obvious, I wondered if punishing and bullying were similar things. In the minds of the teenagers they had taken it upon themselves to punish that other kid because he was gay, and if they were punished it would just be society taking it upon itself to bully them because they were hateful. So, as Charlie was talking about equal rights, I thought about what could have happened to all those other kids, the attackers, to make them so intolerant. At what point did they develop a hatred towards something so inconsequential to them? I sometimes think maybe hatred is just as innate as sexuality. It must be, right? I don't know. I don't know where any of my opinions come from. I don't know where any of me comes from. They

145

say we're an amalgamation of everyone we have ever met, but I haven't met that many people and I'm not very similar to Mira or Iris or Charlie or Frank or Julie. Not superficially, at least. I don't know who they are when they're alone. Instead of talking about that, though, when Charlie quietened and looked at me expectantly, all I said was how it was shame about what happened to the kid who killed himself just because he loved and just because he had hair.

Nothing much else happened this week. Montecore and I have been watching a lot of films. Somehow he knows when another dog is on the screen because his ears spike up, all alert, and his head rests at an angle. Oh, also, I was at Iris' for dinner and Mira told me she had gone on a date with some guy she met at work. Apparently he is very eco-conscious and rides a bike and has a vegetable garden. I said he seemed nice even though that wasn't entirely true. Sometimes I think people do things that make themselves seem good just so they can brag to everyone else. If you think about it, a vegetable patch isn't very interesting; vegetables have always grown and been eaten so really it's entirely unexceptional, but I bet that guy tells everyone about the carrots in his garden. So I told Mira he seemed nice, and I smiled with my eyes as well as my mouth so I didn't look threatening, but she seemed kind of irritated and started acting weirder than usual so I made excuses and went home without dessert.

Myles

Potential last line for a novel:
    It was either yesterday or tomorrow.

Chapter 23
How the Rain Falls
August 1944

John slowly lifted the worn, pallid blue quilt, and slid into the cramped double bed; the mattress was so thin and deadened it no longer begrudged his weight. Lily, who was already positioned the other side of Rose, passed him the extra cushion she had brought to stop his back from stiffening. The three, mother and father and daughter, lay quietly at first. Lily's feet warming against Rose's, her arm folded across her chest, squeezing the pads of her husband's fingertips, which were draped over their daughter's shoulders. This is how they had slept all those nights during the Blitz; this is how they had slept when the bombs fell and no one wanted to be left behind. This is how they slept when they were to die together.

#

Bobby's knees were drawn tight into his chest, his chin tucked down hard against his clavicle. His heart whipped and curdled his blood through his veins. His life now a sprint instead of a marathon. His breath pushed through his throat in shuttling rags and scraps that caught and rattled, his eyes were closed but he hadn't the wits to notice, and his boots and clothes and skin were thick with earth. His arms were raised into the open air, locked and quivering above his head, but he didn't remember putting them there. His palms were sweating against the wood. His forefinger pulling the molten trigger, the magazine from his Lee-Enfield emptying in a punctuated scream towards the Germans, or the sky, or other bullets.

#

Jerry sat once more where, in recent weeks, he had so often found himself. His back was resting hard against the wall and his ankles were sorely folded beneath him, their bones jutting at angles unwelcomed by the hardwood floor. Both his shoulders were compressed, and his arms were caught against his ribcage. The rigidly compact space between the wardrobe and the wall condensed his torso into a tidy cube. His knees bent tightly upwards, he jimmied his elbows between them. The paper weighed heavily between his fingers. He tried to read the words but the grim white of the pages made it too easy to remember Anna's face as she crumpled; her torn expression, drawn and passive, stolen in the beat between apprehension and anguish.

#

'What are you going to read us today, love?' John asked, adjusting the cushion against the small of his back, knowing whatever it was didn't really matter. It was only the voice they heard, the act of storytelling and shared time. The words need not come in any order.

'Oh, it's something special,' Rose grinned and gestured for her father to pass her the box atop the nightstand beside him.

She took the package gently, placing it on the quilt above her lap, lightly lifting the lid and setting it down upon her mother's lap. Smoothly, Rose slid her fingers around the tissue inside, freeing the ends and folding back the leaves, finally revealing a first edition of *Little Women*. Wiping her fingers briefly on the quilt to rid any oils from their tips, she lifted the book from the tissue, nestling it in front of her.

'That's not the copy we got you, where did you magic that from?' Lily asked, pulling the quilt up around her chin, but she already knew.

'It was a present from Bobby,' Rose smiled as she traced a finger across the insignia on the front of the book. Emblazoned into the maroon fibres of the cover, a clean and understated golden oval surrounded the delicate title in a protective halo.

#

A few years before, by way of Jerry's connections about the town, Bobby had been hired to help the butcher ferry pigs and cows from the cattle market, down around the railway bridge, and into his truck once a week in exchange for a half-crown and a pair of eggs for Sunday supper. Bobby, who had been a frugal yet also marginally spoiled child (by both Jerry and Anna, albeit in different ways), began to collect this wage, along with money from birthdays and Christmases, in a small glass marmalade jar above his dresser. Later, when he had too many coins, he added a second, larger jar, and then a third. By the time Bobby had been conscripted he knew exactly what he wanted to spend his teenage savings on. He also knew if he didn't spend them before he left, then, little by little, the content of the jars would be scavenged towards Jerry's alcohol consumption.

Of course, he didn't find it immediately. It took some help from Pete, who had connections with people who lived in larger cities, but before it was time to leave he had managed to acquire a beautiful and rather expensive first edition of Louisa May Alcott's *Little Women*. Bobby had taken the novel, thanked a beaming Pete who was already gratified by completing the task, and ran a grubby finger over the embossed title. He anticipated the smile on Rose's face as he handed his gift to her, briefly grinning at the thought of giving her a pristine edition of *Dracula* instead. He sighed at the memory of them in his bedroom between wars, but the thought was gone as quickly as it arrived, leaving him to recall his gift was just a token; it was no more than a misleading, convivial prelude to his departure, and he knew Rose would likely colour it as dereliction.

#

'He's a good kid, that one,' John kissed Rose's hair softly.

'He'll be back soon, love, I can feel it,' Lily nestled her head into her daughter's shoulder.

'Christmas won't be Christmas without any presents,' began Rose, as the first droplets of rain started to fall.

#

Bobby could hear so much noise he heard nothing at all. It was all one, the bullets and the screaming and the rain and his breathing and the thudding and the engines and the voices and the radio and the rapid fire. He was screaming, too. Between breaths. Tiny screams. Screams with the kick of his rifle and the knock of the soldier next to him, screams with the dirt cascading down upon him like Roman candles, screams with the seconds and the minutes and the never end.

His gun jammed. He screamed. He breathed. He pulled his arms into himself. His makeshift trench was too small to crouch so he twisted onto his back. His fingers were a clumsy mitten of dry blood and wet earth and slippery sweat. The sweat. The yellow and puss and tears. Margarine. His hand was in front of his face in front of the war and he thought of margarine. He had been told a story: troops in Burma had been robbed by naked Indians slathered in margarine. *Can't catch a bloody Indian slathered in margarine.* A hand grabbed his ankle. Nothing quietened. Nothing was heard. The hand was clawing at his calf, a frenzied tugging at his laces.

'My rifle's jammed,' he yelled to the hand in frantic explanation as the face rolled into sight, helmet hung across it's left eye, right ear shedding blood around it's throat.

'I'm fucking scared,' the face shouted.

Bobby heard everything.

'I'm fucking scared,' the face screamed again.

Bobby was lying flat on his black, his feet were pointed away from the enemy, his neck arched looking down over length of his body, his gun clutched against his chest, his fingers numb and flailing at the different parts of his rifle that no longer had names or meanings.

'I've shit myself,' the face was everything.

An explosion. Bobby shielded his face with his weapon seconds too late, but it didn't matter; the grenade had been further along, killing somebody else who was too late. He raised his head again, his blood was smoke behind his eyes and the face at his feet was living terror.

'What?!' Bobby thought he was shouting but he couldn't be sure. Everything was relative.

'I'm fucking scared and I've shit myself.'

'I'm scared, too.'

The boy next to Bobby cried high and short, cut open at the scream, his body rolled against him, hot and lifeless.

'There's no such thing as a brave soldier,' the face yelled up to him, its eyes fitting open and closed at the sound of every shot. 'There's no such thing as a brave soldier,' the face repeated, gurgling, blood running lines down the sides of his mouth, a ventriloquist dummy in a soldier's uniform.

Bobby peeled the gun from the grasp of the body next to him.

'We're just kids,' the face chocked crimson. 'They forced us here and we...' cough, 'we fight in fear and we die in fear and,' the face paused to swallow, its eyes darkening, 'we kill in fear, or we die a martyr. There's no such fucking thing as a brave soldier.' The hand loosened its grasp as the eyes looked directly through him, 'We all end up here.'

Bobby watched as the face took its final shattered breath before nothing happened ever again.

#

The rain came in fierce diagonals across the window. Jerry knew if he looked outside he would see water ferrying down his crooked shed roof and cascading over the edges, creating a ravine in her allotment below, and drowning the life along that shared side. But he wouldn't look out; he would stay cradling the pages of Anna's lifetime fairy tale, squeezed between his past and a blind alley. He had witnessed her blood seep from the crack in her skull and into the rug. Red on red, she disappeared. He noted how many more monsters she had written about towards the end.

#

The rain cried down heavy against the glass, obtuse in its simplicity, as though that was all there was; just rain falling as it had always done and would always do, indifferent to war and horror and hope. Only rain, indiscriminate summer rain. The Hartleys paused their storytelling, momentarily watching the droplets fatten themselves against each other on the glass pane, all chasing the tails of those that had fallen before them. This rain would wash away some of the memories from the dusty streets. It would present the sense of a new start born with the morning, and bring with it the smell of moist, restless potential. They watched through the window as the rain fell like bombs, and they wished to be impassive and untainted. They wished for a time when the rain still fell like rain.

Chapter 24
Before We Were Dead
July 1972

The knocking was gentle but persistent, betraying apprehension.

'I know you're in there, Will,' this wasn't the first time she had said that.

William rubbed his palms around his eyes and down his cheeks, forcing blood through his flesh and rhythmically squeezing at his empty expression. The knocking continued. He was lying on his back on top of the hideous sheets. Staring at the beige ceiling stains, he lent no thought as to how they got there.

'Please.'

He heard what he assumed was her forehead coming to rest against the door. A protracted squeal of fingertips sighed as she slid a hand down against the varnish. *Perhaps she's giving up.*

'Mum used to break Dad's clocks,' Dawn began after a minute of silence had spread between them. Her voice was faint through the wood. William wondered if anyone had walked past her in the hotel corridor, and whether she would have felt embarrassed if they had, but he doubted she would. 'He collects them. He's collected them ever since I can remember. All kinds of clocks: mantle, grandfather, wall, pocket watches... it's just what he does to do something. He buys them cheaply and fixes them up during quiet periods in the shop. Some clocks would lose time, some would get stuck on specific numbers, and others would only work when tilted at certain angles, but whatever was wrong he fixed it. He could fix anything. He never resold them. He'd just put them all around the house. They were everywhere,' he heard her laugh. 'It was so loud, the ticking and tocking, all those clocks chattering away. So many ticks could be heard for every moment that passed it was like time was in fast forward. There were always tens of thousands of seconds to the hour in our house. Mum would systematically go and sabotage them all in some silly attempt to stop the days passing; to slow us down. They played that game for years, Mum and Dad, him fixing the clocks and her breaking them. Stop, start, stop, start.' There was a long pause. William leaned forward, straining to hear if she was still there. 'Mum hasn't broken a clock since last Christmas. All of the clocks work all of the time now. So Dad keeps buying more, and the house is getting so loud, and the time is going so fast... I don't think she loves him anymore.'

William opened the door in silence, promptly returning to his position on the bed without making eye contact. Dawn shut the corridor away behind her and quietly lay down next to him, rigid, staring at the stains in the ceiling.

'Why?' she whispered.

'I spent most of my cash on the plane ticket,' he didn't look at her.

'But you're not...'

'Gay? It's not about that.'

'Is it really better than home?'

'There are different kinds of terrible.'

'That's not an answer.'

'It pays well.'

'Is that it?' she didn't look at him.

'It's less ordinary,' squinting one eye, he raised his left arm straight up towards the ceiling and gazed along its length like a gun. She waited. 'And it's easy when you hate yourself,' he squeezed an invisible trigger. 'I only have to live with my own shit here. I'm all right with my misery; you can't lose too much when you're miserable and alone. But I detest other people's sadness... and not for any good reason either. I just find it tedious.'

'I get it, the bit about other peoples sadness.'

'It's true of their happiness, too,' he could say this now. Nothing he could say could be worse than what was unsaid.

'So what you're really saying is that, in general, you can't stand people?'

'That's not what I'm saying.'

'But it *is* what you said.'

'The same thing can mean something completely different to two people.'

'Not always.'

'Always. Everything from *I love you*, to a shade of red,' he pulled the trigger again.

'I'm not going to argue with you.'

'Arguing is futile. There are as many worlds as there are people, and we all live in a different one.'

'I'm certainly beginning to believe that,' she rolled over to face him.

'I can't do this,' he lowered his arm.

'Do what?'

'What do you want from me?'

'What is there to want?'

'Nothing.'

'I'll take it,' he heard the smile in her voice.

He sat up, and twisted his neck to see her still lying there, staring into the void he had just created. Her hair was fanned across the pillow, her hands tucked up to her chin, her knees folded at opposite angles to her hips.

'What does that mean?' he was up and walking now, pacing, thumbing corners and edges without feeling them.

'Complete honesty?' she propped herself up on her elbow. Her arm didn't shake.

'I don't think honesty should come with warnings,' he turned to the window, staring across staggered distances.

Dawn watched him, back turned to her, as his hand traced around from his throat to the nape of his neck. His fingers knotted into the top of his spine and kneaded his skin, tan and vulnerable under the twist of his hair. She reached back and gently fingered the skin around her own hairline. *The same as his,* she thought, *the same as him.* These would only be words, only words in moments.

'You came here,' she began, knowing he wouldn't turn to face her, 'did all this, this… whatever it is, it was a choice. You wanted something different so you became the opposite of everything you were. You told me your dad stopped being a part of anything and you were there, hating that life you weren't leading. So, what? You came here and felt as much as possible? Right? You felt everything you could, everything, good or bad, you felt it because that's all you wanted. You just wanted to *feel* again,' she sat up, folding her legs beneath her body. Turning to face Dawn from the distances, William knew she was trying to make it so they were occupying the same world, even for just a moment. 'I want to feel, too. I want to feel difficult and complex things, I want to feel apathy and empathy and jealousy and hatred and disgust and hope and surprise and nostalgia,' the words were soaring out of her like a soul sucked from between her lips, 'and bitterness and longing and grief and humiliation and gratitude and respect and panic and shame and…'

'I understand.'

'I don't want a life with someone who loves me now but will eventually consider me nothing more than a reliable comfort, no different to an old couch with a worn depression in the seat cushion. I don't want to be a wife as the word turns from lover to shadow. I don't want to be with someone just to end up in the waiting room of time.'

'Then don't be those things,' he didn't know what else to say.

'Let's get married,' there was wild conviction in her eyes.

'Let's get what?' he didn't hear himself reply.

'Married.'

'Who get married?'

'Us.'

'I'm sorry, I still haven't understood.'

'Me and you. We should get married. We're in Vegas, there's nothing stopping us.'

'And yet I feel like nothing *is* stopping us,' William twisted his tone. It could be a joke, or revenge, perhaps someone had put her up to it.

'Are you attracted to me?' she asked as though it was the simplest question in the world.

'What... I,' flushed.

'You are. What else matters?'

'You don't love me.'

'Of course not,' her smile didn't waiver.

'I don't love you.'

'Well, we've only known each other a few days.'

'Yes, another valid reason not to get married.'

'No! Don't you get it? Why get married to someone *after* all the good stuff. If we got married now we'd be forced to feel.'

'No, we wouldn't...'

'We would! Even if we couldn't stand each other, at least we'd be forced to feel that hate. Feel something. But I like you. I think I could love you, and I'd rather gamble on that and appreciate falling for you, the relief of loving, the coincidence, the luck, the disbelief... I'd rather all of that than wait ten years and marry my best friend, or the man who irritates me least, just because I'm scared of being alone.'

'I'm not scared of being alone.' He looked at her, she was being preposterous. The proposal was absurd, but so was his life now, his choices. Once, if he had spoken them aloud, they would have seemed equally unlikely.

'But you *are* scared of not feeling.'

'No, I'm concerned that feelings aren't enough, not of not feeling them.'

'Then you've got nothing to lose either way.'

'But why marriage?'

The curious nature of the situation calmed him, just as when he did the terrible things. There was no social etiquette to fumble over and no focus group against which to measure the deviations in his behaviour. He pulled the chair away from the Formica desk, picked up a pencil, and drew a small square on a corner of the complimentary stationary. He couldn't sit and draw a square during a date, or in a lift, or when buying a Coke, or waiting for his luggage to appear on the carousel, but he could draw a square here, in no man's land.

'We'll be forced to *live* each other; if we have an argument we'll have to try and reconcile it. Marriage stops us from giving up at the earliest opportunity. The stakes are higher this way. It's the difference between playing poker with matchsticks and playing with your life's savings: you're not playing the same game.'

'I don't disagree,' he drew another square.

'So you'll marry me?'

'What if we never fall in love?' he was here.

'Hey, the last man who said he loved me used to tell me with his fists. We can fall in something else.'

'I'll be a disappointment.'

'Yes or no?'

'Yes.'

Mum, 15/03/2012

I know I haven't written for a while. I don't know why I stopped. I don't know if you read these, either, so maybe it doesn't matter. Maybe you didn't notice and I really write these letters for myself. But I stopped for a while and now I'm writing again and I'm beginning to think everything is cyclical. Planets spin on an axis, day in, day out, all orbiting the sun, year in, year out. We are born, we die. Most lives take on the same shapes. Share the same thoughts. Hope the same hopes and fear the same fears. I think maybe we're all the same, but people have different parts inside them that are louder. An optimist hears their dreams close enough to chase them, a pessimist hears the void. We're the same under that. We have to be. We're all in the same world with the same biology and stimuli. I am you and you are me. And, if I'm right, I'm so sorry.

Iris has been diagnosed with Alzheimer's disease. It feels strange just saying it like that, without the traditional prelude containing a variant of 'There's been some bad news...', but I always supposed that part kind of speaks for itself. Everything exists only in context. Carl Jung said that we can't know happiness without sadness, which is dreadful and wonderful all at once, but sometimes I wonder if we don't just feel either nothingness or sadness. I'm pretty sure someone could be miserable without ever feeling happy but I'm not sure if a person could know they were happy if they'd never been sad. I think maybe happiness is simply the absence of sadness.

Iris keeps making jokes about her Alzheimer's, which is all right because everyone reacts differently to terrible things. When Sam was dying of cancer, or living with cancer, which were both always the same thing for him, his mother acquired a large amount of antique buttons that she would sit and catalogue compulsively. She had thousands of those buttons, and she just threw them all away when Sam finally died. I read that people who don't seem to react to things might just be applying some form of coping mechanism, so recently, when I've discovered I've said something that Mira finds to be insensitive, I've started saying 'Coping mechanism' as an excuse to stop her from moaning. This method proved to have a high success rate when first implemented but it very quickly became inconsequential and, eventually, it just seemed to aggravate situations. Mira is very fickle like that.

Iris is all right at the moment (she's all right in the sense that she could be worse, in the same sense that happiness cannot exist without sadness), and she probably will be for quite some time. Although no one really knows for how long, and even when she gets really sick and can't find half of herself, the other half will still be there. That's the terrible thing about her disease; it doesn't weaken everything at once, which is disquieting. Iris will eventually, unavoidably, witness herself become the illness. I think dementia might be the most tragic thing I know about what living can do to a person.

At first Iris didn't tell us the real reason she was going to the doctor's – she just said it was a routine check-up – but then she had to go to a couple more appointments, which isn't what happens with a check-up, so Mira became anxious and suspicious, and confronted Iris as to what was really going on. Iris caved and told her the truth. The news really scared the hell out of Mira, and since then she has pretty much talked about it constantly. One time, over the weekend, this continual need for discussing Iris resulted in me being introduced to the vegetable-growing eco-male who Mira's still dating. I don't know if anything triggered it, but she had got particularly upset about Iris whilst out on a date with him, and for some reason she called and said she wanted to see me, even though the eco-male possessed all the same words I did.

I arrived at their date and the eco-male was there, and I was very aware of being there, and Mira was crying as though no one was there. We were all seated around a little table in a French restaurant, which was the kind of noisy that is full of sound but on low volume. I ate a lot of bread sticks, and the eco-male said a lot about how he hated the economy and capitalism, and how all the regular people with their jobs and kids and cars were actually suffering from the mental illness of unquestioning conformity. So I said how hating the economy and capitalism and everyone else was a common thing for an eco-male to say, and I asked if all eco-men had the same different mental illness to everyone else. Then he just stared at me as I ate another bread stick with tiny fast bites from one end to the other all at once without swallowing, like a mechanical rabbit, which I find is a fun thing to do.

After the third bread stick the eco-male asked me, 'What the fuck is wrong with you?' before telling me, 'You're not normal,' so I asked him if by his definition that meant I was sane. Then he turned to Mira and asked, 'Are you seriously friends with this guy?' but she was still crying so I said, 'It's a bit insensitive of you to be making generalised accusations about mental illness under the circumstances.' Mira must have been listening through her sobbing because she made a very strange intermission of cry-laughing, before going into a full on hell-bent cackle that was very much at a higher volume than the one the restaurant had been set to. This made the eco-male look at her and frown whilst tentatively patting her shoulder and saying her name a lot. Then, despite our animosity, the eco-male looked at me with an expression of panic that indicated he required help, so by way of explanation for her behaviour I said, 'Coping mechanism,' and Mira laughed even louder even though she was already on maximum, which made the eco-male jump. It was at this point the waiter came over to ask if everything was okay, which also meant shut up, so I said Mira had fallen into a state of deranged lunacy in the face of a sustained shortage of breadsticks, and the eco-male said sorry, and Mira kept cackling.

Frank called, and he sounded what I could only describe as spuckled. I hadn't heard from him for a while so I asked him if he was the one who sent Julie the flowers I found in the kitchen. He went quiet and I didn't know whether that meant yes or no. Then I thought maybe I shouldn't have asked. If they were from someone else then he probably wouldn't want to know, or if they were from him then maybe he didn't want to acknowledge a weakness. Perhaps he didn't want to seem like he missed her. Either way, instead of answering my question, he said a lot of words.

Frank said that when he was nineteen he damaged his knee in London, and that sometimes he still feels the echoes of that pain when he walks long distances. He said he dislocated his shoulder in Florence, landing on it after falling through the floor of an abandoned church. He had his appendix removed in Phoenix, Arizona, and broke his hand in Lima, and knocked two teeth out in Mikhaylovka. Frank said he keeps losing parts of himself to different cities, so his body is becoming a map of his life and the world is becoming a map of his body. He said when he was younger he wanted Paris to have his heart, but instead he just lost it slowly, scattering it about everywhere until there was nothing left. I told him his heart would be really hard to find again, and he went silent for a moment and then he said, 'Too hard,' in a tone that made his heart seem like an exam. After that there was no conversation left, so Frank said, 'I'll see you again soon, I really want to see you again soon, son,' and the 'son' seemed really loud and we both hung up. I still don't know who sent the flowers.

Myles

Potential last lines for a novel:

He didn't believe it was over because he could still remember it.

It was quiet out.

Chapter 26
Bell Curve
July 1957

'Were you brave in the war, Dad?'

'Everyone was brave in the war, kid, we had to be,' Bobby filled a cup of swiftly cooling water from the tin bath and poured it through his son's sun-lightened hair.

'Oh,' he whispered, his eyes pinched from the soapy water. 'Why do you ask?'

'No reason, just something someone said at school.'

Bobby looked up to see Rose, wearing her shimmering coral-toned leotard ready for their performance that evening, slipping out from the back door with a freshly boiled kettle. The bath hadn't been carried from the garden and back into the house since the wooden doorway had swelled in the April rain, and the warped frame had subsequently refused to open wider than Bobby's shoulders.

'And what were they saying at school?' Bobby smiled at Rose as she delicately poured the hot water in with the tepid, carefully twirling the two in concentric ripples with one hand. Tendrils of steam disappeared into the brisk evening air.

'What's this about school?' Rose enquired, leaning over and kissing their son's damp forehead. A bud of red lipstick stamped below his one unruly cowlick.

'Nothing, Mum. There's just a boy in my class, Michael, and he says stuff about how Dad's a magician and then he tells these stupid stories about how his dad shot loads of

Germans. He does this thing where he makes gun noises and rolls around in the playground battling invisible monsters and everyone cheers. Then sometimes, afterwards, he'll be laughing as he looks at me and he'll ask if Dad cast any spells on the Nazis.'

'And what do you do when Michael does that?' Rose squeezed Bobby's shoulder gently, the cotton of his shirt darkening under her wet fingers.

'I tell him Dad was brave too, he just doesn't brag about it.'

Bobby and Rose shared an expertly subtle exchange of pride and relief as she turned back to the house, empty kettle in hand.

'Fancy sticking mine in there next?' a nasal voice sounded from over the fence.

'Had a good weekend, Catherine?' Bobby shouted up to his neighbour who was Cheshire-grinning down at them, pink lipstick clumsily dotted across her teeth.

After she had conducted a particularly laborious and noisy garden renovation two months earlier, Catherine had stacked a pile of superfluous concrete slabs up against the skeletal grey fence dividing their gardens. Since then, she had taken to climbing on the slabs in order to gain enough height to pop her head above the fence and interject in conversations whenever the opportunity arose.

'Busy, busy,' she tittered, raising a pile of damp clothes up in front of her face so Bobby could see them. 'If it rains tonight, and this lot don't dry, I'm sending mine into school tomorrow in their bloomin' pyjamas.'

Catherine stepped down from the fence and disappeared. The visible tips of her washing line quivered. Bobby turned back to his son with raised eyebrows and a wry smile at Catherine's expense, but instead of sharing the knowing look he expected, Bobby saw the boy idly patting the top of the water with his palm.

'Hey,' Bobby whispered. 'I do have one story from the war you might like?'

'Yeah?' hope prickled as light in his eyes.

'Well,' Bobby began, recalling an experience a softly spoken soldier named Griggs had shared with him. 'When I was in India they used to do this thing to try and keep morale up.'

'I thought you were in France?'

'We travelled about a lot,' Bobby briefly threw a glance above the fence, but the face had yet to return. 'Anyway, every month or so, the officers would draw four names out of a hat in a sort of raffle, and the four soldiers whose names got called were granted a couple weeks leave to go home to see their families. There were hundreds of us in India, so the chances of getting chosen were really slim and no one ever expected to be picked,' Bobby fished soap out of the water. 'I'd been over there for almost two years and it was nearing the end of the war, not that we knew that then, when my name was chosen, and I had this friend, Mac, who had a wife back in England. She was terribly sick but the army wouldn't let him go home to see her, so I gave him my ticket.'

'You stayed fighting and let your friend go home?' the boy lifted his arm up for Bobby to wash underneath it.

'Yes, but you see, Mac had children back home just like you, and he wasn't sure if his wife was going to be all right. If I hadn't given him my ticket, he may never have seen her again.'

'Dad?'

'Yeah?'

'I don't think I would have done that.' Not a statement, but a solemn query.

'Well, that may have been for the best, kid.'

'How'd you mean?' he raised his other arm.

'When Mac got back from visiting his wife he came directly to find me. I was on duty in the cook house and he bundled over and hugged me, full of thanks, happiest I'd seen him. He said his wife was getting better and that his kids had already grown up so much. He said his son was just like him, a real funny bugger. He'd smuggled us a couple of fancy beers back, and told me if I came to find him later he'd let me

166

know all about his trip. I didn't see him that night, and when I woke up the next day all the stuff was gone from his bunk.' Bobby could still see Griggs' face as he had told his story; the faded torment of twisted disbelief and guilt were tumours under his skin.

'I ran outside, shouting, asking anyone who would listen where Mac had gone. It was then I saw him. His body was on a stretcher that was packed with ice. He'd caught heat stroke travelling back from England. He'd spent two days crossing India to catch up with us in Burma; we were on our way to burning Mandalay. The heat out there was so heavy it sometimes seemed like the air had dried up with it. He had died in the night.'

Bobby gently washed his son's back, unconsciously counting the vertebrae beneath his fingers.

'So, if you hadn't given your ticket away that would've been you that died, and then I wouldn't be born?'

'Maybe.'

'I'm glad it was Mac.'

'Well...'

'Did they tell his son?'

'His wife wrote to me after she heard the news. I guess Mac had talked about me when he was home and said your dad was a good guy. She was grateful for my friendship to him and asked me for one last favour; to send her a photo of Mac's grave.'

'Did you?'

'Kind of,' Bobby wondered where Griggs was now, whether he still told his story or kept it buried inside with all the other things the war changed in them. 'There were so many killed, mostly from malaria or dysentery as much as anything, so they just buried all the regular soldiers in these huge mass graves. They had no markings or ceremony or anything like that.'

'So what did you do?'

'I lied. I borrowed a camera and sent her a photograph

of an unmarked tombstone that I found above an Indian general's grave.'

'I think she'd have liked that.'

'Me, too.'

'That was beautiful,' Catherine had appeared back in position at the fence, her washing now gently tiptoeing on the wind behind her.

'Thank you, Catherine.'

Rose was patting her wrist wildly at Bobby from the kitchen window, safe from the gaze of their neighbour.

'Right, we'd better get going then, kiddo,' Bobby raised a towel behind his son and wrapped it as a cowl over his head and shoulders, carefully guiding him out of the tub.

'And I should be putting dinner on,' Catherine's head lowered again.

'Night,' Bobby called after her.

'Have a good trip.'

'You looking forward to this evening?' he rubbed his hands roughly over the towel shrouding his son, let go, and upturned the bath. The dirty water fed the dry grass.

'How long are you and Mum going to be gone for?'

'I've told you, it's only two weeks. We've got ten shows booked all the way up to Birmingham then we'll be back. I should expect we'll be able to buy you a pretty special birthday present from there, hey?'

'You are going to be back for my birthday, aren't you?'

'I suggested abandoning you at Nan and Granddad John's so we could travel the world but your mum wouldn't allow it.'

Chapter 27
Our Scars Disguised, Unhealed
January 1990

'I'll just throw myself down the fucking stairs, then, shall I, seeing as I'm that much of a bloody disappointment to you?' Alice screamed, slamming her bedroom door and stomping heavily across the hallway, one hand propped under a five-month swollen stomach.

'Don't be so dramatic.'

'Why? Because you want me to stay here and play happy families when my life is totally ruined?'

'No, because it's entirely unnecessary,' Dawn conscientiously rounded Alice, placing herself between her daughter and the top of the staircase.

'I'll push you, I'll push you down and dive after you and we can just see how fucked up we all get.'

'And what if you did that and then he came back, huh? What if you killed his child or crippled yourself and then he came back, he wouldn't want you then, would he?' she tightened her grip on the banister.

'Oh, come on, woman. He doesn't even know I'm cooking this thing. He. Doesn't. Give. A. Shit.' Alice went to push past her mother but Dawn remained rigid.

'Look. Your dad and I have talked about it, and we think it could be an option for us to bring the baby up.'

'What?' the fight fell from Alice.

'Well, no one knows. And you're fifteen.'

'You don't need to remind me.'

'You're fifteen,' repeated, with intent. 'And, well, we think given your age and your other problems that maybe it would be best if we raised the child as ours.'

'It's all I have left of him.'

'Yes. Well, he's hardly proven to be a great loss.'

'How dare you,' Alice spat, the venom whipping off her tongue as she swept a framed picture from the wall, smashing it to the floor with a scream. 'I loved him, I loved him more than I love you. I loved him more than I will ever love anything!'

'Well, it might seem that way now.'

'It *is* that way now.'

'Regardless,' Dawn remained calm. 'He's not dead, is he? He's just not returning your calls and there's nothing I can do about that, so direct that aggression towards Ba...'

'*Don't* speak his name.'

'Direct your aggression towards *him*. With what we're suggesting everything will essentially be the same as it is now, except you'll have a new brother. Everyone will be told you have a new brother.'

'This isn't a soap opera. That sort of shit doesn't happen in real life.'

'And yet here we are.' A soft crying teased at them from the other room. 'Wonderful, you've frightened your brother.'

'Isn't he, like, meant to have stopped being a needy little cry baby now he's four?'

'He's still got eleven years on you.'

#

'She agreed.'

'She did?'

'Well, not in so many words.'

'Of course not.'

'So, there's that,' Dawn pulled her husband's fingertips up

170

to her lips, gently rubbing their pads against her teeth.

'I don't know what I'd do if we lost her.'

'We won't.'

'I know.'

'Really?'

'No… Every time I look at her I still see the razor in her hand.'

'She hasn't cut in a long time,' Dawn rolled on to her front, freeing her shoulders to the night air.

'Three weeks isn't a long time,' he mimicked her actions, turning onto his back but pulling the duvet up around his neck.

'It is for her.'

'When did all this happen?'

'I don't know.'

'Do you ever wish you could go back?'

'To before we had Alice?' she closed her eyes.

'No…'

'…Before Vegas?'

'I know this is our life. I know this is the one we've been given. But sometimes…'

'You miss selling yourself?' she was emotionless, practised.

'Before that… Before that is too hard to change. With Mum dead I could never stop what Dad became. But Vegas is the last place I could go to before…'

'Before me.'

'Before all this dead time.'

'You were miserable in Vegas.'

'I don't think I was.'

'What were you enjoying so much? Drinking all the time because you couldn't face nights sober? Crippling anxiety? The money you got from indulging self-hate? Letting old men…'

'It wasn't about that. That was just a necessity for me to live freely,' he let her words wash over him. 'I didn't even

171

have to speak to them, it could be a silent exchange. I couldn't
do anything wrong when I did that, I was someone else.'

'You weren't free.'

'I felt free.'

'I still feel you lying awake sometimes.'

'So?'

'I know it's because of that night.'

'It haunted me there, it haunts me here. This hasn't been
a cure.'

'But it could have happened again. It *would* have happened
again.'

'It was all a calculated risk.'

'Do you remember the song that came on the radio that
first morning in my hotel room?'

'I turned around. He dared me to turn around, his shirt
was still on when I'd bent over, and he'd already given me the
money. It was slotted into my sock. I still had my socks on.'

'Will…'

'I turned around. His fingers seemed unnaturally long
although it might have been the angle. They were grasped,
like pincers, into my hips. His bones were visible through
the skin, his knuckles like burnt popcorn. He was thrusting
into me and his face was nothing. It was blank. It was the
expression of someone queuing in the bank, or sitting alone
on a bus. Nothing. Then I saw his chest, the marks.'

'Baby…'

'These welts, this brown mottling like a hundred
misshapen nipples down to his stomach. A machine gun of
scars tumbling down from his shoulders. He looked like a
fucking pizza,' William burst out laughing. Dawn held tears
behind her eyes. 'He looked like a fucking pizza!' louder now.

'Shhhh,' she soothed. 'You'll wake James and Alice.'

'A pizza,' he said again, cackling and wiping his eyes. 'He
looked like a human pizza,' the tears were staggering down
his face.

'It's okay, you're safe,' she curled into him, gently kissing

172

his smooth white skin. 'You're safe, you're safe…'
'I wish I could go back.'

Mum,   11/4/2012

Mira believes in coincidences, not in the usual way a person might believe that a coincidence is just *that*, an adversary to fate, but she believes coincidences occur as a form of universally intervened guidance. She thinks some people are meant to be in each other's lives and that they'll keep appearing in one way or another until you acknowledge them because they're destined to help you either directly, like saving your life, or spiritually, like getting you to realise some sort of potential. Or maybe you're meant to help them. Either way, the fact remains the same; if Mira experiences a coincidence she'll embrace it. I guess that's one of the things that is louder in Mira than in me. Anyhow, coincidence is how I ended up meeting Mira originally and, due to her beliefs, it is also responsible for us becoming friends. After the coincidence happened she made me promise, 'Let's never not know each other,' and because we were absolute strangers the only way for us to never not know each other was to spend an awful lot of time together.

I didn't really know, or get on with, all too many people back then. I still don't. I don't know why I phrased that as though I've been through a period of change. All I mean is that there once wasn't Mira and now there is. I was perfectly happy being able to live my life without the interference of feigning interest, but Mira was very keen on the idea of knowing me for her entire life, and as a person who had no other commitments, I wasn't very well equipped with any excuses to avoid her. So, after it happened, we started hanging out almost every day, and I would maintain the hope she'd have a coincidence with someone else so I could go back to being alone, but now it's now and she calls me to join her when she is on intimate dates in noisy-quiet French restaurants.

I can still kind of feel how the entire time we're together she's waiting for the event that will prove we're an absolute necessity to one another. Sometimes I think she wants it to happen just so she can smugly tell me how her theory was correct. I once mistakenly said to Mira that if there ever was an incident in which one of us desperately required the other, it would only be *coincidence*, and she said 'Exactly,' and I slapped my forehead. So, by way of spite, I mentioned if I ever got the chance to save her from Death's clutches, I wouldn't, just to prove her wrong. She was prepared for this response (because she knows me so well from all the time she has forced us to spend together), and immediately said if I chose not to save her it would mean that if she had survived she would have inevitably ended up with a horrifying disability, perhaps even severe brain damage, and thus a terrible quality of life, and in those circumstances she'd be better off dead. I said we'd all be better off dead because then we'd never know we'd been born, and she ignored me because I say that kind of stuff all the time.

The day I met Mira it was night. I'm not sure what time it was exactly, but it was during the hours that are so black you can't imagine that there has ever been light, and you certainly can't fathom that four thousand miles away it's orange dawn, and four thousand miles away from that it's yellow-white midday and people are wearing sun cream and simmering and squinting and swimming. I had woken up suddenly; it was one of those wake-ups where you're momentarily more alert than during most of the rest of the day: you're sitting up and you can't remember doing it, your heart is bigger than your chest and your body is your lungs. I was too hot and I could feel anxiety stabbing across my skin as sweat came to life through my pores. My bed sheets were wrapped around me like strips of still-moist papier-mâché. It was then that the man at the end of my bed spoke, telling me, 'Go now,' and I woke up again. Sweating. Hot. Papier-mâché. So I went. I pulled some dark grey shapes out of the dark grey pile, and unfolded them to become a dark grey sweater and dark grey trousers, put them on my dark grey body and went.

When I got to the Tiny Cemetery, Mira was there. I didn't know her name was Mira at the time. She was just a girl sitting on the bench that fades into the earth. 'Are we awake this time?' she asked before anything else, and I told her we were. She said she had a dream where the world was ending by never changing, it just kept going on and on and all the people kept filling everywhere up until there wasn't any room anymore, so everybody had to live and work right where they were born. People in offices never saw the people in the coffee shops or the schools or the fields or the factories or the zoos, some people learned forever and some made the same thing forever and some painted on the same canvas over and over again. But then one day the last person was born, and there was no more room, or air, or something, and everyone started dying like lights. The dark was directly in front of her and started expanding in the opposite direction, growing all the way around the world. Then, in the last moments, it started coming up behind her until she was in the final light. She started crying in the final light, and noticed a boy beside her. They were in the Tiny Cemetery, and he took her hand and the light went out. Then she said she woke up, twice. I sat down next to her on the bench that fades into the ground, our sides touching, and told her, 'I know, I dreamed it, too.'

You know how I told you I feel guilty about things a lot of the time, like about junk and other people's lives? Well, I don't just feel guilty about Mira. I feel scared. I'm scared that Iris is going to disappear and because of the coincidence, Mira is going to believe that I'm going be a cure for her sadness. I won't be. I can't be. I don't know how. I was thinking about Mira and Charlie and Iris and Frank and Julie last night until I couldn't breathe. I wonder where all the happy people are. The nothing people.

Myles

Potential last lines for a novel:
He woke up, but it had all happened.
Sometimes it was too much to not be everything.

Chapter 29
A Majestic Creature
August 1964

'I'm going to go down to the beach now,' he informed his father as the last morsels of jam sponge carried down into his gut.

They had been lounging on Southsea Common for the better portion of the afternoon, watching the sun evaporate the tips of the ocean, and he was getting restless to dive into the water and quench the heat from his skin.

'If you wait a moment, I'll join you,' Rose popped a cocktail sausage into her mouth, storing it in one cheek whilst she slid another between her lips, and pressed the open Tupperware lid back down. 'I was hoping we'd be able to see France from here,' she mumbled through the meat.

'It's over 110 miles from here to there,' Bobby answered.

'Sorry,' she offered him the last of the lemonade. 'I wasn't thinking.'

'Nothing to be sorry for,' he eyed her gently, the weight of their past all at once between them. He hadn't been to Portsmouth since they were all shipped across to the beaches; barely out of childhood and yet straight into the fray.

'You coming in for a dip, Dad?'

'I think I'll just stay here, Will. I'd probably just sink after eating all this food. Your mother brought enough to keep us alive for a month.'

'Hey, we're on holiday, no harm in indulging ourselves,' Rose fumbled her hand across the grass, twisted the head apart from a daisy and flicked it at Bobby. 'You could have always made the picnic yourself.'

'And suffered your critique?' he laughed. 'It was all delicious, thank you. Although I don't know if you're going to fit in your coffin after all the buns you demolished; I think the saw might accidentally shave a little something off.'

'Bobby Sinclair!' she pushed him softly. 'I happen to think I look fantastic in my leotard,' she watched him raise his eyebrows in question. 'For a woman of *forty*!'

William stood up, brushed the grass from his legs, and set about vaguely inspecting the patterns left imprinted into his skin.

'I look great, don't I, Will?' Rose persisted, shifting a glance at Bobby, who was smiling coyly and busying himself repackaging leftover sandwiches.

'How would I know?!' William was incredulous.

'Come on, Will,' she pestered. 'You've watched your mother perform a thousand times!'

'Exactly!' he shrieked. 'My *mother*.'

Bobby's laughter shattered through the summer air, catching the attention of other holiday-goers and locals lounging nearby. Bobby hadn't noticed the others slowly gathering since they arrived early that morning, but now a plethora of plaid, chequerboard, and plain picnic blankets covered the common like confetti.

'Will, did I ever tell you what the great Primo Chicane's name was before he met me?' Rose readied the bullet of revenge.

'Yes, Mum,' he sighed in mock exasperation. 'Many, many times.'

'Bobby Baker the Illusion Maker!' she yelped, the words ringing high with absurdity.

Bobby lunged clumsily towards his wife. The almost empty pitcher of lemonade, which had been resting beside him, appeared to leap heroically out of his way and land awkwardly, trickling sticky remnants of liquid onto their picnic blanket. William frowned at his parents, who were now discretely trying to tickle each other; Rose was gasping fragments of 'Bobby Baker Illusion Maker' between shrieks and staggered breaths as Bobby's fingers assaulted the spaces between her ribs.

'I swear I should get paid to babysit you two,' he shook his head, looking evasively around the common in an attempt to dissociate himself from his parents.

Giggling uncontrollably until her gleeful rasps dissolved into a hybrid of hiccoughs and hyperventilation, tears streamed down Rose's face. Bobby ceased his attack and placed two broken breadsticks under either side of his top lip.

'I'm going to drink your blood!' he garbled, in his terrible, best Romanian accent. The breaded left fang immediately dislodged itself, falling into his lap.

'Oh, it's this time again, is it?' William questioned.

Only the day before they had argued, with surprising childish gusto, over the shade of the blanket they'd just purchased:

Fire engine.

No, pillar box.

No, fire engine.

No, pillar box.

No... William, what shade of red is this picnic blanket?

Vermilion.

William had broken down into lone hysteria when, earlier that day, Bobby had spread the fire engine/pillar box/ vermilion picnic blanket out over the grass only to find it was barely large enough to seat one of them alongside their accompanying feast.

'That's it,' he announced to the ocean. 'I'm going to the beach now,' he pivoted from his parents on one heel, and started making his way down to the seafront.

'We made that wonderful, grumpy thing,' Rose smiled, having recovered from her rapturous amusement. She watched him amble awkwardly down the common with his fingers knotted into his hair.

'Yeah, thanks for giving him all of his bad habits,' Bobby kissed her hair. Vanilla, still.

#

Rose drew her toes as snakes through the sand, and watched as the sea rushed hungrily forward to fatten in the newly formed trenches. The smell of salt was much stronger here than on the common; it carried on the wind as a thickness instead of an accent. She felt it clinging to her hair and lining her throat. Rose turned and waved in the general direction of Bobby, who was now blended into the Sillitoe Tartan of distant blankets and grass, and waded into the shallows, the water lapping at her shins eager for attention.

'Will!' her shout faded amongst the torn breeze, rowdy gulls and lotion slathered children playing further along the shore. 'William!'

She squinted towards what she thought was her son; a torso and a pair of kicking feet running parallel to the beach at the edge of the break zone.

'Hey!' Still she received no response.

She laughed with a shock of excitement and ran unsteadily further into the water, the swell slowing her almost immediately as her hips disappeared below the surf, her legs felt as though they were pushing against thick treacle. With each step the wet sand was loose pulp between her toes. She looked up; William had about-turned and was coming back more slowly now, kicking against the longshore current. She couldn't walk out any further, the sea knocked her back with every step, so she lifted her knees to her chest, cautiously treading water in the shallows.

Up until she was eleven, before her parents had relocated and before she had met Bobby, she had lived right against the east coast. For weeks after they moved, being so used to hearing the rhythmic crashing of waves against the cliffs, Rose had trouble sleeping in the new, heavy silence of the night, and had often stayed up until dawn reading by candlelight. She had been a keen swimmer back then, during the days with nights of waves and cliffs, but she hadn't been in the water since she had taught William how to doggy paddle. She was less afraid of the sea than discovering she had lost something of herself.

Rose kicked out gently, pivoting onto her front. She arched her neck awkwardly upwards, supporting her head away from the water as wet hair wrapped around her throat and snatched itself away again with each swell. The sun warmed her back as her toes dug into the coolness below. The crooked angles of her body tended towards the foetal under her trepidation. She floated gently, everything feeling the way it did sometimes when insignificance became joy instead of heaviness.

Rose turned onto her back, her head pointed in the direction she hoped to go, the water washing her westwards, and her feet taking her slowly away from the beach. She was gaining confidence with each kick, twisting her head towards William every now and again to ensure she was still on course. Tentatively lifting her right arm out from the water, she swung it back behind her head. Water droplets dived onto her face, stinging her eyes with salt. Her left arm followed suit as the right circled below her, ready to come up again; her left, her right, they were the hands of a clock spinning backwards through time. She added speed to her purpose, kicking ever harder, her stomach raised, the back of her head resting low in the water.

'Will!' Rose shouted between strokes without looking behind her but anticipating his closeness. 'William!' louder now, it was less crowded here than on the beach. 'Will!'

'Mum?' the voice sounded distant.

'Will!' Her exertion began to cramp her muscles and steal her breath.

'Are you all right?' his voice was strained, fighting the sea breeze.

She stopped. Her knees sighed as they lowered once more. Kicking less vehemently, she twisted to see William swimming only twenty feet from her.

'Mum, are you all right?' he shouted, still swimming, his face submerged face down into the sea.

'What?' Rose, now treading water, forced both of her arms right, her body twisting back towards the beach.

She saw a tall boy running along the sand shouting towards her, one hand busy in his hair, holding something small in the other. William. She couldn't see him clearly in the distance but the mannerisms were his. She startled; cold water splashed suddenly over the side of her face as the unknown swimmer kicked violently past her.

'I thought you were out here,' she yelled.

'What?' he screamed back.

'I thought I saw you.'

'Huh? You okay?'

'Wait there.'

William stood and watched his mother for a moment, her head occasionally nodding behind a wave as she floated near the submerged sandbar. She'd been swept gradually further west whilst they had been shouting and only now, with the absence of familiar landmarks, did she realise he had been slowly mirroring her along the beach. Rose looked up after a few quick kicks and saw her son, satisfied of her return, was settling down on the sand to wait for her.

Recommencing a clumsy back crawl to him directly, Rose cut a diagonal through the blue-grey water. It leapt quickly to scour her throat and sinuses. After two minutes of draining strokes, she looked up to check on her location, only to discover she hadn't moved at all. Her efforts had at best counteracted the longshore current, keeping her in a steady position, and at worst did little but slow it down. Tired now, Rose changed direction, allowing the tide to sweep her sideways as she instead headed straight towards the shore. She would just let herself be carried along with the water and end up further along the beach. She supposed she'd come ashore where the sand tapered out, just before it turned to pebbles and disappeared into the protruding cliff face. No one else was this far across, everyone was swarming around the thick sand and amenities further east.

It was her ankles that slid away from her at first. She was snatched like a slapstick cartoon: feet pulled from behind, hands grappling, nails exaggeratedly scratching into wooden floorboards, only Rose had nothing to slow her down. Her hands grasped fruitlessly at the water that danced and darted and moved along with her, pushed her further, slipped through her fingers and between her lips and down her throat. She had been dragged into the midst of a rip current, her whole body sucked backwards, speeding away from the beach. She wrestled against the water but she was a ragdoll in its gut.

Twenty metres of fight and her legs weren't kicking anymore. She demanded them, implored them to move, but they fell as dead weight beneath her, dragging her down once, twice below the surface, her hands desperately clawing to pull her back up. She gasped in cold air and salt. She wasn't screaming. She couldn't scream. Her breath was spent on the struggle and stolen by the water. Three times. This wasn't like she imagined. She wasn't thrashing around on the surface; she was entombed, her face barely breaking into the air, her arms desperately held out, crucified either side of her. She couldn't wave, she couldn't shout, she couldn't see. Four times. She couldn't breathe. She would die here in plain sight.

There was shouting. Shouting now. William. Somewhere distant. Five times. Choking. Screaming. Six times. Silence. Half air, half water. Swallow. Eyes closed. Yelling. Seven times. Darkness. Heaviness. Tightness. The screaming was internal now. James and Daisy. Her lungs tore and contracted within her burning chest. Mum. Sharpness in her chest, contractions between her ribs. Anna. The way she kept her hair vanilla-ready for when he held her. Which way was the sun? *Little Women.* She had to breathe. When he walked through the door in his uniform after eighteen months of uncertainty. She needed air. William. Her coffin. The boy who showed her something no one else had ever seen. Her lungs filled with water.

Chapter 30
In Our War (After the War)
September 1990

'Eighty thousand years old. Eighty thousand years! That's how old the first known piece of art is. A rudimentary image scratched into rock. That's the first sign of real consciousness. Human cognition is part of that evolution, from passive to active. Before then we were just animals. I mean, we're still animals, but we're on the next level. We don't need that type of creation to survive. It's indulgent, superfluous, but eventually it allowed us to explore and grapple with these ideas and questions we were having about life and values and absurdity.'

'Excuse me,' Dawn bustled past William, an unsteady over-brimming saucepan in one hand and a tray of cheap steak in the oven-gloved other. Sweat was soaking up into the darker roots of her hair, slathering strands in sticky gashes across her forehead and in calligraphic curls down the nape of her neck.

William moved, automatically circling her, vulture and carcass. He kept talking over the clanging, frothing, heat and movement of the kitchen, dodging away from the trajectory of a dirty ladle as Dawn flung it in the direction of the precariously full washing-up bowl. Soapsuds rushed reactively forward to spill across the draining board and down the front of the cupboard door, whilst others catapulted themselves in an eager escape from the heat towards the cool of the steam-frosted windowpane.

'And that was enough for a while, but now what? Death has become so overtly and tediously philosophised that we'd welcome it rather than sit through another existentialist lecture on nothingness. It's this age, too; everything is a disposable commodity, even life. It's too common and banal now. We're devolving. We've sucked the teat of expression dry. We're floundering.'

'Shit!' she spat, dropping the oven tray noisily as a half-cooked steak sighed a lazy somersault onto the back of the oven door.

Pulling off the oven glove, she inspected the burned wrist of her other hand, little pink blisters had sprouted up in a hard line. Satisfied it was just a surface injury, she impatiently pinched the steaming steak away from the door with scant disregard for the unharmed skin of her fingers.

'So what's next?'

'Excuse me,' she laboured, dodging William's wild gesticulation and unsettled pacing, and thrust her scarring arm under the cold tap. She paused only to watch the oil and fat glisten, rejected, in the fragments of visible sink water. Relief circled out from her wrist in waves of pleasant numbness.

'We need to reach the next level. We need that next thing, the next dawn. We need to reach a higher plane of consciousness. Art is eighty thousand years old and we just kept bleeding it dry until we arrived in this Kekuléan nightmare.'

Dawn had already moved away from the sink, slinging four plates onto the countertop as William maintained his anxious dance around her, one hand twisting through his curls, the other open, upturned, hopefully desperate.

'Humanity is just this giant fucking snake eating its own tail: never-ending, impossible,' he flourished.

'Pass me the masher.'

He pressed the object into the palm of her outstretched hand.

'Are you even listening?' he bit curtly, his passion giving a final zealous kick of aggression.

Dawn turned to him for the first time since he had launched into his monologue.

'Are you even *looking*?' she met his eyes directly.

A scream shuddered down from upstairs, followed by a heavy-footed thudding as a voice rumbled through the ceiling.

'At least she's tending to him now,' he said, as Dawn exhaled a curse.

'I'm not sure if this isn't worse.'

They both quietened to listen to a distant Alice impatiently inform her child, *their* child, there was absolutely no need to be screaming.

'I'm going to ask Dad to try magic again,' he spoke quietly.

'Will, it's been twenty-five years,' she softened.

'Twenty-six.'

'Exactly.'

'Exactly… It's been twenty-six years since my mother died, not him.'

'He's old.'

'He's sixty-seven!'

'He's weary.'

'I'm weary.'

'We tried, Will. For years, we tried.'

'I'll ask him to do it for James' birthday.'

'So you can resent him even more when he says no?'

'I'm not who I was when she died.'

'No, you're *more* of that person.'

'I'm not going to run off to Vegas again.'

'I know you're not. The guilt isn't fresh anymore,' she placed her burned hand against his arm.

'I left because of him, not me,' he moved away.

'You still left.'

'I came back.'

The fat red cooking timer screeched out through the steam and smoke.

'Go and call our children, I'll dish up.'

'Thanks.'

'You're welcome.'

'For...'

'I know.'

#

Alice was staring into a blank page, her pencil balanced as a moustache between her nose and upper lip.

'This is ridiculous,' she whispered, dislodging the pencil, which fell with a mute thud into her lap, twisted on her thigh and slid around the curve of her jeans, finally coming to a rest with a gently juddering tap on the floor.

The crying rang out immediately, overwhelming the room in a cloud of sound.

'Oh, for Christ's sake,' she shouted into the scream, throwing her notebook across the room where it promptly crumpled and folded against the Winnie the Pooh mural.

'What?' she yelled over the crib. 'What now? You've only been quiet for fifteen minutes, what the hell can you possibly want?'

The crying persisted resolutely against her reasoning. She hoped one of her parents would come to alleviate her from her duty. Alice knew from the hot smells floating throughout the house that her mother was undoubtedly fussing with unnecessary exasperation over their Sunday dinner, and her father, well, he might come. He'd come if he noticed.

'Shut up, will you?' Alice held the squirming ball of limbs up to her face, inspecting its features as it stilled between her hands, stopping just short of complete silence.

She wondered what it would be like when it eventually became human. Its eyelids were spider-veined blue and red, with a thicker blue worm of blood spiralling around its temple, and fine transparent strands of hair lightly dusting its scalp. Its fat arms were turgid ovals moving mechanically without grace or purpose. Its face was a flat blur of poorly defined yet-to-be features, and its unused feet barely filled the tiny bean-shaped socks. Fat legs curled like fingers from the pallid balloon of its belly. It was a bag of blood and bones, nothing more. It wasn't a person. It was a thing that screamed and shat.

'It's your fault Dr Jackson is making me record my feelings,' Alice stressed the word *feelings* as though it were banded daringly in jest at a time when boys were gross puppy dogs' tails and girls were the painfully boring everything nice.

'Dinner!' William popped his head around the door, feigned enthusiasm poorly concealing his mild trepidation at what he might find. 'Where's your brother?'

'Right here,' Alice smirked.

'Your *other* brother,' he raised a warning eyebrow.

'Looking after himself, I imagine. I believe I recall Mum saying he was more mature than me,' she mimicked his raised eyebrow in derision.

William banged the door shut, spinning away to look for James.

'Perhaps he's writing a thesis,' she shouted through the wall as Myles resumed screaming between her hands.

Mum,   28/05/2012

A lot of nothing has happened this month. Last weekend
was when the most of nothing happened, and as much as I
was there, then, I find that time has already become a series
of vignettes in my memory and I'm not even sure how
legitimate some of them are. This isn't a new occurrence,
I've just been thinking about the nature of memory and recall
and perspective, and thinking about it so much makes me
realise how unreliable it is. Maybe I've never heard a true
story from anyone. I'll try to tell you about the dinner we had
on Sunday, but I have no idea what time it was during which
parts of which course, I don't know who passed me the salt
or laughed hardest or talked longest, I have no recollection
of moving from one room to another, only of being in the
different rooms, and I have no idea how anyone but myself
felt, and again, even that is only an idea. I suspect from this
short paragraph you may, to some degree, be anticipating an
event far more notable than it was, but as I said, it was only
dinner.

I arrived when I arrived and Mira was already setting the
little wooden table. Iris had brought a coffee table in from
the living room and pushed it up against the one Mira was
working on so that the combined surface area was large
enough for all the required bowls and plates and utensils and
condiments. The coffee table was an inch or so lower than
the one already in the kitchen, so each thing had to either
fit entirely onto the coffee table or entirely on to the dinner

table. I remember dwelling on the meaning of that at the time but I don't know what I concluded.

I poured a bowl of water for Montecore, but he was so excited to see everyone that instead of drinking it, he decided to step on the brim and send the whole thing flying. It spun across the linoleum leaving a wave of liquid in its wake, which quickly spread out into a puddle under the dresser. I apologised, and Iris fussed saying it didn't matter, and Mira made a fuss of Montecore, and then everywhere was clean and all the kinds of fussing had stopped and Charlie appeared.

Iris had come to know about Charlie because I know about Charlie, and also because I don't have many other things to talk with her about. I told Iris my perspective of Charlie, which Charlie may or may not consider an accurate interpretation of himself, although I'm not sure if he would be the best person to judge his own character anyway. I don't think any of us can judge ourselves. Then Iris had interpreted what I told her, which was by this point at least twice removed from how Charlie may or may not consider himself, and also twice removed from how Charlie may or may not be.

Anyway, whatever was said, Iris thought Charlie seemed like a good guy and I thought he seemed like a good guy, and we both thought he didn't only need, but deserved, a few more people in his life. I didn't feel I was the best person to be his friend in a complete way, but Iris being old and Iris having lost Paul and Iris living with the dresser seemed like a really good candidate. So we invited Charlie to dinner.

The whole thing went entirely adequately because Iris and Mira and Charlie are all very adequate people. They're all polite and accommodating and empathetic and gracious. It was because of these things and because I already knew everyone that I didn't join in too much. I don't like joining in most of the time in any case, but I thought they should get to know each other without utilising me as a conduit. Whenever I was addressed directly I would try and respond curtly without committing to conversation.

The first course consisted of rolled-up finger crêpes filled with cubes of cheese, something that had the texture of melon that wasn't melon, and a thing that was green and thread-like. My palate was mildly offended by whatever wasn't melon, so I covertly lowered my crêpes underneath the table to where Montecore was lurking, and he snatched them from me happily before promptly spitting them out onto the floor between my feet. This was both disappointing and largely incriminating. Quickly, I devised a plan in which, whilst coughing and without moving my upper body, I would kick the crêpes as hard and low as I could, out from under the table and under the ghost dresser, where they could remain well hidden and undetected indefinitely. So I kicked, no one noticed, and the space under the dresser accommodated the crêpes. It was a success.

Whilst I was preoccupied with trying to extricate myself from the social faux pas I had arrived at by fault of Montecore, Charlie had launched into a story from his childhood. I don't know what triggered Charlie to regale us with the memory, and I had missed the beginning, but Mira and Iris appeared enraptured. After I double-checked there was no evidence of my first course where it shouldn't be, I tuned in to what was being said. Charlie was talking about impressions. How the things that leave a mark on us aren't always the things that are expected to.

Apparently, when Charlie was a kid, his parents had taken him to the Hoppings, I didn't know what that was but Mira and Iris didn't question it so I didn't either. From the rest of his story I think it must have been like a giant fête. He said there were more people there than he had ever seen before, more people than he thought existed in the entire world. Anyway, on account of the whole world being there, Charlie got separated from his parents. He said when he started crying his tears landed on his candyfloss and looked like the opposite of rain. Whilst Charlie was standing alone crying the opposite of rain, an old man came up to him, introduced himself as Samuel and took him to the place where lost things go. A woman announced over the speaker that Charlie was lost, and his parents quickly came to collect him. The woman with the speaker told Charlie's parents that it was a very special man who had found their son.

When Samuel had been as young as Charlie was that day at The Hoppings, he had been to see a play with his own family. He said that he had been finding it incredibly boring, that play, and he had been thinking how he wanted to be home asleep, when a really loud noise startled everyone. After the noise, a man holding a knife over his head jumped from the theatre balcony down onto the stage. Samuel said although he had just witnessed the assassination of President Lincoln, he was too young to really understand, and all he remembers thinking was that the guy with the knife must have been a superhero. For most of the rest of Samuel's life it was his dream to come to Europe, and when he met Charlie he was here living his dream and doing radio interviews, talking about something he probably misremembered anyway.

Charlie had chuckled to himself and wiped the closed end of his last crêpe across his plate, mopping up the remnants of seasoning and oil. He said how the story Samuel told was funny because he completely understood it now. Charlie said that there he was as a child, sitting in front of that old man who had been the last living witness of an incredible event in history, and all he could think of was how old the man's hands looked. Charlie said he would have forgotten the rest of what the old man had said if his father hadn't loved the story and repeated it so much. Charlie popped the final bite of crêpe in to his mouth and we all silently waited for him to continue whilst he chewed and swallowed.

Charlie told us how the old man's hands were so heavily lined that he could remember thinking if he covered them in finger paints and pressed them to paper they would leave blank lines like rivers through the colour. He smiled, telling us that he had been mesmerised at how old that man had been, but now look at his own hands! Charlie held his hands up and we all looked without really meaning to. I saw the same old hands as Iris has, only where Charlie's skin was wood and leather, Iris' was leaves and crumpled paper.

The pasta course was Iris' turn to talk. Being old like Charlie she was able to relay another childhood story, which is customary; someone tells you something, and then you tell them something similar, and then they tell you something similar to that, and so on. Slowly the focus of the conversation morphs organically, all the little similarities start adding up into one big difference between beginning and end. This saves people from running out of things to say. So Iris told Charlie things that were or were not real memories about something that did or did not happen, and Mira listened and worried and looked at me, and I listened and worried about what I was eating, and Charlie listened and smiled because I don't think he's had to listen to another person share something with him for quite a long time.

Time passed, and I separated a fair amount of white meat from bacon from spindly green stuff from pasta, and Mira gently mocked me for it. I was no longer listening to what Iris was saying, but just as she had nearly finished her story there was a moment in which we all looked up. Iris had referred to Charlie as Paul. Mira froze, I felt awkward and everyone seemed so very much more there than they had been before.

I knew it would all be all right so long as Iris didn't realise her mistake, because then she would get sad because of Paul and scared because of the dementia and embarrassed because of Charlie. I could feel Mira still paused as though waiting for Iris to notice, or for Charlie to innocently correct her, or for time to keep passing so slowly, so I shouted. I didn't shout anything specific, I just made a very loud noise, startling Charlie and causing Montecore to spring out from under the table and commence barking at the door. Mira seemed almost as aghast at my behaviour as Iris. Both of them were blinking at me with their mouths open and eyebrows raised, even though Mira knew my intentions exactly. I made a mental note to question her about that but then I forgot about it until just now, and it really doesn't seem important anymore.

Then what happened was this, which I remember exactly. Iris said, 'Are you all right, love?' and I said, 'Just clearing my throat,' and Mira said, 'Can you do it more quietly next time?' and I said, 'Sorry, Princess,' and Iris said, 'What are you two like?' and Charlie said, 'Young love' to no one and I said 'Pardon?' and Mira said, 'Don't be a dick,' to me, and Iris said 'Mira,' and Charlie said, 'Sorry, Iris, what were you saying?' and I said, 'You're welcome,' to Mira and she said, 'Whatever,' and Iris said 'What's going on?' and I said, 'We're all just eating dinner, Iris,' and Mira said, 'Yes, she knows that,' and Iris said, 'Yes I know that, dear, but what else is going on?' and I said, 'That would take an awfully long time to answer,' and Charlie said to Iris, 'I've never met anyone quite like Myles,' so I stared at Charlie, and Mira stared at me, and Iris stared from one of us to the next, and the Paul situation was averted.

The last thing that happened was we all went into the living room and Charlie asked Iris what the time was and she looked at the clock for a long time before saying how it wasn't time to leave yet. I looked at Mira with an expression that conveyed I had noted that Iris couldn't read the clock face, and Mira smiled at me and whispered how sweet it was that Iris didn't want Charlie to leave.

Myles

Potential last lines for a novel:
This couldn't be the end.
He had lived a thousand lives and none at all.

Chapter 32
Cryptobiosis
September 1990

The phone had been ringing for four minutes with no sign of relenting. He could always lift the receiver and immediately hang up, although then they'd know he was home. But of course he was home; he never went anywhere and that's why they had already let it ring for four minutes. They were trying to smoke him out. It was working. He didn't like being reminded he belonged to a network of other people with other priorities and other lives. He was alone, and he was happy alone so long as he could forget that twenty-six years had passed and the world had changed. He was happy whilst he could still pretend he was sitting on that sun-laced common having just watched her slip away from him, never saying goodbye because it wasn't. It was just her floating down towards the sea, getting smaller and smaller until he couldn't see her anymore. *That's all that's happening now,* he told himself. *William never came back up that hill ragged and defeated, William never uttered those words I couldn't understand... I am still sitting on the common watching the sea, waiting for my family to come back together, salty and exhausted. My son isn't calling me from his own life with his own children. I'm just sitting out there waiting for my Rose to come back.*

Bobby answered the phone after seven minutes.

'Hello?' the sound of his own voice surprised him; he

hadn't spoken yet that day. Then again, maybe he hadn't spoken the day before either, or the day before that.

'On top of the wardrobe,' William's voice was distant.

Bobby hung up, a moment passed, the phone rang again.

'Hello,' he sighed.

'Dad, sorry, I got distracted waiting for you to answer,' William's voice strained at normalcy.

'Evidently.'

'Unsurprisingly.'

Silence.

'James is five next month,' his son continued.

'It seems time is a train for which we do not all have a ticket.'

'What does that mean?' William was used to this, he expected this.

'Oh, nothing, just that little James has done so much in four years; he's turned from nothing to something. I could not say the same.'

'It doesn't have to be that way, Dad.'

'Time is for the young,' softly.

'Time is for the living,' thoughtlessly.

Silence.

'I'm sorry,' William.

'Still?' Bobby.

'Please.'

'I didn't mean to.'

'You did.'

'Only in that moment.'

'The brevity of time doesn't measure the weight of the action, Dad. Nor does it excuse it.'

'You'd make a terrible lawyer.'

'You're making a terrible grandfather.'

Silence.

'I bought him a magic set,' still William. 'He loves it. I told him his granddad is a magician.'

'Was.'

'Is. He can't do any of the tricks yet. He thinks he can; he's started doing shows for us. He'll stop in the middle of a trick and put his hands under the table, fumble with the cards for a few minutes arranging them how he's learned, and shout "Ta-daaa" triumphantly showing them again. Even then he doesn't always get it right,' he laughed. 'Sometimes we'll tell James he's made a mistake, it's important he learns humility, but other times we cheer right along with him.'

'I tried to get you interested in magic once.'

'I remember.'

'It was never your thing. You were always too preoccupied by the details of reality to concern yourself with illusions.'

'I guess the magic skipped a generation.'

'I guess so.'

'Why don't you teach him?'

'I'm not a teacher.'

'You don't have to be.'

'I'm not a magician.'

'My childhood begs to differ.'

'Not without her I'm not.'

'Mum was your wife, not your craft.'

'She was my life.'

'Exactly, Dad. She *was* your life. She *isn't*, but she was.'

'I'll never forget her.'

'For Christ's sake, living isn't forgetting!' William's voice spluttered out of the receiver, incensed and breaking.

Bobby slowly placed the phone back down until he heard the tiny click of disconnection. He stared at his hands. Strange hands. Hands she wouldn't know if she were to see them. He was a stranger to her now. He was a stranger to everyone. He thought how people who spend a lot of time together grow alike; couples develop the same lines in their faces, the same mannerisms, the same subtle, private languages, natural motions to give and receive one another effortlessly. Then they break up, through betrayal or misunderstanding or one heart being more full than the other, and they stop speaking.

They enter new lives alone, with all their learned gestures and tics going unmet. They fade, they change and they become different people. Five years pass without a word and they both meet again, happenstance, on a train, in a restaurant, at a new job, on holiday, and the pain is deadened, the grudges lost and they are strangers.

He picked up the phone, dialled his son's number and waited.

'Hello?' William.

'She doesn't know me anymore.'

'Mum?'

'Mum.'

'She doesn't know me either.'

Tears crept silently down Bobby's face.

'I'd like someone to know me.'

A pause.

'I can know you, Dad.'

Chapter 33
Towards Us, Impossibly
September 1990

'Should I get anything special in?'

'He'll be here any minute.'

'But I can pop to the shop,' Dawn fussed about in her faux-leather handbag, fingering the satin lining for knotted up change.

'He's been here before,' William paced from one side of the kitchen to the other, five steps in total, about-turned and retreated, remaining unsettled at every juncture.

'What? Seven Christmases out of the last eighteen? That time after he thought he saw her across the street, and to babysit Alice whilst James was being born?'

'He's no stranger, Dawn. You've been over there, too.'

'Two Christmases, and when he didn't answer his phone for three weeks so we had to go and check he wasn't hanging from his throat above an upturned chair,' she stopped rummaging and returned her handbag to the kitchen table next to an amalgamation of party foods.

'Dawn.'

'Well, I just don't want him running away because he feels ill at ease.'

'He's not a sick dog.'

'He's not a *dog*,' she exhaled.

'He's not si…'

'Just because you can't see something doesn't mean it's

201

not there,' she looked at him for a moment too long.

'What?' although he knew. 'I'm fine.'

'Are you?'

'Must you be cryptic?' he adjusted their mug tree.

'Must you play this game?'

'Dreaming of a different future isn't a sickness.'

'There's nothing wrong with the future you have,' she watched him carefully.

'Isn't there?'

'Is there?'

'Well, I can name one thing: the fact that we both seem so absolutely clear as to what my future might be that we haven't even considered arguing about the details,' he scuffed his toes along the grout dividing their kitchen tiles. 'There hasn't been a flicker of suggestion towards the fact that I might not know what's in store, just a discussion of whether or not my *given* life is any good.'

'Tell me what's so wrong with that security?'

'If my future is so knowable, it might as well be my past.'

'You can't keep running.'

'I've been living between these walls for fifteen years,' he spread his arms dramatically, forced disbelief at her accusation riding high on his tone.

'Physically.'

'This is all I have,' he gestured to his chest. She looked at him, silent, waiting. 'If you've got something to say, say it.'

'You were running when I met you.'

'I had escaped him… You knew I didn't want that life; the life he wasn't living,' William heard the truth in his own voice, and with it the dishonesty. The dishonesty of everything withheld. The dishonesty of trying to do nothing but nothing being too much.

'You were running when I met you, and then you met me and I became your new Vegas, and then we had Alice so she became me, and then everything settled down and I hoped you would too, but you kept running. You're still the

202

guy in that hotel room. You're still concocting different lives; wherever you are, you aren't.'

She tucked at his collar, studying his movements as he twisted away from her, pushing his thumb through a cotton belt loop.

'I'm right here,' he said, propping up the lid of the sugar jar and inspecting its contents.

'No, you're not,' Dawn took his wrist in her hand, turning him into her. 'You're in there,' she looked directly into his eyes as they darted between her and his stolen wrist. 'You've always been in there,' she traced a finger around his hair line.

'Where else can I be?'

'You've lost yourself in there.'

He squinted at her, she was saying things with no conclusion and he had no contribution. He twisted his arm free and her fingers fell loosely away.

'Dad's ill, Alice is ill, I'm ill… anyone else you want to diagnose?'

'You didn't kill her.'

'I didn't save her.'

'Couldn't.'

'Didn't.'

'*Couldn't.*'

'I can't have this conversation again. Three people died that day.'

'*One* person died that day.'

'Three people died,' William paused. The broken tap dripped its regular thud into the sink below. Dawn frowned. 'And what the hell?' he bit. 'You knew who I was when you married me. That was *why* you married me… what's happened to *you*?'

'I grew up, Will.'

'That's not enough of an answer.'

'We couldn't live that way for ever. We've got kids now, a family. I had different needs back then, it was the dream of a twenty-year-old.'

'It was the dream of someone living.'

'It was implausible.'

'You lied to me.'

'The truth changes.'

They stared at each other, years screaming between them. The tap dripped. The clock ticked. The fridge hummed. All so loud. All so rhythmic. William opened his mouth, but a new, gentler beat pattered across the kitchen window. Turning abruptly, he saw his father's face appear through the glass, old and haunted. Bobby smiled weakly, raising a hand in greeting.

'Dad!' William welcomed, already at the door. 'Come in,' he manoeuvred Bobby into the kitchen. 'James is getting ready with Alice upstairs, and Myles has been dropped off with a lovely woman up the road.'

'Oh, I was hoping to see the littl'un,' Bobby's eyes searched hopefully between them both.

William looked at Dawn.

'He gets restless,' she proffered. 'This is James' day. We felt it was best we gave him our full attention on his birthday. I think he's felt slightly neglected since the baby arrived. You know how kids can be.'

'Just as temperamental as adults,' Bobby smiled.

Mum,

You've got to wonder at the point of all this, as fruitless as that may be. Today I am in the coffee shop where Mira works, even though I don't like it, because Iris wanted to come here. Iris has wanted to go for coffee everyday this last week or so, not always here but always somewhere. I don't enjoy being near these people, and I feel neutral towards coffee, but as Iris feels better when we go, we go. Iris hasn't said anything much since we arrived today, but she's happy when she's quiet. I think she feels safer in silence. Especially in public. In silence she can't make any mistakes, and if she can't make any mistakes there's a part of her that can pretend she isn't getting any worse.

She has started saying one thing, though. She keeps saying how all she wants is to see Paul one last time. At first I thought it was the illness; that she was getting forgetful and repetitive. I know that's what happens. I watched a documentary on the effects of dementia and this woman just kept walking around a care home all day every day saying one word over and over again in different pitches, as though she was background noise in a movie of someone else's life. Iris started saying the Paul thing a lot, and I wasn't sure if it was a kind of prayer or because of the illness, but she must have known I didn't understand because she turned to me and said, 'I know I'm repeating myself, dear, I'm just trying to get something important to stick even when everything else has gone.' That's probably the closest I've ever felt to crying.

Personally, I'm kind of getting sick of my own thoughts. It's like I am haunting myself. *Wherever you go, there you are.* That's what people say. It doesn't really matter where I go or what I do, because I'm always telling myself the same stories, talking to myself in the same words with the same opinions and experiences and knowledge and aptitude and perspective...

Even before I think a thought I must already know what I'm going to think, you know? Like how there's a signal sent from my brain to my fingers to tell me how to move this pen, and it seems instantaneous, but an imperceptible amount of time has still passed? Well, that must be the same for thoughts. There has to be a bit of time when by brain tells itself to think something, and in which case – just like it knows my finger is going to move before it moves – it already knows what it is going to think before it thinks it: a pre-thought. Then what about that pre-thought? My brain must have thought something to know it had to have that pre-thought too, right? And thought about that pre-pre-thought, as well? And on and on and on for ever?

When you work backwards like that, from the final thought, you can never meet the trigger. If I saw an image and it triggered a thought, and before that thought was a pre-thought, and before that pre-thought was a pre-pre-thought, then 'pre' could be added indefinitely and I'd never get back to the image. Kind of like Zeno's paradox, like Achilles and the Tortoise. But that way, when it's backwards, instead of never being able to finish you'd never be able to start. I'd never see the trigger in the first place because there would always be another thought – another division of time – between the image and the first thought. And if I could never have seen the image, how could I have the thought in the first place? I don't have an answer about that and it kind of makes me feel like I'm drowning.

I look around these places. Every coffee shop we go to is always the same, full of these junk rats. Iris and I call them the milk flock, not that we're any different. I think Iris wants to go now. She never says she wants to go in case I don't want to, and because she's polite, but I'm always ready to leave.

I'll write more tomorrow.

#

We're in Starbucks today. Iris has ordered some sort of chai crème concoction because she's of the perfectly respectable belief that if we're going out to drink she might as well have something she can't have at home. I have a filter coffee because I don't want to spend an entire hour of minimum wage on a drink when I have drinks at home.

Through the window I can see Ms. Ex-Art Teacher sitting at one of the outside tables. She's wearing a black sun visor, closely shading her bronze rimmed reading glasses. Her hair is roughly dragged away from her neck in a cheap clasp, and the brittle ends have been lightened by the sun. I can see little of her face, but the traces of liver spots and bulging veins on the back of her hands place her at sixty, the Rizla-thin skin falling down her forearms and concertinaing at her elbows adds another five years. She holds a broadsheet in front of her, I can't tell which it is as one of the corners has curled inwards, but I can get a good enough view to see an article entitled, 'People of the Week', and beneath it is a photograph of a man in a business suit holding a banana.

The people walking past on the street, today's extras, are adorned in both coats and vests; as usual, no one is entirely sure of the English weather. The coats and vests are floating on a sea of denim. I don't own any jeans. Maybe I should. I saw a quiz in a magazine the other day, something that proposed to categorise the type of person you were based on what kind of jeans you wore; skinny, baggy, ripped, boot-cut, faded... there wasn't an option to not own any jeans, so instead of finding out who I was, I sipped the dregs of my coffee and watched the fizz dancing away from a nearby glass of Coca-Cola resting in the sun. Beauty in everything and all that.

207

We've come to Starbucks again today. I guess Iris really liked that chai crème drink. Or at least that's what Mira would say, but Iris probably just forgot that we were here yesterday. Mira has developed an incredible ability to ignore Iris' illness. I'm not sure if Mira believes what Iris says or if she is just trying to make it seem like everything is still all right, that it might always be all right, but she has started to do this a lot. Iris will say something that really makes very little sense and Mira won't question it, not even to herself, as far as I can tell. She just accepts it. It could be denial or it could be ignorance. Maybe it's both. Maybe everything is always just both. Mira will relish the absurdity as a moment of abstract clarity, as though Iris has suddenly become a conveyor of these philosophical and artistic truths. Mira is behaving like Iris is finding herself instead of losing herself, and I'm really beginning to think she believes it.

In other news, Mira has got us all tickets to this art show next month. She's been looking forward to it for ages because one of the exhibiting artists comes in her coffee shop sometimes and she wants to show support, which I think is a poorly veiled excuse for her desire to be ingratiated into their world of linseed oil and vacant pretension. The show is a collection of one work from each artist, but it's meant to be their *magnum opus*; each artist is to present a work which has consumed them. They've called the exhibition *(yclept)*, which has predisposed me to dislike everything before I've even seen it. At least it's something to do, I suppose.

(myles)

Potential last line for a novel:
  When we were alive.

Chapter 35
Ace of Spades
September 1990

He was sitting on a child's chair. His legs folded up stiffly, his left knee providing awkward support for his elbow as his arm twisted back inwards, his chin resting upon the outside of his wrist, hand curled into his neck. He was captive.

Bobby graciously received a party-orientated orange juice and lemonade mixture from Dawn as she whisked by to ruffle James' hair and ask him if he was nearly ready.

'We don't keep alcohol in the house anymore,' William whispered from his own tiny chair. 'We thought it was best to ensure Alice didn't have access to any,' his ankles were pinned together, his hands neatly placed on his kneecaps, heels tapping urgently.

'Oh, did she have a problem?' Bobby tried to recall a mention of alcoholism in any of their recent snatches of conversation, but he could remember nothing. Had he been so poorly attuned to his son's life that he hadn't listened at all, or had he never been told? It amounted to the same thing.

'Well, you know, she has *problems*,' William hushed. 'That actually transcend character,' he added tersely, watching Dawn help James spread a flush of ripe pink fabric over a stout wooden table.

'Sorry?' Bobby took a sip of his fizzy orange. The tang immediately disagreed with the remnants of mint left between his gums from when the taxi horn had screeched at him whilst he was brushing his teeth. He sucked at his tongue and rooted the tip around the uneven flesh of his cheeks, excavating all the residual taste and swallowing it away.

'Oh, nothing.'

'No, it was something,' he stretched a leg out cautiously, the joint popping in relief and contracting again as he returned it to position.

'It's just difficult sometimes,' William paused. 'How are we supposed to judge between difference and dysfunction?'

'I think those things end up judging themselves,' he thought about the two of them, sitting cramped into the chairs of children. His son, a man, an individual, a life that was so invariably linked to and yet so separate from his, and himself; a man, a life so long and yet so short, a sixty-seven-year stream of consciousness. Sixty-seven years of being defeated by fears, only to rename them and start all over again. The fear of nothingness, the fear of living too little, the fear of living too much, the fear of happiness, the fear of remembering, the fear of change. The fear of living without fear.

'He wants you to help him, you know,' William looked from his father to his son.

'I don't know if I remember how.'

'That's not the part that really matters.'

Bobby was reminded of Jerry then. Not the residual husk of a man he discovered when he returned from the continent to find his mother dead and his father nothing but guilt and whiskey, but the father who had built him a coffin. The father who stood first to cheer him, the father who welcomed Rose as a daughter, the father who bought him a wand and told him that sad things could be beautiful, too. For eighteen years, Jerry had loved him as a man would love a child in a world without war. Bobby had mourned the loss of his father long before his liver surrendered and rotted him away.

'Ladies and gentlemen!' a little voice announced from across the room with as much gusto as possible. 'I'm going to start in a minute so can you all sit down and watch?'

'Oooh!' Dawn exclaimed, grabbing a third tiny chair and levelling it alongside the men. All three were now facing James' little set-up. His room had been swathed in great, tent-like folds of cheap, glittery fabric until the walls were barely visible. Little glow-in-the-dark stars had been tacked onto the ceiling in lazy constellations. It was mid-afternoon, and the omnipotent light outside was largely ignoring the thin shield of James' curtains, which cut away only the yellow of the sun, so instead of sparkling, the stars were simply suspended in off-white stains against the uneven stucco.

'Where's Alice?' James asked, lips pinched.

'Where *is* Alice?' Dawn spat at William.

'Alice!' William yelled moving only his mouth, his body relaxed, expression neutral, staring directly at Dawn.

'I'm coming!' an exasperated shrill volleyed up the stairs.

'That's a nice little assortment of props he's got there,' Bobby addressed Dawn across William, nodding his head towards James' table.

'It is,' she gushed. 'My dad gave us a whole bunch of stuff from the store when he shut it down. This was before James was born, but Alice didn't have any interest so we kept it in the loft just in case. I think James had a wand in his hand before he could walk!'

'Ah yes, you'll have to excuse me, I forgot your father had a magic shop. He was never into the performing side, though?'

'Not Dad. He'll chat to just about anyone easily enough, but put him on a stage and he freezes stiff.'

'Why did he sell?'

'The store wasn't doing too well. In fact, it hadn't been doing too well for about fifteen years, but then Mum left him for a solicitor with a terrible bowl cut so he just sold everything; went into total liquidation, house, business, car, everything.'

'What did he...'

'He's living in Spain now. Always wanted to live in Spain

but never did because Mum didn't fancy learning a new language. She left and he replaced her with a country.'

'Right, let's get this over with shall we?' Alice stomped across the room and threw herself down onto James' Ninja Turtles beanbag, crossing her arms and hooking her heels up on the bookshelf. 'All right, Granddad?'

'I'm fine, thanks, Alice,' he leaned forward to look around William and Dawn until his chest pushed up against his knees. 'You?'

'Super.'

'Glad to hear it.'

William looked from Dawn to Alice, chewing his bottom lip.

'Get on with it, sprout,' Alice heckled James.

'I am!' he shouted back, clearing his throat for effect. 'Ladies and gentlemen, may I present to you, me!' James bowed with an ungraceful flourish. 'Amazing James!'

Bobby smiled, long unused creases drawing up around his sallow lips. Alice groaned in pantomime. Dawn cheered. William closed his eyes and hoped this could be enough.

'For my first trick, I will show you spring, summer, autumn and winter!' James pulled a bunch of cotton flowers from his gaping cuff, which promptly blossomed and folded in on themselves, before appearing to shrivel and disappear up his alternate sleeve. 'Ta-daaaaa,' he announced wildly, committing to another awkward, elaborate bow.

The adults cheered with varying degrees of enthusiasm and authenticity. Alice fingered a slither of gum from her mouth, twirled it around her finger and sucked it back between her lips.

'Next, I will pull a rabbit from a hat!' he waved his arms above the table and pulled a glossy black top hat out from one of the hidden compartments. 'This is the hat!' he waved the hat in the air.

'No shit,' Alice contributed.

'Alice,' Dawn snapped.

'As you can see, there is nothing inside!' James held the hat at a miserly angle, gesturing to the barely visible interior. 'Now watch!' he placed the hat top-down onto the table and waved his plastic wand above the rim. 'Abracadabra!' he cheered, twirling the hat around, reaching inside and withdrawing a stuffed white rabbit. A cardboard tag was still attached to one droopy ear. 'Ta-daaaaa!' he repeated with the same elation as before, knocking into one side of the table as he swept a dramatic bow so low the momentum forced him to take a step forward. Flushed, James uprighted himself to see his family cheering dutifully and Alice slow-clapping in a pointed lack of enthusiasm.

Bobby's back was hurting. The pain was on both sides of his neck, and he could feel blunt knives slide into his lower spine. He reached over to the slowly de-fizzing orange and lemonade, his body protesting in jolts of discomfort and sighs of relief. The drink tasted pleasant this time, the flavour of his own mouth had overwhelmed the mint, and the freshness of the beverage was satisfying, running coolly into his stomach. The dying bubbles greeted the top of his mouth before being washed along by the next wave of liquid. *This is quite something*, he thought, *this act of tasting*. The textures and flavours and temperatures all competed for attention and subtlety. He took another sip, rolling the mixture around on his tongue and draining it across the front of his gums, the tang alerting them to life and purpose as it rushed away into his throat. He smelled the zest, ripe against the cold glass, and the sugary sweet fragrance lightly dissipating into the room.

'For my third, and second-to-last trick, ladies and gentleman, I shall need a volunteer!'

Bobby felt all eyes immediately fall upon him. Weight where weight wasn't. His grandson shuffled his feet, either with apprehension or impatience, Bobby was unsure which; he was out of tune with children. With everyone.

'Dad?' Bobby wasn't so absent as to leave the hope in

William's tone undetected.

'Yes, yes. James, I volunteer. Where do you want me?' he stood, unsteady for a moment as his blood rushed to fill the places it had been denied.

'Excellent, if you could come over here please, sir,' James gestured to the space beside him.

Dawn beamed at the exchange. William watched his father hobble across the room, his back still curved from sitting, legs slow to recover, body thwarting mind. His dad was suddenly an old man. William stared in silence as his son bounced to receive Bobby, his body moving faster than he could think, limbs clumsily falling over one another, speed without clarity. Energy before purpose.

'Please be so kind as to pick a card,' James thrust a half-splayed pack of cards towards Bobby, his little hands too small to fan the pack cleanly.

Bobby went to take a card but noted James' grip was too tight for the card to slide out with ease; the dry shine of the plastic coating could stick cards together as sturdy as glue under a tight hold. He looked up to indicate his card was stuck, only to see James' eyes wide, ready to catch his, pleading mutely. Bobby, recognising the look of fear and fragility, winked at his grandson, who smiled and squinted back at him.

'On second thoughts,' he announced, 'I think I'll go for this one.' He took the only card in the pack that was almost entirely visible.

'Now!' James gave a flamboyant flick of his wrists, slowly shuffling the rest of the pack with plain and steady concentration, tongue peeping through the corner of his mouth. 'Show your card to the audience!'

'*Audience*,' Alice laughed.

Bobby showed his card, the ace of spades, to William and Dawn. Alice announced she was going to get something to eat and sauntered out of the room.

'Now, if everyone has seen it, please slide your card back

into the pack anywhere you want,' James held the cards out flatly in a neat pile that dwarfed his palm.

Bobby tentatively lifted a few cards, careful to observe any cues of direction from James, but upon receiving nothing but a showman's grin, he slotted the ace of spades into the pack, which subsumed it eagerly.

'Please feel free to return to your seat, Granddad,' James waved towards the tiny chair and Bobby felt his body tense. 'Sir!' James spluttered as a punctuating afterthought.

He was received uncomfortably by the small wooden square of the seat, but smiled widely as James grinned at him from his magic table.

'One... two...' James staggered the count with dramatic pauses, 'three!' he screamed, throwing the cards vehemently towards his family.

The pack caught on the air at once, breaking apart and cutting in sharp angles through the space, cards erratically darting behind shelves, into corners and under chairs, others twirling screwdrivers and helicopters floating slowly down to land atop the desk, the cheap foam mattress, or upon untidy shelves. Each person clenched their lungs to witness the moment of suspension in which the air was thick with clubs and diamonds; the apparent stillness of each card simultaneously fulfilling its parabolic trajectory was a snapshot of a flock of birds, before they landed with the dead speed of stones.

All three adults stared up at James, who was smirking behind the gauche confetti now littering the room. He gave a small twirl, the softness of his movements elastic and tender.

'Now,' he smiled. 'Your card,' walking over to Bobby, James wrapped his tiny fingers around the back of his grandfather's neck and snatched his hand back, the ace of spades proudly displayed across his palm. 'Ta-daaaaa!' he spun his arm into the air before bowing this time, his wrist still flailing emphatically as he dived to bend in two.

They all cheered, Dawn most loudly, standing from

her seat of torment to raise her hands above her head and mutter idioms of praise. William patted James on the back as he returned to his table, one small arm still extended in performance. Bobby clapped gently, smiling at the sight of *his* ace of spades lying conspicuously face up in the middle of the room.

'Are you ready for the big final super trick?' James shouted, as though to a room much larger and more eagerly filled.

'Yeah!' Dawn maintained admirable enthusiasm as her son ducked out of view and began rummaging under his table.

William stole a glance at Bobby, who met his eyes and nodded. It was all right. James was all right. They had a hope now; James wasn't them. William understood, moved to squeeze his father's knee, hesitated, and redirected his gesture towards Bobby's glass.

'You want another drink, Dad?'

'I'll go get it, you stay here,'

'You sure?' William shifted to stand.

'Yeah, yeah. I won't be long. I'll check on Alice,' Bobby smiled.

'Thanks, Dad. Don't worry if she says any…'

'I'm not delicate,' he reassured, standing with the inadvertent sigh of exertion that had found him a few years earlier.

William exhaled heavily as Bobby moved towards the door. He was all right. His dad was going to be all right. He might live again. Years were lost but there was a salvageable flame, he hadn't drowned so completely. And James had none of their burden, he wasn't like Alice. Dawn had a son. And Myles. James and Myles. They were the future now. He was free.

Chapter 36
To Become Suddenly Quiet
September 1990

His show had gone brilliantly so far. Everyone had been completely surprised by the card trick. If only they could have seen the looks on their own faces! He'd known that one would go the best, well, until the final trick, so long as he could pull it off. He believed he would too, because although he had only practised the beginning quickly he'd done the rest in his mind a gazillion times.

'Are you ready for the big final super trick?' he asked confidently, looking for his parents' reaction.

'Yeah!' his mum shouted.

Grinning, James crouched under the table, his mum's cheer still in his ears as he rooted around in hidden draws. His excitement was beginning to boil under his skin and a short giggle came from his lips, his smile snapping even wider across his face.

'You want another drink, Dad?' he heard his dad ask his granddad. Good, that would give him time to find everything he needed without being rushed.

'I'll go get it, you stay here,' his granddad replied.

From under his table, James peeked through the pink fabric covering and snorted at the sight of the adults crammed into his play chairs.

'You sure?' his dad had his hand in his hair as always.

Uh oh, James had absently put a finger in the drawer

217

containing his cloak and gloves, and it came out damp. He felt around, everything was soaked. 'Shit,' he whispered, quickly clamping his hand over his mouth and holding his body scrunched in case his parents had heard him. They hadn't. He was safe. He breathed out. He must have knocked it over during the show. He picked up the fallen bottle; he couldn't have turned the lid all the way closed after his practice. Unless this trick went really well, he was going to be in a lot of trouble for wasting his mum's stuff, especially as she didn't know he had taken it. He hoped it didn't cost a lot of money, but at least she would be less likely to shout at him whilst his granddad was here.

'Yeah, yeah. I won't be long. I'll check on Alice,' he heard his granddad announce. James smirked; Alice was going to be so amazed by this he would almost bet she might even say something nice for once.

'Thanks, Dad. Don't worry if she says any...'

'I'm not delicate.'

James hoped Alice wasn't mean to his granddad because he seemed nice and he wanted to ask him to teach him magic, and he would only do that if he wanted to come back to visit again. He heard his granddad stand up with a *humph*. Old people were always *humph*-ing.

James, still crouched under his table, fumbled around for the box of long matches he had stolen from the kitchen. Luckily, they weren't wet like everything else so they'd still work. He selected his trick candle from the draw, it was a bit wet but it didn't matter because getting – he read the label on the bottle – kerosene oil on the wick would just make it burn easier, and that's what he wanted; a show-stopping flame like the real magicians had. He heard his granddad shuffling out of the room just as he lit the match.

The world screamed.

Mum,   22/08/2012

I haven't got cancer. It's been eighteen months since I first started writing to you and I've been afflicted with no life-altering disease. No terminal illness to encourage me to try and live at terminal velocity. That's the problem with living. It's too open-ended. There's no urgency. Living is too banal, too common. Seven billion people are living. In fact, I read somewhere that there are 3,000 quintillion living things on earth. I googled how many zeroes that was: 3,0 00,000,000,000,000,000,000,000,000,000,000 in the UK or 3,000,000,000,000,000,000,000,000 in America. Apparently even numbers are hard to agree on, but quite frankly, either way, that's too many zeroes. And I'm just one of those. Living is eating and shitting and breathing and working. The tedium is exhausting. *Dying* though, that's something a little extra. A little special event for each of us. Dying is when you're the most alive because you only ever get to do it once, and then nothing. For ever. A lot of people are living until all of a sudden they're dead, and they never get the chance to be alive. I'd like to be dying, if only for a day; I want to know what it is to be alive. Just once.

Remember I told you we were going to go to that art exhibition Mira was excited about? Well, we've been now. I said we were going to go, we went and now I'm writing you a letter no different than before. Sometimes it feels like all time has happened at once. The entirety of my past is only a tiny compartment of time, and no matter how many years I add to it, it feels as though the length is constant. My past felt as long at nine as at it did at fifteen as it does now at twenty-two. The future has the illusion of being longer but only because of impatience and the unknown. Once it has been experienced it will all filter into the same minuscule space of time as the past. And in that respect, I am already an old man.

I didn't think too much of most of the exhibition. One piece, entitled *Fifteen Years*, was just a clear Perspex box in the middle of the room, and in it was a collection of dust and hair and sweat and finger nails and snot and wax and tears... I mean, some of these things had dried or amalgamated, but essentially the artist had collected the dead and rejected parts of his body for fifteen years. He'd shaken the bed sheets to collect his old skin, scraped vials under his armpits after the gym, cried into glasses, and saved hairs from his clothes. He did this every day for 5,475 days before decanting everything into a clear box ready for people to look at for a few minutes over one weekend. It wasn't much of anything really, that box, but then I imagined seven billion boxes and how much that would be. And I realised how inescapable people are.

Another room was just a really big piece of paper that was completely filled by a grey square so large it folded out across multiple walls and spilled out over much of the floor and ceiling. It was entitled *My Secret*, and the leaflet said it was a single pixel from a photograph of the artist's most guarded secret, magnified until it dwarfed the field of vision of the human eye.

My favourite piece, the only piece I really liked, was entitled *SHE*, and in simple terms was just a one-year study of a young woman. What interested me most about the piece was that whilst the artist was documenting this girl, she was creating, too. There's a whole wall of his exhibit dedicated to video clips and photographs of her spending an entire month doing nothing but painting a huge canvas. She wasn't supposed to be an artist, this woman. One day she had just decided to paint. She painted a giant face in the dirty greys of heavy shadow as a layer on top of a faded, washed out city. It was the face of an old man with the eyes of a child, and then, in a delicate translucent white lace, she had painted a final layer over the whole thing: a flock of birds. This painting was exhibited in the final room as part of *SHE*. No one took all too much notice of *SHE*, but Mira told me that after the exhibition, the untitled painting was bought for thousands of pounds by an important collector, and how that woman was going to become famous and the man who documented her was still just an artist trying to be more of an artist.

I took an extra leaflet from *SHE*, so you can read it if you're interested:

SHE, 2011

SHE began two years ago when I met my muse in an art gallery in East London. It was the day after she had been released from psychiatric care in relation to her suicide attempt in April 2009.

I was exhibiting in the gallery with three other artists and silently observing reactions to my pieces when I saw a girl looking at my painting entitled *First and Last*. She immediately stood out to me; she was draped in old thin gym clothes amidst a room of those who had dressed in an attempt to fit into the cultural art aesthetic, and I thought how she belonged more than any of them.

I walked over and asked about her reaction to the piece she was studying. Without looking at me she said, 'It is everything.' So I told her it was my work, to which she replied, 'Then you must be everything,' and walked away.

I followed her and offered to buy her coffee, which was when I noticed the scars down her wrists, and she told me about her depression and hospitalisation as lightly as remarking upon the

221

weather. I asked her why she had visited the gallery that day, and she told me it was because it was her first day of freedom since she had tried to kill herself and she hadn't been allowed to feel for so long. I fell in love, she moved in with me, I started work on *SHE*.

I created this piece as an examination of perception for her. I spent an entire year cataloguing everything she was: her awkward frown, her birthmark, the way she was quick to blush, the way she held a book like a flower, the way she whispered when she asked you to wait – I kept it all. I documented each little thing that builds up to make a person because I thought if she could see herself through my eyes then, if she once again found herself in a position where she wanted to take her own life, she'd never be able to take the life of the girl I showed her.

After a year of paintings, photographs, quotes, video footage, sound bites, sketches, frustrations and hope, I collated everything into the exhibition you see today: a celebration of the girl who would be dead. When I finally brought her here to see herself so complete, so rigidly and sycophantically dissected across eight white rooms, she looked around silently, and when she came to the end I asked her what she thought. It is what she said then that is written across the final wall in six-foot-tall black letters, concluding my year of *SHE*:

'You can't tell me apart.'

Two really bad things happened this past week that made me feel so terrible in so many ways that I called in sick to work. Work wasn't happy about this because it was only last month I took a week's holiday and sat in all those coffee shops with Iris, and also because Charlie had called in sick too, so they had no one available to sit in the basement all day. I said we must have both caught the same thing and hung up.

At the weekend, Iris invited me and Charlie over again, which went almost exactly as the time before except everybody used different words to tell similar stories. The hours passed, slowly and unstoppably, and as the sun died and the electricity began to fizz in more and more bulbs and Montecore got more and more restless it became time to leave. Charlie said his gracious goodbyes first, kissing Iris and Mira on their cheeks, squeezing their palms between his perpetually shaking fingers, thanking them in the genuine way that only occurs when someone gives you something you could never have given yourself, and then he was gone.

I turned and looked at Mira and Iris in the silence that always follows a departure, and smiled. This was the unspoken time for us to discuss Charlie, to assess any odd behaviour or quirks of character, but he had been entirely amiable, as always, so there was nothing left for us to say. I simply nodded in indication of the afternoon being free of incident and turned to leave, which was when Mira stopped me half way out of the door with a pair of glasses in her hand. They belonged to Charlie; he had forgotten them folded up on the armchair. I thanked her and said I'd return them to him at work.

As I was walking home I realised it was Saturday night so I wouldn't see Charlie until Monday, and I thought how he might need his glasses before then, especially seeing as he doesn't watch the TV so I assume he probably reads a lot. Or makes those little models of ships or aircraft. Or draws. Or whittles. Whatever it was Charlie did, it seemed to me it would be something he would need his glasses for, so I decided to drop them off on the way home.

I knew where Charlie lived because I asked when I invited him to Iris' the first time, in case he wanted me to come by on my way to show him where to go. He told me his address and said it would be too far out of my way and not to worry, he'd get a taxi. I had looked his street up when I got home from work and it is kind of near the Tiny Cemetery, which isn't very far at all, really, and I wasn't sure if Charlie knew where I lived anyway. Anyhow, when I got to Charlie's house, I knocked, but the door was already ajar and Montecore ran straight in. I whispered for him to come back as loudly as possible, but he didn't reappear so I pushed the door open a bit more and called Charlie's name. He didn't respond either so I stepped inside.

Charlie's kitchen was so full of things I couldn't see the appliances. It was stacked full of newspapers and trinkets and books and candles and toys and lamps and paintings... there was so much stuff it looked like a storage room for a whole variety of shops. I twisted my way around the floor, which had only one, thin available path through all the stuff, and followed it into the hallway. The hallway was even worse. I had never seen so many things in one place. Open cabinets spilling bead necklaces and watches and earrings and notepaper and CDs and hats... everything layered upon everything else. The people from the junk TV shows wouldn't have known what to do with themselves. His house was like the house of a hoarder from one of those documentaries, only it wasn't full of rubbish and dirt and disgust, it was full of things; real things that *should* be kept, but kept by tens of people over lifetimes, not by one person all at once.

Charlie had so many things it was hard to breathe. It was then I saw a teetering pile of all the books he had taken from the library. The books he told me he had donated to kids. It was also then that I saw Charlie watching me, tears rolling silently down his face and collecting along his jaw like heavy condensation. I placed his glasses on top of the stack of books, turned, and screamed Montecore's name as I darted through the Charlie's maze and out into the street. I didn't stop running until I heard the screech.

The sounds all seemed to come at me at once: the screech, the cry, the horn, but I knew they were really in swift order. Horn. Screech. Cry. I was frozen. I already knew. My feet slowly twisted my body around to face the direction from which I had just ran. I looked up. Tears already in my eyes. Montecore was lying in the middle of the road, unmoving, glowing in the headlights of the car slowly reversing away from his body. It was going to drive away. I started sprinting back down the road as hard and fast as I could. Everything was both silent and deafening. All I could see was Montecore. My body slammed into the driver's side as the car was still slowly reversing, its angle changing in preparation to manoeuvre around the stillness of my Montecore. I fumbled for the handle and opened the front door as the car switched gears to pull forward, and I heard a man's voice yell at me to get away. I didn't get away.

I couldn't see because of the dark and because of my tears and because Montecore was on the ground instead of bounding over to see me, but as the car began to drive forward, door still open, I ran beside it. I ran as fast and as far as I could, which wasn't very far at all because the car could accelerate and I couldn't. Just before the car kicked in some real speed, I reached in to where I thought the driver's face was and clamped my hand down. The movement of the car almost immediately threw me off, but at the last second of contact I squeezed with all my strength. I forced my nails into the man's face, and felt my ring finger plunge between his teeth and tear through the skin of his cheek. I tripped, sprawled out onto the tarmac and listened to the engine roaring away down the empty street. My hand was covered in blood.

Getting to my feet, I could feel a split in my trousers and bruises forming under the skin all down my left side. I didn't care. I was already running back to him. I fell to my knees beside his body. There were patches of black soaking through his golden fur. Patches that I knew would turn red in the light. I felt utterly powerless as my tears fell so helplessly onto his side, and all I could think to do was close my eyes and scream. So that's what I did. I screamed until my throat buckled, and gently lowered my forehead into the softness of his neck. It was then I felt the hotness of his tongue against my cheek, cleaning my tears away. I looked up. The parts of his face that would have eyebrows if he was human were raised and he tried to lick me again. He was straining to comfort me but he was too badly hurt to move. I kissed his muzzle and told him he was going to be all right. That I loved him. I love him. I love him and it's too much. How can something so overwhelming be so useless?

For the past couple of days I've been thinking a lot about how people would remember me if I died. I mean, for the most part I'd be forgotten, I don't know that many people and I've never done anything of note. But I don't care about that. Everyone will eventually be forgotten. I just wonder about those people I do know. Even little things could mean I'm misremembered, like maybe sometimes I've looked really pissed off even though inside I'm fine, but that's just how my face looks. There are so many things I think and feel and don't say, and some things I don't think and feel that I do say. I guess what I'm really getting at is how we all die as strangers, leaving a different version of ourselves in the memory of each person who knew us, none of them accurate. No one really lives on in memory like they say; shadows and characters and images of us are remembered, but never us.

Iris once told me about this guy, Jasper Maskelyne. He was the youngest in a line of magicians from his family, and in World War Two he became sensationalised when the British Army employed him to help the troops. To prove himself capable of the job, he had concocted the image of a German battleship on the Thames. Then, during the war, Maskelyne made both the British-occupied Alexandra Harbour and the Suez Canal completely disappear so the Germans weren't able to deploy an attack. You can't bomb something that doesn't exist. Later, as the war was beginning to draw to an end, he devised a plan to create 2,000 fake tanks and use them to feign movement towards battle, drawing attention away from the real invasion, which had, in turn, been disguised.

That whole story about Jasper Maskelyne, 'the great war illusionist', is really famous, but in reality, Maskelyne didn't do any of those things. It's true that he was a part of the war effort, but his actual contribution is questionable at best, and certainly doesn't include the feats listed above. That part about making entire places disappear is completely fictional. Fake tanks *were* created and successfully implemented in the diversion of Afrika Korps' attention from the real British threat, but Maskelyne wasn't behind it. The effort was claimed in his name after the man believed to be responsible was killed.

I think that's what is so incredible about Maskelyne. He didn't need to do those things to be a great magician, his most incredible feat was the false memory he created in the public consciousness. It reminds me of that quote from Baudelaire's *The Generous Gambler*, 'The finest trick of the devil is to persuade you that he does not exist.' I think that's the greatest illusion any of us can pull. No one knows who we are, not really. And in the truest sense of that, to everyone else, none of us exist.

Myles

Potential last lines for a novel:
    My fear fell away and I was no one again.
    I was never here.

Chapter 38
Everything Unordinary
September 2012

Bobby ran a dirty fingernail around the edge of the worn bundle of papers. They had been folded and unfolded so many times the creases were soft fabric. He thought briefly of James and Daisy and the Castle at the Beginning of the World, and then of Henry Fraser. After the war he and Rose had toasted Fraser's life with a bottle of Shiraz. Bobby could taste the ocean again, and looking down, he saw his hands as they were that day in the boat; his palms were soft and dark with dirt.

The letters weighed barely anything, and yet they were heavy between his fingers. His hands, now the roots of trees, were ragged and gnarled. He peeled up the topmost page one final time: *Mum, I haven't got cancer, not that I know of...* He closed his eyes and brushed his cracked lips against the words, folding the letter away, and placing the small bundle carefully inside an old tin box.

'I'm sorry,' he whispered, placing the tin into a shallow hole and covering it over with the soil he had just unearthed.

Bobby stood, his left knee cracking as the right momentarily gave way. He angled his leg awkwardly under the wooden seat and pressed the soil down neatly beneath his shoe. The flora would grow back over the bare patch soon. He turned to sit on the bench shielding the new grave.

Six lives were remembered in his Tiny Cemetery: three

skin and bone, three paper. They had never found Rose's body, so instead he buried Daisy's letters, just as his mother had been cremated by his father before Bobby had returned from war, so he buried the gargantuan fairy tale of his childhood. Now Myles' words joined them, all three concealed and safe under the little bench. Bobby could feel them whenever he rested there, his feet hidden in the tall grass.

#

Bobby washed the soil from his hands and checked the clock; it was almost half past ten. This didn't give him much time to get ready before the next duty he had to fulfil, and he had yet another appointment after that. This was the busiest he had been in years. Once his hands were clean, he changed his trousers, folded the ones with dirty knees on top of a small pile of washing, and walked over to his bathroom cabinet.

Staring at his reflection in the cabinet door, he did not recognise himself, not even in the untouched side. He was not just gaunt, a marionette where a person once was, he was an utterly hollow man. The other side of his face, the labyrinth of scar tissue that had claimed his left eye, was more recognisable. His past was a monster and he wore it always.

Bobby opened the cabinet and took out a small bottle of light beige liquid. Weary hands shaking, he unscrewed the lid and poured the creamy fluid onto his left palm. Placing the bottle and lid down, he padded the tip of his finger into the pool of make-up and began applying the colour over his burns. He built up multiple layers of foundation upon the ugly, ruddy divots and tight strings of darker skin. When the chewed-up tissue had arrived at a roughly homogeneous colour, he brushed a setting powder over the top. Next, he took an eye patch from the cabinet; it would help to hide what wasn't there. Finally, he added a woollen hat, pulled as far down as his brow, and a scarf behind which he could hide his mouth.

For her, the last Friday of every month was visiting day, and so every last Friday Bobby would complete this routine. She was still delicate, but climbing closer and closer to the surface, closer to being found. For two decades she had been somewhere unknown, but over the last couple of years, with the aid of a new medication, she began to experience weeks of lucidity at a time. She started to read, to teach herself science and history. She would laugh loudly and converse freely but, like a wild animal, if scared she would suddenly bolt back inside of herself. This was the only fear Bobby had left. He feared he would die before she came back completely. It had been Alice who had pulled him away from that room as the insensate howl escaped his lips, as he tried to claw his way to his family, or into the fire. He was never sure which. It wasn't until hours later, when the final time was announced and all uncertainty quelled, that Alice, having lost everything, lost herself.

#

6:80 flashed red on the meter. Bobby passed the taxi driver a trembling twenty and extricated himself from the back seat, cautiously placing both feet onto the pavement, pushing himself up and out of the vehicle.

'How much change, sir?' the driver shouted through the divider.

In response, Bobby shut the door quietly and took a step towards the house; his last objective of the day. He thought of Alice as the taxi slowly pulled away. How almost normal she had finally seemed. She had been timid and careful with her movements, but she was bright and, encouragingly, she seemed enthusiastic. Excited about each and every thing. Excited to see him. Excited to touch and taste and feel. She was thirty-eight now, but both a woman and a child. Her body knew a weariness that her mind did not. He was told she might soon be ready to leave. Bobby did not know what 'soon' meant: soon in comparison to the twenty-two years she had been in psychiatric care, or soon when compared to the weekly television schedule? He dare not hope for either.

He looked up towards the house in front of him. Bobby hadn't attended Myles' funeral, but he had spoken to Julie on the phone after the adoption agency contacted him. After the suicide. He had asked Julie for the address. He was unsure why, but he best guessed it was to explain. To explain for Alice. To let somebody know why Myles had never heard from his real mother. He should have done it earlier, when the letters first arrived, but he wanted to wait for Alice, he wanted… he had expected there to be more time.

Bobby reached up and pressed the doorbell. His pallid wrist extending from its loose sleeve. He had worn a suit. It was slightly too large, but he had hoped it would ingratiate him. He had hoped it would help to compensate for the rest of his appearance. The door opened.

'Can I help?' the man looked at him inquisitively.

'Oh,' Bobby glanced up to the house number. 'I thought, sorry, that is to say, I thought someone else lived here.'

'Who were you looking for? Maybe I can help.'

Bobby could feel the man's eyes on him, on the three visible inches of his left cheek, but when he met his gaze he was smiling. Bobby coughed.

'I was, Iris and Mira? A grandmo…'

'Then you're at the right place!' the man stepped backwards. 'Would you like to come in?'

'Oh, I didn't expect,' he stammered slightly, squinting at the man. 'Charlie?' he proffered.

'Paul,' the man put his hand out.

'Bobby,' mouth slack and open, he shook Paul's hand.

'Come in, Bobby,' Paul walked back inside the house, gesturing for him to follow.

Bobby could feel the warmth from inside already, it smelled of cinnamon.

'I didn't expect…'

'Bobby?' a female voice called.

Bobby stepped into the kitchen, shutting the front door. An old woman, still fifteen years his junior, was walking toward him.

'Iris?' he allowed her to embrace him and delicately patted her shoulder.

'Julie told me you were coming,' Iris stepped back, one hand squeezing his forearm. 'She said you had been in contact with Myles before…' Her eyes welled, 'Sorry.'

'No, I'm sorry…' Bobby didn't know what to say. 'Maybe it's too soon.'

'Don't be silly, dear.' Iris swallowed, and slid a chair out from under the tiny kitchen table. 'It's a pleasure to meet you.'

'You, too,' he realised Iris hadn't reacted to his burns. Most people usually did a second take, or tried to look without looking. Maybe his disguise was better than he had realised. 'I just wish it could have been under…'

'Please, sit down,' she gestured to a chair.

He lowered himself onto the seat, his joints screaming then sighing.

'Sugar in your tea?' Paul called over his shoulder.

'Oh, erm, yes,' Bobby looked around at the cluttered kitchen, and from Iris to Paul. 'Thank you.'

'I'll have one if you're making,' a young woman appeared beside the dresser. 'Bobby?' She looked at him, expressionless.

'Hello, Mira?' he was cautious of being over-familiar.

'Nice to meet you,' there were dark smudges around her eyes; either old make-up or lack of sleep.

'You too, I've heard a lot about you,' she made him nervous.

'Really?' Mira's face weakened.

'So much,' Bobby smiled as the girl lowered her stare, her hand held to her mouth.

'Here,' Paul placed a precariously full mug in front of him.

'Thank you,' he nodded, feebly.

Iris joined him at the table, their knees almost touching as she accepted her own cup from Paul, who then manoeuvred himself around the thin walk space to Mira.

'Here,' he gave the girl a tea and kissed the top of her head. 'I'll be upstairs if anyone needs anything,' Paul gave a reassuring look to the room and disappeared. Bobby exhaled.

'Sorry about my husband, he's taken it really badly. He can put a brave face on but he hasn't spoken about it since it happened. It's his way of coping,' Iris cupped her hands around the hot tea.

'Oh, I quite understand,' *I should have waited.* 'Like I said, I shouldn't ha…'

'*I'm* grateful you're here,' Iris interrupted, a hand moving to touch his. 'Where's your brother, dear?'

Bobby shot a confused look to Iris.

'I don't…'

'He's coming down now,' Mira replied.

'I'm here, Nan,' a voice shouted from another room.

Bobby frowned, his eyes darting around the kitchen, he had not been prepared for this many people. There was only one dresser. Iris must have let go of one after Paul came back. He wondered which one he was looking at, the living or the ghost. A young man walked in.

'Nice to meet you,' the boy came directly towards him, arm extended in greeting.

'And you,' Bobby lifted a weak hand to meet his. 'I'm Bobby.'

'Sam,' the boy nodded, slipping into an empty space.

'*Sam?*'

'Yeah?' Sam answered attentively.

He hesitated, staring down at the table. There were stains in the wood. He was hot. The room was so small and full.

'Excuse me,' he tried to stand but, unsteady, fell back into his chair.

'Are you all right?' Before he knew what was happening, Iris pulled his hat up and placed her hand on his forehead. She was touching his skin. Touching his scars. He braced himself for her repulsion. 'Sam, get him some water. You're running awfully hot,' she took her hand away, placing it comfortingly on his arm. 'Do you want to take your jacket off?'

Bobby grabbed his hat back down, slowly daring to look towards Iris. Her eyebrows were raised, eyes looking deep into his, questioning.

'I'm fine, thank you,' everything was so close. Sam placed a glass of water next to his tea, 'Thank you.'

'You get that down you,' Iris instructed.

Bobby drank the water in small, slow mouthfuls. No one spoke.

'Iris,' the water was gone. 'Can I ask you a question?'

'Of course.'

'Who is Charlie?'

'Charlie who, dear?'

Bobby swallowed thickly, staring into the empty glass.

'Oh, nobody. Just somebody I never knew.'

We hope you enjoyed *When We Were Alive*, a striking debut from a promising young author. At Legend Press, we pride ourselves on publishing original, thought-provoking fiction, and so if you'd like to find more compelling reads…

Come visit us at
www.legendpress.co.uk

Follow us
@legend_press